The Hard Way

The Hard Way

Julie Luongo

A Tom Doherty Associates Book
New York

This is a work of fiction. All of the characters, organizations, and events portrayed in this novel are either products of the author's imagination or are used fictitiously.

THE HARD WAY

Copyright © 2008 by Julie Luongo

All rights reserved.

Book design by Spring Hoteling

A Forge Book
Published by Tom Doherty Associates, LLC
175 Fifth Avenue
New York, NY 10010

www.tor-forge.com

Forge® is a registered trademark of Tom Doherty Associates, LLC.

Library of Congress Cataloging-in-Publication Data

Luongo, Julie.
  The hard way / Julie Luongo.—1st ed.
    p. cm.
  "A Tom Doherty Associates Book."
  ISBN-13: 978-0-7653-1667-7
  ISBN-10: 0-7653-1667-6
  1. Self-actualization (Psychology)—Fiction. 2. Self-realization in women—
Fiction. 3. Single women—Fiction. 4. Chick lit. I. Title.
  PS3612.U64H37 2008
  813'.6—dc22

                                                          2008005246

First Edition: June 2008

Printed in the United States of America

0 9 8 7 6 5 4 3 2 1

This book is dedicated to
Alice Luongo,
my mom.
Thanks.

Acknowledgments

I've gotten by with a little help from a lot of people. My friends all know I appreciate it. But this is as good a time as any to thank them and the outstanding people in the book business who support new writers.

For the people who helped make this book a book: Nikki Van De Car, Paul Stevens, Dave Dunton, Natasha Panza, Nicholas Flagler, Nanci McCloskey, and the Petersons for the loan of Ridge Road Camp, especially Lydia Peterson, and David Powicki for the shower.

To all of my friends who asked for, read, and commented on drafts, especially Kristen Kellogg, Sarah McCarroll, Julie Powers, Alice Luongo, Rachel Peterson, Jeanette Peterson, Anne Fetherman, Danny Oh, Joe Trunzo, Debi Webster, Stephanie Powers, and Saundra Gleisberg. A special thanks to the people who went public with their praise, including Jason Schossler, Juliet Latham, Stephanie Lessing, Daisy Fried, Jim Quinn, and Discouragement Kitten.

And much love to the people who supported me along the way, providing inspiration, money, jobs, fun, and love, especially Dan Luongo, Sandy Luongo, Rose Luongo, Lisa Luongo, Goldy, Jim McCarroll, Donna Webster, Gerald Kielpinski, Dave

Ascuitto, Jenn and Jeff Fritzen, Megan and Chris Smith, Gage Kellogg, Mandy Zateeny, Chris Simms, Christy Klopfenstein, Michael Williams, Jen Desberg, Roger Bird, Dawn LaFeir, Kathy Stevens, Steve Bunche, writers and professors from Temple's writing program, and my former students at Rowan.

A special thanks to Matthew Costello at www.onekindact .com, who made www.julieluongo.com possible as one of his many kind acts.

Contents

Beach Bar with Tequila
(Watercolor on Paper, 1990)

The death of Lucy's father marked the moment when three women began their lives as new people. Lucy heroically forged ahead, imagining her dad cheering her along. Her sister, nineteen years Lucy's senior, fell gloriously apart. And their mother, after the grief, started dating a dynamic entrepreneur. It was the sort of coupling that everyone looked at and said involuntarily, "Of course."

Lucy was the collegiate quasi-feminist who was studying journalism and demanded to be called a "woman." Nancy, her sister, was the black-clad pharmacist who lit a candle each night in remembrance and cried herself to sleep. And Margaret, their mother, was the global excursionist who was renewed by adoration and basked in the extravagance of new love.

Margaret, in what Lucy figured was a postcoital moment of sentiment, decided to rent a place in Mexico for Christmas break. She and Eli, the new boyfriend, would stay two weeks—his kids would come for Hanukkah and hers for Christmas. "It couldn't have worked out more perfectly," Margaret told Lucy, "the holidays butting up against each other this year."

"Thank Jesus," Lucy said, "and those tricky Romans for their acute sense of timing."

"Nancy's coming, without Bob, just for a couple days. But you're on break, right? I can book your ticket for the whole week?"

The thought of Nancy without Bob was unsettling to Lucy. She only knew them as a unit. A matched, however mismatched, set. NancyanBob. BobanNancy. It had recently occurred to her that her sister might be gay. This was a default theory Lucy and her roommate Jayne brewed when Lucy admitted that she couldn't conjure an image of BobanNancy ever having an intimate, sexual moment. Her own sexual moments were no inspiration, but still, she couldn't even place NancyanBob in one of her awkward fumblings that passed for sex.

Amorphous, dumpy Bob and compact, muscular Nancy. They didn't make sense. Jayne was bisexual and said she could imagine Nancy having sex, only it was with her. She was forever categorizing people as "doable" or "avoidable." So, instead of studying for their economics exam, Jayne and Lucy began the saga of BobanNancy's elaborate cover-up scheme.

Bob and Nancy married in the 1970s, when being gay was something newspapermen accused politicians of as if it were akin to being a murderer. So, under this pressure, they married and happily conducted their private affairs.

The only problem Lucy had with this theory was, if they were cohorts of that sort, then they'd most likely be better friends than they were. They would share stories. "I almost slipped at work and said that Sharon and I were in Barbados," Nancy would tell Bob over a cup of morning coffee. "I covered up by saying '*sharing* an eye . . . for beauty, Bob and I really enjoyed the sunsets in Barbados.'" Bob would laugh, rub his

stubby hands together, and tell her that no one would ever suspect a thing.

Nancy's considerable grieving over their father's death confused Lucy even further about the forces that motivated her sister. Nancy would call Lucy at college and wail into the phone,
"I just miss him so much."

The first time Nancy called crying like this, Lucy asked,
"Who?" It had been over a year, which Lucy knew was not a
mile marker of any significance when it came to the personal
process of grieving. She was ashamed of herself. Why did she
feel okay about his death? Why didn't she know her sister better? Why did she wish her sister had called someone else?

Nancy called repeatedly to cry to Lucy, who was usually
typing furiously to make deadline for the campus newspaper or
finish a report due the next day. The phone crimped between
her shoulder and ear, she would say, "Uh-huh . . . I know . . .
uh-huh . . . I know," only half listening.

Jayne would mouth "Nancy?" and, not cruelly, more in-
quisitively, put her fists to her cheeks in the universal sign for
boo hoo.

Lucy would nod and roll her eyes. Sometimes she would
motion for Jayne to take the phone from her while she ran to
the bathroom. Jayne would dutifully "uh-huh" and "I know"
in Lucy's stead.

Lucy arrived at the airport in Mexico to a grand reception by
Carlo, the cabdriver Lucy's mother hired for the week. He was
holding Lucy's high school photo and smiling that island smile
that said, "Welcome home, finally."

"Oh, Lulu," Carlo said in his heavy accent, calling her by

her childhood nickname, "shoo are so mush prettier than this pick-ja."

Lucy adored compliments, so she and Carlo were instant friends. Lucy's college weight gain had been a topic of conversation and open speculation among her family, and she hadn't been expecting to hear any compliments on this vacation. In fact, she was glad a stranger was there to greet her.

She had unnecessarily braced herself for repeats of the past year:

At her father's funeral, her mother had said tentatively, "You look . . . healthy."

"It's just college weight," Nancy had said, making it clear what everyone was thinking. "You'll take it off."

That Christmas, her mother had said, "It's not as easy as you thought. You really have to watch what you eat. And get out there and move around a bit."

Her sister, with a sniffle, had said, "Daddy used to gain weight like that."

The truth was that Lucy liked the extra weight. She was more the milk-fed farmer's daughter than she was the Czechoslovakian immigrant anyway. But she played along and listened to their suggestions, and then ate whatever she wanted. It wasn't too much of a strain to pretend she had the same standard of beauty as everyone else.

They were constantly cheering her on to "get moving." But she'd always been something of a drowsy child, which suited everyone just fine back then. But even Lucy had a sport; hers was tennis. On the ride to the bungalow, she asked Carlo if it was possible to schedule a daily match with someone at the tennis club. His cousin would make the arrangements, he said.

Then he got on his radio and spoke in Spanish for a few minutes about *la gordita* who wanted *jugar al tenis.*

That would please her mother and Nancy, she thought. It was her preemptive strike against the inevitable bombing she was to get for her pants, which were stretched across her butt, and the oversized button-up she hadn't buttoned up too high so as to show off her cleavage. It was the feature that benefited the most from the extra weight.

Lucy had met Eli only once before, for dinner at the best restaurant near Lucy's college in Philadelphia the night before he and her mother flew to Athens. She arrived at the bungalow expecting to find the two of them leaning close, holding hands, and sipping champagne, which was their standard position the evening Lucy spent with them. In fact, Lucy realized that she only ever pictured Eli and her mother eating in that restaurant. Lucy often wondered why her mother didn't look as "healthy" as she did with all of that eating. But her mother, at sixty-one, was as trim and beautiful as ever.

What she arrived to was a house of sullen thirty- and forty-somethings hosted by teenagers in their sixties. Her mother and Eli were in the kitchen—Margaret was cutting cheese and Eli was unwrapping poppy-seed crackers. They were giggling and grab-assing, from what Lucy could tell from her mother's swivels and jerks behind the counter that separated them from the sitting area.

To Lucy's shock, Eli's adult children were still in tow. Son, Ezra, daughter, Maura, and her husband, Joe, were glowering in the living room, ignoring each other and the antics in the kitchen, watching local news. Why would they care? Lucy wondered.

Who watched local news on vacation? The woman on TV was speaking *muy rápidamente* about a fight that had broken out in her neighborhood. Lucy figured they all understood Spanish, because they were so engrossed that no one stood to greet Lucy when Margaret introduced her. But Margaret was unfazed. She just happily hustled Lucy off to the bedroom she was sharing with Nancy.

"Settle in, dear, and come out for cocktails," her mother said as she pushed her into the room and shut the door.

Lucy heard the news droning and her mother saying, "Eli, don't you dare," followed by muffled giggles.

Nancy was sitting at the end of one of the twin beds, face puffy and eyes red.

"Isn't it just awful?" Nancy rose and embraced Lucy.

Lucy had never felt much sisterly camaraderie with Nancy. There was the age difference and the impenetrable Nancyan-Bob alliance. But she hugged her and asked, "What?"

Nancy looked at her, stricken. "Oh, you'll see. The way Mother and Eli carry on. It's disgraceful."

"What are they doing?" Lucy had an image of her mother topless on the beach alongside Eli in a thong, passing a joint back and forth, drunkenly cursing at small children.

"They're just so . . ." Nancy burst into tears again, plopped her butt on the edge of her twin bed, and buried her nose and mouth in a crumpled tissue.

"Unhygienic? Drug crazed? Unsuited?" Lucy ventured.

"How would Daddy feel if he saw this?" Nancy asked.

"Happy to be alive?"

Nancy glared at Lucy. "She and Aristotle Onassis are carrying on like—"

"Lovers?"

"Mom's just lonely. This is the product of that and nothing else."

"First of all," Lucy said, "if Eli resembles anyone famous it's Mel Brooks, which is an insult to Mel Brooks. Secondly, if Dad could see this, he'd probably say what everyone else is saying, which is 'yeah, that makes sense.'"

Nancy stiffened. Lucy knew she was supposed to be her sister's ally. But she barely knew this blubbering thirty-nine-year-old woman sitting on the tropical-print bedspread who was begrudging her mother happiness and begrudging herself a nice vacation.

"You'll see," Nancy sniffed. "I've only been here a day and I give you that long to abhor his kids and Mother's antics."

"Let's just have a good time." Lucy put her arm around her sister's taut body, stiff with overworked muscles and tension. "Just us, and forget everyone else."

Nancy smiled a little, and Lucy was fully convinced that it meant Nancy was imagining her next step in the plot against her mother and Eli. "That would be nice," Nancy said, "but I'm probably going to change my ticket."

There it was. The plot. Lucy thought she should be so lucky to have Nancy leave. So she just shrugged, stood, and unpacked. Lucy stuffed bathing suits and beach wraps into a musty drawer.

"And those kids," Nancy said. "Eli and Mother wanted us to overlap." Nancy went to the connecting bathroom and splashed water on her face. "They should have checked with us, but Mother said she thought it would be fun."

"What are they like?" Lucy asked.

"The daughter is the worst. Very unkind to Mother. Her husband is nice enough. Drinks a lot and doesn't say much. And the boy, Ezra, is a complete waste. Never married. College instructor. He might be gay."

"What makes you say that?" Lucy listened with renewed interest. She thought she might make some headway with her admittedly wild theory about NancyanBob.

"He's sort of effete in that academic way. And he reminds me of someone I know who's gay," Nancy said.

"Oh?" Lucy tried to sound casual. "Who?"

"What difference does it make?" Nancy huffed. "You wouldn't know him anyway."

Lucy wasn't any closer to understanding this steaming creature that was her sister. Her half-joking speculations about sexual orientation aside, she really did want to know about this gay acquaintance of Nancy's. Or any friend, for that matter. Her sister had become someone Lucy knew only through her histrionics: "This is terrible . . . that is awful . . . you should have seen . . . can you believe . . . ?" Lucy knew Nancy's annoyances well enough. She pictured her huddled with Bob in her far-too-big-for-two house, huffing about the injustices meted out to her that day. "The cashier shorted me five cents. I just stood there with my hand out and waited. . . . I do not have the cannoli for tonight because I got to the bakery and they told me that the woman who makes the filling was in the hospital. I told the girl I ordered them a week ago. Couldn't they have gotten them from another bakery? . . . If they block the driveway again I am suing them!"

Lucy thought of her sister as one of those hateful women who lost her looks and took it out on everyone because she thought she was being slighted for it. Lucy scolded herself for this decidedly unfeminist thought. Plus, it couldn't even be true. Nancy hadn't lost her looks. Damn, another unfeminist thought. Lucy was terrible at being a feminist. She was considering abandoning it. She read a women's magazine on the plane and felt like shrilly defending the regular women of the world who didn't have time to take oatmeal baths and ponder the erotic secrets of the Orient in order to please their men. But she didn't like either scenario—being the defender or the half-wit.

While she was revamping her opinions about things, she decided to abandon the homosexual theory about Nancyan-Bob. She was being far too generous to her sister by making her life somewhat interesting via this scenario. Nancy was really just a fuming little beast whose superpower seemed to be the perception of mythic injustices.

"Lulu," Nancy said, watching Lucy dress, "you're not wearing a bikini, are you?"

"I was going to," Lucy said, tying a wrap around her waist.

"Still can't shake those extra pounds? Have you been drinking a lot of beer?"

"I'm going to play tennis tomorrow." Lucy pulled a purple tank top out of her drawer and slipped it over her bikini top.

"Beer will put it on faster than a diet of chips and burgers." Nancy was energized by her zeal for developing a weight loss plan for Lucy. "There are some great new drugs out now. I've seen a lot of women lose with them."

"You think it could be the beer?" Lucy said mildly, just to keep Nancy interested in the topic. It was a safe distraction— better than Eli and Mom or, God forbid, Dad. Nancy controlled her own little world through the strict management of her weight. Diet, exercise, pills—these were topics Lucy found women with no other discernible interests could discuss with passion and expertise. As her sister prattled on about success stories, Lucy wondered what could be accomplished if women stopped obsessing about diet and exercise. Total world domination? It was possible.

"Tennis is a good idea." Nancy looked Lucy up and down. "Now, let's go make the best of this situation," she said, as if it were her idea, and banged out of the bedroom.

Margaret and Eli were sitting on the bamboo-framed loveseat. A pitcher of something white and frothy was sweating on the glass-topped coffee table. Joe and Maura were on the matching sofa, and Ezra was on the remaining chair with his feet up on the footstool. Nancy stood with her arms folded and Lucy dragged two chairs from the dining table to form a circle with the rest. Nancy harrumphed and sat.

"You're welcome," Lucy said brightly.

"So, how was your trip?" her mother asked while Eli rose and poured two more drinks.

"Well, I suppose it was much like yours." She smiled at the dour adult children of her host for a beat and then said, "Utterly terrifying."

She was faced with silence. Her mother was looking at Eli. He was pouring Nancy a drink, which she declined. And the others were staring into their glasses.

"It's really the only reason to fly, though," Lucy continued. "For the adrenaline rush during takeoff and landing."

No one agreed or disagreed.

"And that three-hundred-pound gorilla we were transporting had our tiny plane listing dangerously to the left," Lucy deadpanned to see if anyone was listening.

More silence.

"And the wrecked planes on the runway didn't inspire confidence."

"So, despite their best attempts," Eli said, "you made it anyway," and her mother laughed.

A little slow on the uptake, but she was grateful to them. Lucy figured that she was more like her mother, and Eli, for that matter, than she liked to admit. The three of them would forge ahead, make jokes, and tell stories just as if they were all having a great time. It was something she'd occasionally despised in her mother. As a child she thought her mother's brightness was a denial of Lucy's misery. Evidence of her inability to empathize. But now it seemed more like a clever survival mechanism. Or maybe it was an overriding philosophy to be happy in each present moment. Either way, Lucy appreciated it.

"Your mother told us there are more paintings of you than would fill the Met." Maura said this with an acid tone and raised eyebrows while giving Lucy an obvious once-over.

Similar signs of disbelief over Lucy's past as an artist's model were common with the very beautiful, which Maura certainly was. If Lucy was a sheepdog, Maura was a mink. A bejeweled one at that. Maura reminded Lucy of the Tibetan women who sewed all of their jewels and gold pieces into their clothes to show their wealth. She was weighted down with gold and platinum. She had so much sparkling ice on her that Lucy wasn't surprised she was so cold. And she had the kind of skin, olive and smooth, that Lucy thought only an airbrush could accomplish. She wasn't sure if even a magnifying glass would show a pore. Maura had delicate, angular features and silky hair. Lucy longed for silky hair. She smoothed her frizz down in an unconscious gesture.

"Probably a smaller museum than the Met," Lucy said.

"*My* parents," Nancy said, as if she were pitting them against Maura's, "sponsored an artist when Lulu was young."

Lucy cringed at the nickname. It was worse than being a Muffy or a Babs. Lulu. Skip to my Loo. Yes, folks, skip to the toilet.

"Painted nude, as a child?" Maura said, and wrinkled her little nose.

This was getting worse. Lucy could just imagine the conversations they'd been having about her. "I was cherubic," Lucy said as a joke. No one laughed and she felt her skin flush.

Maura drummed her fingers on the bamboo arm of the sofa and cut her eyes at Lucy. She didn't seem to realize that she was doing this, so Lucy took a sip of her drink and emerged from behind her glass with froth on her upper lip. Maura averted her eyes.

"If you *know* art, you *have* heard of this artist," Nancy said, sounding like a schoolmarm. "Do you?" She didn't wait for a response. "He lived with Mum and Daddy until Lucy was born."

Mum and Daddy? Lucy wondered if Nancy had been watching too much *Masterpiece Theatre*.

"My father," Nancy continued, "was a preeminent professor of art."

Preeminent? Good grief.

"Daddy," Maura said, ignoring Nancy and addressing her

father, "what ever happened to the portrait of Mother you commissioned?"

"Right, Margaret, you found that artist for us," Eli said, turning to Lucy's mother. "What was his name?"

At that, Ezra, who until that point appeared to be napping, leaped out of his chair in one fluid motion. "I'm going for a walk," he announced. He grabbed his baseball cap from a peg on the wall and was out the door.

Lucy jumped up. "I'd love to get the lay of the land. I'm going to tag along," she said to no one in particular.

Lucy hadn't consciously wanted to befriend Ezra. She just wanted to remove herself from the my-father's-better-than-yours war Nancy and Maura had started. It was bound to reach epic proportions before the lovebirds noticed and did something to diffuse the bombs. Plus, Lucy didn't think she could stand another mention of Lulu. She already had that song in her head—a continuous loop—*Skip to my loo my dar-lin'. Skip to my loo my dar-lin'. Skip to my loo my dar-lin'.* It just got faster and faster.

Ezra was thirty-five, which Lucy, at twenty, thought should have looked older than this man-boy appeared. His hair was black and hung in shiny loose mullet curls out of the back of his baseball cap. He walked in a droopy, round-shouldered lope. It didn't take long to see that Eli's adult children suffered from the kind of arrested adolescence that came with extreme wealth. She was going to be vacationing with overgrown teens. Lucy suddenly felt like the oldest one of the group.

Lucy and Ezra ended up at a beach bar for happy hour, which started at three in the afternoon and went until midnight.

Happy, indeed. The bar was still fairly empty as the two hoisted themselves onto well-worn bar stools.

"I've always loved the name Ezra," Lucy said, which was true, but alas was not much of a conversation starter. It was the best she could do. They'd covered the basics on the walk, and now she was searching for some common ground of the "oh, I've always hated my name" variety. Then she'd curse him with the skip-to-my-WC-my-darlin' song.

"They named me Ezra so Dad could pass his monogrammed stuff on to me." He smiled at the bartender, asked her name, started a tab, and they were off. Common ground: drinking!

Nearby, two tanned sea dogs were playing the ring swing game. It was a simple concept. There was a metal ring on a string and a hook on a post. Lucy watched the men play. They stood a few feet away from the hook then swung the ring toward it. Swing and hook, swing and hook, swing and a miss. "Ohh." Lucy sighed in defeat and she and Ezra both took a swig of their tequila drinks.

The ring reminded Lucy of the brass ring on the carousel in Asbury Park. It was where they used to go on rainy days at the Jersey shore. The carousel was inside a cavernous, round building that had elaborate murals both inside and out. When Lucy picked her horse, she only cared that it was within view of the sleeping giantess that was painted on the inside wall of the building—green, scaly, and dressed in rags. Her head rested on a red, heart-shaped pillow. Lucy had never seen a giantess. It was only after Lucy was older and she went back to Asbury Park that she realized the pillow was actually blood surrounding the giantess's head and the background was filled with retreating villagers, their torches and pitchforks raised in victory.

Kate, Lucy's best friend, had always joined them at the shore. They would lean out from their steeds and try to pull two rings at a turn to increase their chances of getting the brass one. Halfway around, they'd discard the plain steel rings into the reject bucket and position themselves to pull again.

When Lucy's mother would finish a chapter of her book, she'd sit back on the bench and call out, "This is the last ride, girls." Lucy and Kate knew if they got the brass ring on that turn, then they could convince her to stay. And if they stayed for one more ride, it would turn into one more chapter's worth of rides. More evidence that Lucy didn't mind her mother's obliviousness when it benefited her.

Y ou hold it like this," said Jimmy. Ezra called their "ring swing" teacher Jimmy Buff, because he looked like Jimmy Buffett, only bigger. Much bigger. Lucy wasn't sure if it was the drinks or a happy distraction from talking to her, but Ezra came alive with their new friends. He instantly made up nicknames for both men and spoke with authority about boats and obscure ports of call. He reminded Lucy of Jayne, who was the only young, active alcoholic she knew. Sullen one minute, charming the next. She was really beginning to like him.

Jimmy pinched the ring between his thumb and index finger. He handed it to Lucy first to try. It felt like a treasure, like fortune, pure luck.

Jimmy's opponent, "the Skipper," as Ezra dubbed him, loudly disagreed. "Don't hold it like that. I'll show you." Skipper leaned conspiratorially over Lucy. "Look at the gum on the floor and swing it over that, just to the right." He must have been a bowler before he took to the sea.

Lucy was slightly off balance by that point. Nevertheless, she positioned herself behind the white line painted on the bar floor. She held the ring taut at the end of the string. She closed one eye, looked at the gum on the floor, and swung the ring toward the hook. "Score one for the good guys," Lucy yelled.

Skipper gave her a high five. "We got a shark here," he said, walking to the hook to retrieve the ring for her. "And you go again." He swung the ring back to her.

Lucy hooked another, then threw an "air hook" that came right back to her. While Ezra took his turn, Lucy, Skipper, and Jimmy all did a shot.

On Lucy's next turn, Skipper stood behind her with one hand on her hip and the other guiding her arm. He turned to Ezra and said, "You don't mind, do ya, Gilligan?"

"Touché," Ezra said into his rum and Coke on hearing his new nickname. He and Jimmy were deep into what seemed to be a passionate conversation about drinking. It was serious business. Ezra looked up, then waved his hand to dismiss Skipper's question. "I only mind if you do that to me on my turn."

Normally Lucy would have protested this exchange, saying that even if she and Ezra were together he certainly wouldn't have claim on her body and on and on. But she was rethinking her feminist tendencies. Okay, she was abandoning them. She wasn't completely sure that they'd let her back in the club, but she was on vacation. And there was no such thing as a "party woman." Plus, she was not above a little ring toss coaching by a slightly paunchy but handsome yacht owner. No siree.

Ezra slid off his bar stool and lurched toward them. "Let's make this interesting."

"What are the stakes?" Skipper asked, taking the stool next to Jimmy.

"Drinks?" Lucy asked to no one in particular, concentrating on the hook, on the trajectory, on the gum spot on the floor, on not falling over.

"Too late," Skipper boomed. "All drinks are on me, for everyone!" There was a couple at the other side of the bar and they raised their glasses to him. "Happy anniversary," he called over.

Ezra brightened at the mention of free drinks. He pulled off his hat, looked at the front, BU, and said, "How about this? Dad's alma mater." He shrugged and added, "I have a few of them."

Lucy offered her cheap white shell necklace that she'd grabbed as an afterthought on her way out the door to catch her plane. She got one every year at the shore. This one was from the summer after her father died. "Lord of the Ring gets this," she said, pulling on it.

Jimmy and Skipper stayed out of it, and everyone was too drunk to notice.

Lucy beat Ezra, then Skipper beat Lucy, then Jimmy and Skipper battled.

"Has my sister been horrible to you?" Lucy closed the paper umbrella from her drink and placed it on the sticky bar with the others.

"I can't really blame her." Ezra was still drinking tequila and juice, quickly.

"Our parents seem to be happy together," Lucy reasoned. "So who are we to judge?"

Ezra took a thoughtful pull on his swizzle straw. "We're the ones . . ." he started, then looked flat at her. He poked his straw in her direction to punctuate his words. ". . . who can foresee the cost of this happiness."

"Which is?"

Ezra jammed the straw back through his ice-stuffed drink. "My mom's bound to find out. And then he'll have to choose." He spoke into his cup. "My mom would never tolerate it."

There was more. He went on. He liked to talk, as it turned out. There was something about Margaret being a nice lady and all. But Lucy was stuck at "My mom's bound to find out." And the giantess inside Lucy rolled over onto her lungs, her heart, her stomach. Her mother was the other woman. And without asking, Lucy was sure that her mother was fully aware of this. Of course she was.

Then Lucy saw the three of them in their new roles. Her mother as the other woman, her sister as her shrill defender, and Lucy as the nude child model who waggled her wide can into jolly strangers who bought her drinks.

"Lonely." That word her sister spoke lodged in her heart. It was the soft spot where the giantess lay her head. Lucy smoothed her hair and said, to no one in particular, "Let's make the best of it." And then Ezra said, "How about another game? Tiebreaker?" And Lucy nodded as if it would sort things out for them.

Crime Scene
(Photograph and Ink, 1994)

PHILADELPHIA LAWYER KILLS WIFE AND BABY.

Maybe you read about him in the paper? I wrote one of those articles. I first heard about the deaths on the radio. I usually had one on in every room of my small apartment, as if one radio wouldn't be enough. But I liked to keep them low, so I didn't disturb my neighbors. Their favorite thing to do at about midnight was yell, all together now, something that sounded like "You son-of-a-bitch-whore-motherfucker-what-were-you-thinking-I'll-hit-you-with-this-I-swear-I-will-SHUT-UP." I'm sure they appreciated my respectful, quiet consideration of their lifestyle choices.

I lived in southwest Philadelphia in a three-story apartment house. My microscopic, first-place-after-college had tabloid-thin walls, and the acrid smell of pot, cigarette, and probably, although I wouldn't know, crack smoke seeped into my bedroom late at night. I comforted myself with the fact that it was late-night partying and not all-day partying, which was much more dangerous. Really, statistics showed this to be true. I looked them up for a story, not because I was paranoid. Well, I might have been paranoid, but I could justify it. Either way, I chronicled crime, but I didn't invite it.

My kind of reporter didn't get paid much, so I painted the apartment myself. The small space I called my own was supposed to be deep rose, and ended up being blood orange red. In it, I had a twin bed with a salmon-colored comforter, which was supposed to complement my walls. Instead of living in a warm, womblike glow, I was living inside a bubble-gum wrapper. I managed to lug an old navy blue filing cabinet up the three floors without any help. It supported my little television in the office/bedroom. The nightstand held the most important books of the moment, the police scanner, the phone, and the alarm clock. And last, the card table held my computer. It was a tight fit.

The man I was dating didn't help me set up my apartment. Gary was pushing fifty and I was straight out of college, so we had different ideas about the meaning of do-it-yourself. For him, doing it himself meant calling someone and paying. Not doing it himself meant he told his assistant to call someone, which was usually how things went with him. He also introduced me to my first vibrator, so technically he didn't do *that* himself either. I wasn't complaining. As far as I could tell, this sort of sex play was the echo of the sexual revolution. This guy grew up with women who wanted sex, so when he experienced technical difficulties, he had a convenient understudy. Men who were adults in the 1970s really were more sensitive.

"I feel bad for people who don't experience sexual satisfaction," he said one night, possibly as a substitute for "That was great, baby."

"And they feel bad for you," I said.

"Yes, we're just a bunch of apes making obvious jokes and playing with ourselves." He scratched under his arm and grabbed his crotch.

"And killing each other and making more babies, as if passion were the barometer of all existence." I knew how to kill a good joke.

I met Gary outside a newspaper office after I'd bombed a job interview. He was the paper's publisher. He didn't believe in favoritism, so I still didn't get a job after we started sleeping together. I didn't believe in it either, so I appreciated his standards. He was also seeing other women. It was the favoritism thing again, I supposed.

Gary came to my place one night—made a special trip, just popped in. He told me that my apartment was enough to make him consider antidepressants. "We have to break up," he said. He didn't like giving up the sex. He truly hated the color of my comforter. He had to leave. The neighbor's secondhand smoke was so pungent it might be giving him lung cancer. "And, hey, let's stay friends."

There were some drawbacks to the sensitive man.

Coincidentally, the breakup came after he saw my beat-up hatchback with fast food wrappers and paper coffee cups tossed in the back. Usually I'd have suspected the forty extra pounds I'd been carrying around since college. Although I'd been carrying them since the first year of college, so I was beginning to think that they couldn't really be considered extra anymore. They just were. But he had a pretty soft physique himself. As I watched his immaculate BMW speed down my street, I concluded that he broke up with me because I was a slob. I thought I caught a glimpse of blond hair in the passenger seat. With that kind of investigative reporting, I should have been getting the big bucks.

Who cared about him or his little paper anyway? There

wasn't time with all of my scrambling. I was desperate for a staff position at *The Philadelphia Inquirer*. Now, I was weaned on *The New York Times*. But the *Inky* had comics, and every week I'd begged my parents to pick it up. And that was how I got hooked on Philadelphia. It was a small-town city. People weren't indifferent. Guys and gals still did good.

I listened to the sounds of my city as I typed a story on my computer, a 1989 Tyrannosaurus Mac. There was the scream of one police siren; a lilting "motherfucker-son-of-a-bitch"; rhythmic footsteps thumping up the bare wood stairs; the staccato knock of a fist on my neighbor's hollow door; and the wail of the child who once bit me when I offered her a fast food child's-meal toy that had been sitting in my car for months. The City of Brotherly Love. They must be talking about the Menendez brothers.

Since I didn't get an offer to cover real news, I opted to freelance for whoever would buy. I was hopeful. The trick was to write stories similar to the ones you intended to write for your career. No one would hire you for a crime beat if all of your clips were about *Hello, Dolly!* Gary told me this while I was writing about the arts in the suburbs.

I was glad to give it up. They were fluff features. It wasn't so easy to give up, though; that kind of writing could really snowball on you. I got calls and pleas and demands from directors and producers and publicists. An actor's mom called me once to interview her son—the kind of woman the term "pushy broad" was invented for. I said yes, of course. The story was about this precocious actor whose first gig was as the baby Jesus in a church production. That led to the principle role in *Waiting for Godot*. A very good play indeed. And he was already cast in

Equus, which began after *Godot* ended. No wonder, with a mother like that. The transcript of our interview read something like this:

> Jeffrey Tanner: Is that thing on?
>
> Lucy Venier: Yes. Just ignore it, though.
>
> JT: Testing. Testes. Testes. Do you know which president had the largest shoes?
>
> LV: No?
>
> JT: The one with the biggest feet.
>
> LV: Oh, a joke. I gotcha.
>
> JT: What bone will never have meat on it?
>
> LV: Mmmm. Hold on.
>
> JT: You're supposed to say you don't know.
>
> LV: I might, though.
>
> JT: It's a trombone.
>
> LV: Okay, I have one. What month has twenty-eight days?
>
> JT: February.
>
> LV: All of them.
>
> JT: *(Laughter)* I like that. What pets make the best music?
>
> LV: What?
>
> JT: Trumpets!

He told all of his instrument jokes. Then he went through his storehouse of knock-knock jokes. We were like the premier act on a weekday in the Poconos. I was the straight man. The best quote I got out of Henny Youngman was when he said the play was "really existential." I asked him what he meant, and he shrugged and said that was what his brother said. I figured that any interview after that would be "like the easiest dessert there is to make." A piece of cake.

I didn't mind the theater world so much. But I really had to watch what I wrote because theater people were vicious. One director screamed into my answering machine, his voice got high and shrill, then higher and shriller. At the end of the tirade I think he said he felt bad for the air I breathed. Or that he felt bad for the Arab breed. Either way, I was rattled. What if he became a city employee or a member of the Parking Authority? Clearly he wasn't cut out to direct. He was going to have to change careers sooner or later. I thought of the actor who, before the French Revolution, was booed off the stage in Lyon. During the Revolution, he went back and sent six thousand people to their death. Encore! It was safer to cover crime. I knew who was dangerous on that beat.

When the lawyer killed his wife for the stripper, I called Gary at work. We were friends. Right? Right.

"I'm chasing the story about the lawyer and the stripper."

"Lucy, you know why I broke up with you?"

"My car?"

"What? No. It's because you're depressing. All of this talk about chasing stories. Nobody says things like that. It's boring."

"Really? I was sure it was my car. So, you don't really want to be friends?"

"I am being your friend. I'm trying to get you to ease up."

"Tweeze what?"

"I know this job is all you care about, so I'll tell you that when I was a reporter I retraced the subject's steps."

"What do you mean 'all I care about'? I can talk about other things."

"Next time, Lucy. We'll have dinner next week. I'll call you."

Everyone was on this story. Strippers and prostitutes sold. Unless they were killed. Dead kids sold, so did dead white women and dead rich men. Forget dead people of any ethnicity, unless it was done by kids, white women, or rich men. I didn't tell people what to care about; well, in a way I did, which was why journalistic ethics was alive and well in universities. But I was just trying to sell stories to editors. They were just trying to sell papers. Ah, the vicious cycle that it is.

Anyway, the system had its own balance. There were the celebrity reporters like Barbara Walters who reported on anything they wanted to report on. There were salaried beat reporters who covered what they were told to cover and what they knew they'd soon be told to cover. And there were the people like me picking up the crumbs of big stories or cobbling something out of the less exciting leads. So, really I was lucky. Free reign was something only the top and bottom of the totem pole allowed for. At the bottom, I talked to everyone, and anyone, who wanted to talk about the murder.

Mike, a transient stationed at a southwest Philadelphia corner store, called the shooting "craziness, crazy, hey, what, are you calling me crazy?"

No, I kid. Mike didn't actually say that. He wasn't that lucid. He had a prophet complex, so he pitied me because I couldn't see what was coming. Sometimes he got confused about why he was condescending to me—he had slight, but permanent, brain damage from a severe beating he'd received. But Mike was a happy guy. He believed he was John the Baptist reincarnated. And he had an audience of faithful transients who also believed he was a prophet. Shelter encumbered his life's work and I was not to mention it again. He wanted me to know that the apocalypse was upon us, he appreciated my dollar, and I shouldn't eat mac and cheese from a box because it supported the evil empire. I told him I chronicled the apocalypse, he was welcome, and I was doing PR for the evil empire. He understood.

My corner store, where I chatted with Mike, was the sort of place that I suspected was a front for drug dealing. It only ever had a few grocery items, all with a layer of dust, which didn't deter me from buying the mac and cheese. In the back half of the store there was a weight bench and a glass trophy case with incense holders and wigs. Wigs?

The lack of good food in my neighborhood may have been why I ate a lot of fast food in my car. The reason I left the fast food wrappers in the foot wells in the back of my car was to discourage car thieves. Really. I did this on purpose. It was proven that to dissuade thieves you should either have nothing in your car or leave it a mess.

I drove to the suburbs to retrace the killer's steps. I stopped at a gas station near the murderer's house and talked to an attendant. The lawyer was from New Jersey, the only place left where someone was still required to pump gas for you. This attendant said he filled up the murderer's Diamante on a regular basis. "I see him all the time," he said. "Nice dresser. Manicure. Pays with a credit card."

I also went to the strip club. I was nervous to go there. I

liked to blend. I'd never been to a strip club and figured I wasn't their usual client. I consoled myself by reasoning that they'd probably seen a fair amount of traffic from nosy reporters since the story broke. But that could backfire on me. Maybe no one would talk to me and I'd get kicked out.

I sat in my car looking at the faded mural of a woman in a bikini on the side of the old warehouse-turned-strip club. I was frozen. Doubt was the reporter's worst enemy. I had to go into every situation believing in the human need to talk. They don't love it. They need it. We all do. It's cathartic. I opened my car door by rolling down the window and lifting the outside handle. I was going to get kicked out, I was sure of it. To eclipse the fatal doubt I was harboring, I threw my chest out and embraced the nothing-to-lose posture. If it didn't pan out, I still had the manicure thing. No one else had the manicure. I'd have to find the manicurist.

Probably more important than confidence was timing. I got there before clothes came off and the women, the stripper's coworkers, were friendly and open. "It's such a coincidence. We were just talking about him."

Indeed. Who would have guessed you'd have been talking about him at this very moment? Eerie.

I thought I hit the motherlode when one of the strippers agreed to call the victim for me. But the poor girl was still in shock. She wasn't quite as street-smart as some of the other strippers. *They* saw it coming. They knew his type, that stripper-stalking, spouse-slaying solicitor. No, I didn't write that for the paper, but I wanted to. That was the problem with reporting. Everyone was a type. Stereotyping was a survival tactic. I'd spent four years in college fiercely defending the exception to the rule, and here I was in my first job faced with rules without exceptions.

He was a cliché. She was a cliché. I was a cliché. The whole story was a cliché. She was the innocent-stripper stereotype who would become the streetwise-stripper stereotype in due time. Anyway, the lawyer told her he loved her. They had sex. She found out he was married with a kid on the way. She left him. He followed her around. So he was the stripper-stalker stereotype straight from a TV movie of the week. It turned out that the victim didn't give me anything quotable, but I quoted her anyway: Former girlfriend of prominent Philadelphia lawyer accused of fatally shooting his wife and infant late Friday night said, "He'd been stalking me for months."

When I submitted the story, my editor looked at it for three seconds then said, "Well-written. A real scoop." Or he might have said, "I'll read it, now scoot."

I got every newspaper I could get my hands on. There were stacks of papers in my apartment piled to the ceiling on either side of the card table where I worked. I cut out the stories I wanted to follow up on and put them in the roasting pan my mother gave me as a housewarming gift. A roasting pan? I could have used the ten bucks for lunch and more newspapers.

When funds were critically low, I devised a system to get free newspapers. First, I called Gary. "Sure, I put my papers out on Wednesday morning. Just come by and get them." That worked. We were friends. Or, at the very least, I was his favorite little garbage picker. I also went to the train station and scooped what papers I could from the benches. Occasionally, I would get one or two of the smaller, community papers that were mixed in with the city standards. One day I even stood near the exits for the trains coming from the suburbs and politely asked, "Are you through with that?" to all of the paper holders. It didn't go so well. Most of them veered or sneered. A small woman in a suit either told me to back away or called me a hack by day.

At dinner Gary told me I was trying too hard.

"I didn't know there was such a thing." I had just gotten out of college, where trying hard was rewarded.

"Let's talk about the menu for a second," Gary said. "How did you decide on what to have?"

"I looked at the choices," I said. "I narrowed them down, and then I went with the cheapest one."

"What?" Gary looked at me like he'd just sniffed his old gym socks, which I'd seen him do. "Why the cheapest?"

"When someone is treating, I feel rude ordering something expensive."

"You're worse off than I thought." He shook his head as if to rattle the idea into his brain. "Here's how I ordered. I was hungry for steak. I opened the menu, looked at the beef choices, and picked the one I thought would be the best."

"And doing that means you'd make a better reporter than I would?"

"I went into it with a purpose. It just makes life easier."

"Okay, so why did you ask me to dinner?" I said. "What's the purpose here?"

"Sex."

"But you broke up with me."

Gary shrugged.

"I guess we'll go to your house then," I said.

I tried to approach each new story with a purpose. Crime features needed a hook. I looked for opportunities to find the "model citizen" or the "happy ending." Not easy. My best attempt came from a police blurb about "two held on rape charges."

Ron, the hero, was a grad student at Penn in the psych program. He also worked a day job with the severely mentally ill. I met him at a Penn hangout, Smokey Joe's. It was early and the bar was cold and smelled like dirty ice. The night two were held on rape charges, Ron and a female friend drank a few mugs of lager, then he walked her home. He doubled back and headed to his apartment.

Shortly after midnight on a Friday night in April, Ron Mackenzie detained two rapists attacking a woman just west of Penn's campus.

We walked together through the streets at dusk in a neighborhood where big shade trees arced over the streets and Philadelphia felt safe. There were only small indications of possible danger, such as bars on first-floor windows and little red lights blinking inside cars to indicate armed alarms. I looked at the FOR RENT signs and scribbled down locations while taking notes. *Ron: Tall, handsome, long strides, sneakers—Apt: Pine & 40th, looks cute, porch.*

While we retraced together, Ron told me about his job. I found myself wanting him to be interested in me. But it got so I couldn't tell if people were charming for my benefit or for the article.

"I like the schizophrenics the best," Ron said. "They're usually smart and when they talk, they incorporate outside influences into their stories."

"You mean like how you work phone ringing into your dream?" I asked.

"Only with a schizophrenic, it's considered delusional. One of my clients—I shouldn't tell you this."

"Off the record," I said, but kept taking notes. It was a habit.

"Well, she believed that when the phone rang," Ron looked from side to side then whispered, "the FBI was remotely installing a wiretap."

"Can the FBI do that?" I whispered back.

"Oh, Lucy," he said dramatically, shaking his head in disbelief, "anything's possible, especially where the FBI is concerned. In fact, schizophrenics would probably be an asset to the FBI."

"They could head up a special paranoia task force," I said while I scribbled *smart, cute, fast walker, 3rd floor, Spruce & 41st.* Of course I couldn't use any of this for the story, but I always kept writing. It kept interviewees talking and focused. It was a subtle reminder that everything they said was being recorded. I found that when I stopped writing, they stopped talking. And I definitely wanted Ron to keep talking.

As we rounded the corner, Ron's body went rigid. We were at the scene.

Walking to his apartment, Mackenzie approached the scene. Behind a metal trash receptacle, amidst litter and crushed glass, he saw the assailants.

The woman's eyes locked on Ron's. He knew there was no

time to get help. One of the men charged him. Ron, with his "poor man's karate," put the guy on his knees and dislocated one of them in the process. The other man then charged him with a knife. Ron took him down as well, disarmed him, then sat on his chest and banged his head into the ground whenever he tried to move.

"I'm not a ninja or anything. It's a simple move. Plus, they were big and clumsy." He shrugged. My editor cut that quote. I liked it. I thought it would be an incentive for people to take self-defense classes. I also thought it showed Ron's humility. But the story isn't mine once I sell it. Ron went to the hospital with the woman, and he said that once he was in the squad car he wished he'd peed at the bar. See, charming for my benefit.

I sent the story to my mother, who called and tried to convince me to do something else with my life. "Why are you even doing this? I thought you were going to get a job in advertising? Something creative?"

"I like it," I said, doubting my words. "And you'll like it when I bring Walter Cronkite to the house for dinner."

"I could sell him art." My mother brightened. Since my father died she had thrown herself into her career. She was an art broker and didn't even read stories about crime, unless it was about an art thief. And how often did that happen?

"Yes, I've heard he's in the market for a good art dealer," I said.

"Couldn't you at least write funny stories like Dave Barry? No one ever dies in his stories."

"Yes, but people *have* died laughing."

"Not literally."

"Philemon did," I said. "He was a comedy writer and, ironically enough, he died laughing."

"He may have been laughing, but he probably choked on something," she said. "A peach pit, maybe."

"It's not an expression for nothing."

"Just be careful. I don't like this one bit."

Ron's story sort of freaked me out. After I wrote it, the police blotter seemed to be filled with rape stories. RISE IN REPORTED RAPES. DREXEL WOMAN RAPED AT FRAT PARTY. RAPE KITS TAMPERED WITH AT LOCAL HOSPITAL. Suspected rapists, serial rapists, convicted rapists. What was I doing?

Find a purpose, retrace steps. Gary's advice was my new mantra. Or maybe it was my first mantra. Either way, I started to see what he meant. I *was* depressing. In my stifling bedroom, sitting on my twin bed listening to the screech of the police scanner in a secondhand-smoke haze, I had a crazy thought that I might be able to effect a *decline* in reported rapes. Why not? I was renewed, and dug in with that thought in mind.

I found Jeremy Carter, a spokesperson for an awareness group called Safe Kidz. Jeremy and other victims of violent crimes gave programs on personal safety to schoolkids. He was an eighth grader when a man had pulled him into an arcade bathroom and raped him. Jeremy described him as "that sleazy guy who always hung around." The perpetrator had given Jeremy quarters and smokes here and there. Jeremy was a pretty boy. Pageboy blond hair. Delicate features. He said that his "look" is one that's seen a lot in victims of pedophilia. I didn't believe him.

"Violent criminals don't discriminate by age, race, or social class. They are predators, and their victims are anyone they can lure away from the safety of the public eye."

I went to Jeremy's apartment in a high-security complex in Roslyn—guard, gates, buzzers, cameras. He invited me in, didn't frisk me, and had me play with his pet rat while he got us some iced tea. The rat shit on my pants, which were brown, so I couldn't really see the stain, and I wasn't going to tell him. I was going to be amiable. Maybe he'd tell me something interesting if he thought we were friends. And these were the things I did for a story. When I couldn't sell it, I called Gary to pretend I wasn't asking for help.

"I hate to encourage you," Gary said with a sigh. "Why don't you try the teen tabloids?"

"But I like to encourage *you*," I said, cheered by the suggestion. *Teen tabloids, of course.*

"You're not cynical enough. Which means you'll become cynical."

"Do you have a name for me at a teen tabloid?"

"I'll have my assistant call you with one. You want to come over tonight?"

"I don't know." I twirled my hair around my finger. "Okay."

I sold the story to Gary's contact. It ran with a sidebar piece I also wrote about a high school girl who was raped at a party. "Karen" was passed out for most of it. I concentrated on the part alcohol played in putting her in a dangerous situation. PARTYING SAFELY, the splashy red headline read. I gave the paper to my neighbor who had teenagers.

"Hey, Lucy," her daughter Janina called from the stoop as I

lifted the day's haul of papers out of my backseat, "read your story."

"Oh, yeah, thanks," I said.

"That's a load of crap, though," her sister Lauren said.

"Which part?" I didn't doubt that anything I wrote for teens would be considered a load of crap.

"Drinking doesn't lead to rape," Lauren said.

"Mostly rapes happen when moms get new boyfriends," Janina clarified.

"I'll look into it for next time," I said, knowing that Lauren and Janina were probably closer to reality than I was.

"You wanna talk to my friends who were almost raped?" Janina opened the door for me.

"Sure," I said. "I'll leave my number with your mom so they can call me."

I met Janina's friends at the lunch place on my corner that had fried food in chafing dishes under red lights. The girls told me they were passengers in a car going to an after-hours party. From the backseat they discovered that they were being driven to the suburbs to be raped. How did they know? The two men in the front seat casually chatted about it.

"What did they say?" I asked.

" 'We're gonna stick it to them,' " the one girl told me.

" 'You bitches better get ready,' " the other girl added. " 'We're gonna fuck you and you'll like it,' " she said even louder.

I looked around to see if anyone heard that last comment. Of course someone did. The owners, the counter guy, and the mother and daughter behind us. Yep, they were all looking at us. Great, I guess that made me a submissive lesbian with a penchant for threesomes with teenagers. Didn't every neighborhood have one of those?

"One of the guys," girl one continued with a mouthful of french fries, "the one in the back with us, wasn't into it."

Apparently, at a stoplight he reached over the girls, opened the door, and shoved them out. He got out with them, and they all ran to the nearest Denny's and ate pancakes and smoked cigarettes. The girls knew the backseat guy, and he knew the front-seat guys. And kids, that's how you can find yourself in a car going to a late-night party with rapists who like to talk about their pending crime on streets with traffic lights and stop signs.

That story didn't make it to print. It was just too unlikely. It could have happened. I'm not saying it didn't. It's just that people, especially teenagers, made stuff up. One thing I came to realize was that people wanted to be famous. I didn't know why they thought I could help. Maybe they would have had better luck if they slept with their mothers' boyfriends. Jerry or Ricki would be glad to have them fight about it.

Janina knocked on my door at nine on a Saturday night. "You gonna print that story about my friends or what?"

"I don't think so." I stood in the doorway with a clipping in one hand and scissors in the other.

"Why not?" She put her hand on her hip.

"No one believed it. I couldn't get any editor to buy it."

"You know, you just ain't trying hard enough. That's bullshit."

"Okay, Janina. Well, see ya then." I shut the door and she pounded on it again. I opened it up to see her stomping down the hall. "Did you knock?" I asked.

"No, bitch, I punched your door and now my fucking hand hurts."

I went to Gary's. His condo was clean and modern and big and beautiful. He had just gotten in from playing handball or squash or some such game when I arrived. He jumped in the shower and I sat on the closed toilet lid and yelled to him over the noise of the spray.

"You say I'm trying too hard, some teenager tells me I'm not trying hard enough."

"Lucy, you have to let criticism roll off of you. Like water off my bald spot." He thought he was hilarious.

"When you broke up with me, why did you make me think it was because of my apartment?" I asked.

"I can't make you think anything," he said. "But I do want you to move out of there."

"I can hardly believe anything you say."

He turned off the water and stepped out of the shower. I threw him a towel and he dried himself with a rub-a-dub-dub flourish that annoyed me.

"You just like yourself so damned much. It's irritating."

"I knew it," he said. "The cynicism would start creeping in." He wagged his finger at me.

"Are we going back out with each other or what?" I demanded.

"Well, we go to dinner and have sex. And I don't care that you sit on the toilet and talk to me when I'm in the shower." He looked in the mirror and considered a mole on his collarbone. "But, officially I'm only dating Carol."

"Are you kidding me? You have a girlfriend who doesn't know you date other women?"

"She wouldn't understand."

"I don't understand," I yelled. "Are you completely insane? Do you even own this house or are you some sort of criminal who rooks people into believing you're normal?"

Gary sighed. "I knew I'd lose you to the profession. Now with the conspiracy theories, thinking everyone is a criminal. Lucy, you've got to get out of the business."

"Lose me?" I threw my hands in the air. "You never even tried to win me."

"It's not lose and win, Lucy," he said, shaking his head. "It's lost and found."

I stormed up the stairs to my apartment. Janina was in the hall in her standard position, with her hand on her hip. "My friends are pissed."

"Yeah," I yelled without stopping, "next time, tell them to get themselves killed and then I'll be able to sell their story."

I slammed my door and kicked over a stack of papers. I threw myself on the bed and then reached over to my answering machine and pressed *play*. I got a call from a girl from Germantown who had gotten my contact information from the teen tabloid article. I called her back. I was fired up. I was ready for the best story of my life. I went back out to meet her.

The neighborhood was primarily clapboard row houses and burned-out shells. There were also a good number of dirt lots where the shells had been demolished and never replaced. We met at the park where a man who was masturbating and exposing himself had chased her.

"I was just minding my business."

"What time of day was it?" I asked.

"Midnight, one."

Of course, the park, at night, in the city, minding her own business. Quite naturally. I didn't know why I suggested we meet. I might have just wanted to get away from my apartment and Janina, who was probably plotting some sort of revenge. And Gary had really steamed me. The girl continued, and I didn't even bother taking notes. She went to the police station to file a report and was struck with a fit of the giggles.

"I didn't mean to laugh. It was just a nervous response. Some people laugh when they shouldn't. I didn't think it was funny. And then the police f'in' yelled at me."

Her innocence had been corrupted and then she was treated like a child by the police. The irony. She was angry. She wanted satisfaction. It was too bad she was also going to be disenchanted by the press, who didn't care about her petty humiliation. When she called to find out when the story would run, I told her that the editor couldn't find room for it and didn't like to publish anything too long after an incident. I think she called me an f'in' bitch while I was hanging up, which made me chuckle, the genuine kind. When she started calling me every night to call me an f'in' bitch, I started laughing the nervous kind of laugh.

It was like the theater thing. I couldn't get away from these teen girls. I didn't even like teen girls when I was one. Well, that wasn't quite true. There was Kate, my best friend, whom

I hadn't spoken to in three weeks. The worst trouble she and I ever got in was when we were caught drinking by her mother. But maybe my memory was bad. Maybe I was revising our history to distance myself from these people I was starting to hate, starting to blame.

I called Kate. We didn't see each other much even though she was living in Ardmore, which was close enough to Philadelphia to make dinner together a possibility and far enough away to make it inconvenient. We were finding life after college to be exhausting and expensive. Plus, she had started dating Scott, which made scheduling harder. Scott worked at the pizza shop in her development and it seemed to be the kind of romance that was more about easy takeout than anything else.

"Here's a crazy story for you. Scott got Maced last night," she said.

"Did you say wasted?" I asked.

"No," she said. "Mace, you know, like tear gas. Pepper spray. He was leaving work and had a cheesesteak tucked under his arm. He turned a corner and startled some woman who Maced him."

"It gets so good people can't run through the streets with cheesesteaks anymore," I said.

"To top it off," she added, "as he's lying on the ground choking and gagging with his eyes slammed shut, he hears her clip-clopping away yelling 'fire, fire.'"

"Nothing gathers a crowd better than a fire."

"They come with marshmallows," she said.

I told Gary the story when he called to apologize. He said he didn't believe Scott was innocent. He said he probably got what he deserved. I made a note in my day planner to call Kate and let her know.

"Did you break up with me when you stormed out the other night?" he asked.

"Are you severely unbalanced, or are you just trying to give me something else to talk to you about besides work?"

"You always talk about work. You started the conversation with the story about your friend's boyfriend who got Maced."

"That's not a work story," I said.

"Yes, Lucy, I want you to talk about me and if you don't, I'll pick a fight to bring the focus back to me."

"I don't know how I could have broken up with you if you're officially only dating Carol."

"That was a joke. How was I supposed to know you'd go crazy about that? You never cared before that I dated other women."

"Because I thought they knew."

"What's the difference?"

"It's the female code."

"There's no such thing."

"Maybe when you were growing up there was no such thing."

"Oh no," he said, "the trump card. Our age difference."

"You are enraging me."

"Sex is good for rage."

"I'm not talking to you for a week," I said. "Call me then."

I went back to the police blotter, the scanner, the neighborhood papers. MORE WEAPONS IN CITY SCHOOLS. Janina was leaving hate mail under my door. SHOTS FIRED. Janina's mother was snubbing me. WOMAN STABBED. Someone keyed my car. FRANTIC 911 CALL UNANSWERED. I was losing my enthusiasm. VIOLENT CRIMES ON RISE. The crank calls were coming in waves, with high tide on weekend nights. VICTIM TREATED FOR BROKEN NOSE. I considered following up on the man who said, "I hit him because I didn't want to get dirty wrestling around," but crawled into bed, unplugged the phone, turned off the scanner, and pulled my salmon-colored blanket over me.

When I woke to the thumping bass from a car outside I turned on my little TV and watched news programs. I started to think the anchors were all lunatics. They had to be. I needed a new job.

I found the Web site of a company based in New York that wanted "gritty urban stories (but nothing too heavy) about brushes with danger." I had stories like that. The site sold self-protection devices—security systems, pepper spray, and deadbolts mostly. And the original purpose reared its head—to effect a decline in rapes.

I revamped the Mace story—made it pepper spray, told it from her point of view, made the cheesesteak a weapon. And they bought it. I was a Web content writer.

When Gary called, I told him I had a new job. He told me he broke up with Carol.

"Why?" I asked.

"I'm really starting to like you."

"Gary, we've been sleeping together for months and you're starting to like me?"

I was still getting harassing phone calls, but I didn't want to change my number in case an editor wanted to offer me a staff position. I didn't expect it to happen, but I was a little disappointed that none of them ever called to find out what happened to me. I could have been killed researching a story and no one would have even reported on it.

I couldn't complain, though. Mr. Safety was an excellent boss. I never saw him. He sent me money. He never fact-checked. He never called me. Or maybe he called when the phone was off the hook. It was possible. More likely he was busy running his personalized seminars on safety. His Web site had links from questions like:

"What do you do if your house is being robbed?"
"What do you do if you're mugged on the street?"
"What do you do if you get abducted in a car?"

I knew the answer to that. You wait until the guy in the backseat with you reaches over, opens the door, and shoves you out. I clicked the link to see if he could use that story. As it turned out, it was hard to find people who had been abducted in a car and lived to tell about it. Mr. Safety said that if you found yourself in a car with an assailant, you were as good as dead. Mr. Safety was not an alarmist. That aside, here was the drill. First, put on your seat belt.

"Do you mind? I always wear my seat belt, makes me feel safer."

"Oh, not at all. I'm going to slit your throat and leave you for dead pretty soon, so consider it a last request."

Once your seatbelt is on, grab the wheel, yank as hard as you can, and crash the car. Preferably into a police station. But it doesn't matter where. It's your best way out.

———

Gary sent me flowers. Or, more likely, Gary told his assistant to send me flowers. Lauren asked who they were from and I told her that my father died and she should tell Janina and her mom to be nice to me because I was grieving. My father was already dead, so I could say that about him. I didn't know why I cared about Janina and her mother and the other people in the apartment building who were ignoring me. But it was getting so I couldn't even get a polite nod from anyone.

Gary and I went to dinner. I ordered seafood because I was hungry for it. He was allergic to seafood so we couldn't share.

"How's the new job?"

"Well, I got an e-mail from a woman who bought self-defense tapes because she was beat up at a mini–grand prix racetrack after she clipped some woman's go-cart."

"Maybe she should have gotten defensive-driving tapes instead," he said, then laughed at his own joke.

"And I downloaded a wedding picture of a guy with bruises on his face from a bar fight he got into at his bachelor party."

"You know I didn't mean to say I was starting to like you."

"You're not starting to like me?"

"I've always liked you. I left Carol for you."

"Do you think you could get her back?" I asked.

"Yes," he said with just the littlest hesitation.

"Why didn't you ever help me get a job as a reporter?"

"I thought you wanted to do it on your own," he said.

"There's no such thing, and you know it."

"It's creepy," he said. "It's like directors casting their girl-friends in roles."

"It's only creepy," I said, "if the girlfriends are bad actresses."

"Okay, I didn't think you were cut out for it. You're not the type," he said with a shrug. "I've been around long enough to know that your type makes a terrible reporter."

"I wanted to be a *journalist*."

"See, Lucy, only bad reporters insist on being called journalists."

"You should probably try to get Carol back."

"I'm not doing that."

"I think I'm going to resent you for a while, until I get a job that I like."

"You don't like the content writing thing?"

"No, now it's just the violence without the bylines."

"I know an advertising firm that's looking for people. Did you tell me you were interested in creative?"

"If I don't like it, I might still hold a grudge."

So, with some of the money Mr. Safety paid me, I ordered my own can of pepper spray. Then I submitted my last article before I started my new job. The story was about a woman who moved out of her red apartment where people fought nightly and smoked crack. She moved to a safer neighborhood. Studies showed it was a good idea. She looked them up. She thought that was the best way to avoid the violence of her everyday life. To move away from it.

Study in White
(Casein on Canvas, 1995)

Lucy was finally making some money at her first "real job" in advertising. She had a 401K and everything. So, she splurged on a rental share on Long Beach Island. She felt like a grown-up having her own place at "the shore"—which is the accepted name for the New Jersey coastline—while the rest of the coast-line is just "the beach." Never mind that she was sharing it with sixteen other people.

The place slept eleven, uncomfortably, but the bed Lucy laid claim to was all hers on alternate weekends. In retrospect, it hadn't been the wisest use of her vacation fund. She could have stayed at her mother's place in Avalon for free or with the man she fought with, which approximated dating. But the shore life was all about the people, and her most fun single friends talked her into LBI that summer.

Kate had advised her strongly against it. "You don't even like that scene anymore."

"That's ridiculous, I love the whole movie—*Lucy Does Long Beach*."

"More like *Sardined Sin-Gals*," Kate countered.

Kate was newly married, which meant she had also recently finished a year of painstaking insensitivity training. Some called it "Wedding Planning—the Happiest Time of Your Life." Lucy tagged it "the most self-centered time of your life." It gave birth to Kate's annoying new personal habit. "I told you so" became an acceptable and oft-used response in almost any situation. However, Lucy knew that even though Kate always had the right answer and she almost always disapproved of Lucy's choices, she secretly liked vicariously living the single life. Who wouldn't? It was fun.

It's my weekend with the bed," Lucy told Kate from her cell phone in Friday-evening Atlantic City Expressway traffic.

"Do you think the bed likes you or the other girl better?" Kate asked. Lucy heard the scrape of metal on concrete and could tell that Kate was settling into her "talking chair" in the breezeway of her new house in the suburbs.

"Actually, on alternate weekends, the bed comforts Ben," Lucy said. "I think it likes him better."

"Because his last name is Dover?"

"Everyone likes Ben better," Lucy complained for Kate's benefit. "The full-timers are genuinely disappointed when I arrive. 'Oh, that's right, Ben's not coming this week.' And then all weekend I have to hear, 'Ben did this, Ben threw a party, Ben's so funny, Ben, Ben, Ben.' "

"Why did you get that place to begin with?" Kate asked.

Lucy braced herself for it.

"I told you it was a bad idea."

"Yes," Lucy sighed, "you told me so."

But Lucy was determined to usurp Ben's reign. She would be the cult of personality. She wasn't sure how to do this, but she began with a stocked trunk of booze and mixers. It was a start. Maybe it would lead to drugs—pot, cocaine, crack, crystal meth, pills, heroin. She'd be the jovial supplier spreading dependency wherever she went. People would want her around way more than Ben.

The downside, of course, was that they'd look back on the Ben days with nostalgia. The wonder weekends when they weren't consumed with madness. It was pointless to contemplate. Lucy didn't have the first idea how to buy drugs except for the deadliest of them all, alcohol and cigarettes. The few times she did try to buy dime bags of pot in college she was overcharged or flat out ripped off. She was as likely to become a benevolent drug supplier as she was to inspire Ben-like admiration.

Lucy opened the car window as she neared the shore. The air was thick and salty. It whipped her hair into springy southward curls. For all of her complaints to Kate about the "Ben situation," Lucy did love her two weekends a month at the shore. Mostly because two of her housemates, Tami and Trina, had become the best new friends she'd made since college.

Even Kate liked Tami and Trina, although she maintained a mock rivalry with them. Once, at their weekly lunch, when Lucy complained about the shore, Kate said, "It couldn't have been that bad. Your secret best friends were there, right?"

"Yes, they were," Lucy said. "But they badgered me all weekend to slip poison into your drink this week." Lucy shrugged, then raised her glass solemnly. "Cheers, good ol' buddy."

At first, Trina and Tami reminded Lucy of those catty schoolgirls who tried to pit their friends against each other. Lucy half expected to get a note from Trina that said, "You're my best friend, just don't tell Tami."

As was generally the case with the interminably cute (Tami) and the breathtakingly beautiful (Trina), they had been misjudged (manipulative and bitchy). They turned out to be Lucy's only reason for enduring Ben's Fan Club, which was what the rest of the housemates had been deemed by Lucy and the Two Ts. This was the name they gave themselves—it was their fantasy all-female beach band that they convinced drunk men they were in.

Trina and Tami were already mixing drinks when Lucy arrived loaded down with a box of liquor. Tami squealed, as Tami was apt to do.

Trina stopped what she was doing and took the box from Lucy's arms.

"Do you need help with your stuff—how was your week—that boy from two weekends ago keeps calling me, I'm dying—your hair is wild and fabulous—what do you want to drink?"

Tami mixed daiquiris for everyone in the house. Two housemates did yoga in the living room and sipped their drinks between poses. The screen door banged shut in an endless stream of roommates, friends, and the occasional random person off the street who thought he knew someone who lived here but couldn't remember her name.

Lucy and the Two Ts, with a jump start on happy hour, went to their room to primp. Lucy had always liked primping. All through high school she and Kate were roughly the same size, so they swapped clothes. Since then, Lucy had packed on the curves and Kate had discovered aerobics, so they'd stretched the spectrum of their builds considerably. Lucy kept to her own wardrobe these days. Tami and Trina exchanged short shorts and tank tops. Lucy endlessly scrutinized her body, confronted by the living, breathing reality of the two most popular female ideals. Tami was short, perky, and compact. Trina was tall, lanky, and model-like. Neither had to shave above the knee on a regular basis. Neither had a stomach to suck in. Both had blond, silky hair that looked good without a fuss.

Lucy felt like their unruly doll. They tamed her frizz with their curling irons. They tied wraps around her waist. They squeezed her into tank tops that covered her belly and bra straps. They openly marveled at Lucy.

"What I wouldn't do for boobs like yours." Tami sighed.

"Pendulous?" Lucy asked, adjusting. "Sloppy?"

"What you'll do is go under the knife," Trina said, dusting her cheeks with bronzer.

"And your hair, you can do anything with it." Tami jumped on the bed behind Lucy and twisted her hair this way and that. "I can put it all up in one bobby pin."

"Ah, yes," Lucy said, "all the runway models envy the wiry-haired for that very reason."

"It would be so sexy to have hips," Trina said, turning her fat-free body this way and that in front of the mirror.

Lucy felt like a fertility statue. She was the Venus of Willendorf, who, Lucy was pretty sure, had at least a dozen babies before she posed for that sculpture—big boobs, round belly, wide hips, thick thighs. But Tami and Trina wore Lucy down, and she eventually let their admiration cheer her. For the most part, Lucy had always liked her body. What was she insecure about? She threw the women's magazines onto Tami's bed and vowed not to look at them anymore, no matter what promises they made on their covers about getting better orgasms or thinner thighs.

At the bar, Lucy was the ugly cousin again. Men swarmed the blondes. They sent them drinks. They pulled up chairs. One creative suitor dropped to the floor and did an impressive, albeit outdated, break dance move. Lucy was woman to their girl. Stepsister to their Cinderella. Dollar draft to their wine spritzer. The parade of men nodded politely to Lucy and then stopped in front of Tami and Trina's grandstand to salute and perform.

Lucy had never been the ugly one, or the funny one, or the bitchy guard men had to get past to get to the princesses. In fact, through most of her flirting life, Lucy had Kate standing guard. It had nothing to do with the hierarchy of looks, though, just Kate's conviction that Lucy was a menace to herself. It made Lucy feel special.

Here she felt like a sketch that had been poorly erased—a fuzzy mess on ragged paper—almost invisible. Lucy guessed that her insecurity was partly because of her position in the house—not just second-class citizen to Ben, but the reason Ben was missing. And then there was her appearance next to Barbie and Kewpie. Don't forget all of the women's magazines lying around the house. They told her how to be a slut and how to catch a man, as if these things were desirable and similar. She felt woefully behind the game because she hadn't considered the virtues of the smoky eye and the tongue stud.

Her sense of humor felt nasty and transparent. Her sweetness seemed disingenuous and desperate. Her beauty was cartoonish in the world of the fit and perky. Fluffy hair, big boobs, ample hips. She still felt smart and creative, which only made matters worse. It was a rare occasion when knowledge of René Magritte came in handy at the shore. If only she'd boned up on the finer points of bikini buying and tittering.

Lucy knew why those birds of a feather flocked as they did. Tweetie, the Swan, and Big Bird. That's what she wanted to rename the band.

She played along, though, flirting as if the men talking to her weren't just trying to get closer to the goddesses. But by the middle of the summer, something in Lucy snapped, and she became the worst version of herself—cruel and intimidating.

"Hey, what's your name?" a paunchy man yelled much too loudly directly into Lucy's ear over the din of the band.

Lucy watched him stare at Trina.

"Nunya," Lucy said, without raising her voice to talk at bar volume.

He heard her anyway, proving Lucy's point that you didn't have to cause hearing damage to talk in bars. "That's interesting," he said and looked at Lucy, possibly to see if she was of some exotic nationality. "What is it?"

"It's short for Nunya Business," Lucy said with a terrific smile and a tilt of her head.

"Oh, you got me there," he said. "You're a pistol."

"No, I'm sure I'm not." Lucy kept her eyes on the band. She was fascinated with the ham-handed lead guitarist who was successfully mucking up every song. She shouldn't have been mean to the paunchy man. He seemed friendly enough.

"Are they friends of yours?" he asked, jerking his head toward the Two Ts.

"You are chatty, aren't you?" Lucy said, before she realized he was talking about the band members.

"I used to be in a band."

"Polka?"

"Polka, she says. No. But I can polka. Wanna see?"

And Lucy finally knew what it was like to have the grand-stand seat at the shore. In fact, she became the ice queen of the grandstand. She didn't mind the attention at all. So maybe she was a little cranky. It was working for her. Maybe all of the other women were reading the same women's magazines that said you should toss your hair and say something about liking to give oral and men were getting sick of the same old line. It was the latest version of "Don't I know you?"

Instead, Lucy doled out backhanded compliments—when she was feeling generous. Otherwise, she spewed every sharp-tongued comment that popped into her head.

"You wouldn't like a date, would you, beautiful?" said an unsuspecting suitor.

"In fact," Lucy said sweetly, "it tops the list of things I wouldn't like."

"You're just magnificent. Howja get so beautiful?"

"I got your portion."

"You wanna have a good time?"

"Yeah, I do," Lucy said. "So, move along."

The phone started ringing at the shore house for Lucy and she noticed that this somehow gave her new status with the others. It was ludicrous. She wanted to write her own women's magazine. "How to Win Friends and Get Dates Without Being a Total Tart" would be her lead article. The housemates begged

Lucy to come down on her off weeks. They thought she was hilarious, sassy, a riot. They thought she was kidding.

Because Lucy deigned to have drinks with some of the more interesting men she insulted, Lucy ventured to the shore on her off weekends. By then Tami and Trina had both coupled up with men who, conveniently, were housemates. Even better, their house was big and beautiful with a spectacular view of the bay. Lucy stayed with them when Ben was lording over the bed, and she and the Two Ts triple-dated. They had cookouts and went boating. At night they played card games and got drunk on good beer.

Lucy, Tami, and Trina were having a blast. It didn't necessarily matter whether they were in their tatty shore share or the rambling bayside house, with men or without. But the bayside house had a hot tub. And the bayside house meant that Lucy didn't have to meet Ben. Okay, so she was still a little jealous of him. She didn't even know why. The housemates had formed a fan club for Lucy and she suspected it had more members than Ben's. It wasn't all she'd imagined it would be, though. In fact, she decided that her housemates lacked any interior identity. So, in a way, she and Ben were the same. Just figureheads for the amorphous swing voters. Lucy comforted herself with this thought because it was inevitable that she was going to have to meet Ben. The roommates wanted their two favorite people around. Good-guy Ben and wry-witted Lucy. Lucy pretended not to notice, but there had been a campaign afoot for weeks.

It was unavoidable. Ben met them at the bar on one of Lucy's weekends with the bed. He entered and clapped people on the back as he approached Lucy's table.

"Ben's here. Lucy, that's Ben. Look, everyone, Ben, Ben, Ben."

Fickle housemates, Lucy brooded. No one noticed. She usually kept a pretty straight face at the bar—it encouraged men to ask the original, "Hey, aren't you having a good time?" ("I was," she said to this.)

People stood. Ben hugged and shook hands. Then he pulled up a chair next to Lucy.

"I've heard so much about you," Ben said, then leaned closer and mock-whispered, "from those gossipy dust mites in our mattress."

"I told them not to talk about me to you," Lucy said without making eye contact.

"Well, they didn't mention how beautiful you are."

"You don't have to use that line on me," Lucy said, trying to be flip. "I'm already sleeping in your bed tonight."

And there it was. She used a line. On Ben. She was mortified. She might as well have flicked her hair back and asked him if he thought she should get a tongue stud. But he was a Dean Martin. Okay, maybe a slightly dorky Dean Martin. She shook it off. He was a Jerry Lewis. He was just a Jerry Lewis. She would not join the fan club. She would not. But she liked Jerry Lewis.

So, Lucy did her best to disregard Ben, which was not easy. He told stories, engaging the whole group with his warm brown bedroom eyes that always seemed to catch Lucy's whenever she tried to sneak a peek at him. He bought trays of shots from the roving waitresses and overtipped them as a matter of course. He danced with their housemate Mia when she squealed, "They're playing 'Brick House.'"

After Ben left the table to dance, the rest of the group dispersed to his and her normal bar activities. A foursome went to the dartboard to resume an ongoing feud. A couple of the men trolled the bar for the women they were pretending to ignore. Lucy stood with a few of the women in their standard position—produce in the marriage mart, aisle three. Lucy was talking to a forty-something lifeguard when Ben got off the dance floor. She had just said to him, "Oh, so you're a *lifer*-guard?" He didn't get it. He cocked his head to the side in the universal sign for "Huh?"

Ben sidled up and put his arm around Lucy. "So, did you close the window above our bed before you came out? It might rain," he said.

"Our bed" successfully scared off the lifer-guard, and Lucy tried to be livid. She wasn't ready to admit to herself that she liked Ben's attention. Besides, it was only right to take offense.

"That was my dad," she said.

"That was why he was staring at your breasts, I suppose."

"He has dementia. He forgot I was his kid." Lucy wanted to give Ben a hard time, so she tried unsuccessfully to suppress a smile.

"Sadly, what he doesn't know is that you sleep in *our* bed without me," Ben said.

"Sad for him or for you?" Lucy asked.

"Oh, I don't give a crap about him," Ben said. "Unless, of course, he really is your father, and then it'll be awkward when I ask him for permission to marry you."

"Yes, that aside, I should mention that the bed, technically, is mine right now."

"Splitting hairs. Fine-print stuff," he said, waving his hand in the air to dismiss the distinction. "Plus, I'm not clever enough to come up with another way to scare men away from you. In fact, I even stole that line from you, that's how clever I am."

"Why don't you just stand next to me with a big club and grunt when men come near?" Lucy offered.

Ben smiled, and she watched a laugh roll through him. He was a full-body guy. Lucy had met them before. They weren't just smiley or beaming. Their joy came out through their open hands, through an almost imperceptible shudder of glee, a spark above the crown of the head. They laughed from the belly. They were the types who didn't squeeze or lean when they hugged. They held. They encompassed. Oh, man, this guy wasn't a goofy Dean. He was a shining Buddha.

"About the bed," Lucy said. "You can have it tonight. All weekend, in fact."

"Don't tell me you've agreed to go home with ole leather face the ancient mariner?"

"He has leathery skin," Lucy explained, "because he's been a lifeguard for his whole working career."

"That's not a career," Ben said, "that's an excuse to have sex with sixteen-year-olds for three months out of the year. It's a job for men with a statutory rape fetish."

"Your grunting scared him away before he found out I was twenty-five."

"Let's get back to this bed situation." Ben put his hand to his face, faking a thoughtful gesture. "Will you be in it?"

"No." Lucy took a sip of her drink and watched over the rim of her glass as Ben sighed in disappointment. "I'll be nearby, though, in either Trina's or Tami's empty bed. They're both staying in more luxurious digs on the bay all weekend." Although the Two Ts had offered, Lucy had just then decided not to stay in the spare room at the bay house.

"Luxurious," Ben said, "will be the view from my bed."

"I'm beginning to like you," Lucy said, telling the absolute truth.

And shortly thereafter the bed they shared separately became the bed they shared together. Ben told people that he wore her down by calling her Lucy Goosey and only agreed to stop if she kissed him. The real story was that one night they sat on their bed and played cards, Spite and Malice, until three in the morning. When Lucy got up to get into Trina's bed, Ben asked her to lie down with him and tell him a story, something he should know about her.

She told him about how her dad taught her Spite and Malice. And craps. That was her favorite because they would yell out bets—"Gimme eight the hard way." "Dollar yo." "Lay the ten." Yelling was a novelty, as Lucy's family members were generally quiet people who loved art. In fact, Lucy had always wanted to be a painter because of her father's admiration for it. He had been cremated because he believed it was irresponsible to bury bodies in the ground. Ben pushed Lucy's hair back off her face and said that he was sorry she lost him.

Then Ben told her that he learned the card game from his uncle Louie, who was in the Mafia. The family found out about it when there was a big bust for illegal gambling. All of the wise guys were hauled out of the makeshift casino covering their faces. All except Uncle Louie; he strutted to the police cruiser like he was going to breakfast. Lucy laughed. Ben looked square into her eyes and told her that he wanted to cheer her up whenever she was sad. But if she ever just wanted to be sad he wouldn't jump around like a clown. He'd let her be sad. And then he kissed her.

After a month of weekends and calls from their respective weekday beds, Ben told Lucy he felt as if they had been having the same conversation, which was occasionally interrupted by space and time. He loved it. He loved her. She was a crossword puzzle he was noodling. No, he had a better analogy, one he knew she'd make fun of. She was like one of the long-running Dungeons & Dragons games of his youth, when his powers were strong and his character enviable. He could do no wrong. She didn't tease him. He loved her.

Ben? As in the Cult of Ben?" Kate asked. Lucy had been keeping Ben all to herself, but couldn't hold it in any longer.

"It's Ben's Fan Club, actually. But he sort of deserves the fans."

"Oh, thank God, Lucy. I told you that you'd meet someone if you just opened yourself up to it," Kate said.

"You told me so?" Lucy smiled.

"If you opened yourself up to the right man, not all of those losers you normally date."

"Well done, then."

"So, tell me everything," Kate said.

"Well, he's fun, sweet to me, we never fight."

"How long have you been seeing him?"

"Over a month."

"And you're just telling me now? We'll forget that. I

understand. Let's fast-forward to the problem. You've never had a fight?"

"Sorry," Lucy said. "And no, no fights."

"Well, that just shows a lack of spirit," Kate said. "I'll have to meet him."

"Yes, as soon as the summer's over, we'll plan something."

Lucy tried to picture it. Ben in her life. In her real life. The one where she got up late for work and went to bed with the TV on. The one where she left her dishes in the sink and socks on the floor. The one with her friends who didn't know Ben, and her dinner parties where she boiled pasta and everyone drank too much red wine and told gross stories about sex and toilet accidents.

Ben lived and worked in Manhattan. She imagined that. Taking the train to see him. Taking the subway from Port Authority. Meeting him at his office and walking to a restaurant in the East Village. He owned an Internet start-up. His conference room had an air hockey table and a mini–basketball hoop. There was beer on tap on Fridays. Every day was casual day. It was doing well. And he was thinking of selling it.

"I don't think that selling nothing for mad quantities of money will necessarily last," he told Lucy on the beach, his chair facing hers, a beer in hand.

"Seems like a good idea then," she said, shielding her eyes from the sun to look at him.

"I'm thinking about taking a job with my buddy in Philadelphia. He needs a chief technical officer."

"Chief technical officer?" Lucy nodded. She wanted to joke with him about it. Come up with a special salute. But it wasn't the time.

"You know, I never warmed to New York." Ben pulled a hat out of his bag and offered it to Lucy. "I miss Philadelphia. My mom and dad. The Sixers. So, I've been thinking about it seriously."

"Oh, yeah," Lucy said, arranging the hat on her head, trying to sound casual, "since when?"

"Oh, for a while." Ben dug his heels into the sand. "Okay, I've only started considering it since I met you. But, still, it's a good time to sell."

Ben prepared his company for sale and visited Lucy when he could. She was living in a roomy apartment in a neighborhoody-neighborhood in Mount Airy, which was still technically in Philadelphia for tax reasons, but was in the suburbs as far as rush hour traffic was concerned. In those sleepy postcoital moments he'd tell her about "going public" and "IPOs," which Lucy thought might be roughly the same thing. She watched him and thought he'd be better suited dating someone who understood what the heck he was talking about. Being supportive was the idiot's version of being helpful.

"So, after I'm done with the sale," Ben asked, "what do you want to do?"

"Do?"

"I was thinking about buying a house down here, you know, for us."

Lucy was glad it was dark because she was sure she went pale. "I've never been a fan of the idea of living together," Lucy said.

"Fair enough," Ben said, "but I still want you to help me pick it out. I mean, you'll stay over once in a while, right?"

"It'll be fun," Lucy said, relieved he took the rejection of his offer so well. She didn't know why the mention of it made her arms numb. "We'll house hunt and then have dinner in the neighborhood to see if we like their cooking."

Lucy and Ben firmly believed in supporting the restaurant industry. They agreed that deferring to the experts on matters of cuisine was always the best idea.

"Yes," Ben agreed. "If there are lots of Chinese buffets to choose from, we'll know we've ventured too far into suburbia."

"And if there are only restaurants that sell dishes with sun-dried tomatoes and pine nuts, we'll know that our neighbors are bound to be snooty and suit-clad."

Lucy came from a split family, not divorced, not Democrat and Republican. Worse. Her dad was a New Yorker and her mom a Philadelphian. When she unfolded the map of the city to get a lay of the land, she was glad she'd sided with Mom on the feud. The housing possibilities in Philadelphia were vast for someone with Ben's budget. Their real estate agent, Betty, started them in Cherry Hill. They followed her to each location. Betty preferred to have her clients with her in her car, but Ben told her that he and Lucy were going out to eat when they were finished, so it was really best to take separate cars.

"I didn't want to tell her that we fight over shotgun," Ben said.

"What she wouldn't believe is that we both try to force the other one to take it."

"I like the backseat," Ben said.

"But you have longer legs," Lucy said.

"I want you to be comfortable," Ben said.

"Besides, Betty went a little heavy on the Estee Lauder," Lucy said.

"It came out of her showerhead this morning."

"Do you think all real estate agents are required to be named Betty?" Lucy pondered.

"Or Cookie?" Ben added. "Did you know that telemarketers change their names to have the *ie* or *y* ending because it's friendlier?"

"Yes, when I call you Benny, I like you better."

"And when I call you Lucille, I like you less so."

"I'll bear it in mind," Lucy said.

When they got out of the car, Betty came at them with a preemptive strike. "Show me a nice area that doesn't have bad traffic at this time of day and I'll buy every property myself."

It was a good ploy. They liked her. Which helped since they blanketed the city—Chestnut Hill, Mount Airy, West Chester, Downingtown, Manayunk, Conshohocken, Society Hill, Old City, Center City, University City, South Philly, Queen Village, the Main Line, the New Main Line. They looked at condos, doubles, apartments, penthouses, Victorians, colonials, pre-colonials, post-colonials, and even farms.

Lucy extolled the virtues of each. She *ooh*ed and *ahh*ed at great views of William Penn, the Delaware River, or Boathouse Row. She, despite herself, imagined where she'd hang her art. She mentally decorated and nested at each new place.

"I feel like Negative Norbert," Ben said over dinner in Kennett Square.

"Because I like every place?" Lucy asked.

"I hate being bad cop."

"Benny, it's your money. I'm just playing house here. It's easy for me to love every place."

"Lucille," Ben said, "would you play bank instead and pretend it's *your* money?"

"Deal. I'll be more discriminating, I promise."

"That last one was pretty cool, though, wasn't it?" Ben leaned in.

"Do you have any idea how bad that whole town smells during mushroom season?" Lucy asked.

"Wait," Ben asked straightening, "are you playing bank now?"

"Yes," Lucy said, then leaned forward. "For real, wasn't that view spectacular?"

When they settled on a place in Bella Vista, Lucy was thankful that she didn't really have to play banker. When the time came, she gracefully backed out of the negotiations. Inspections, points, mortgages, escrow. Again, Lucy agreed with Ben's decisions and nodded thoughtfully when he explained the complexities of the transaction. She loved him for taking care of it all without her help. She was pressed enough at work, stretching the limits of her natural tendencies by slaving in the workaday world. She really just wanted to spend her days painting and gluing things. She thought collage art would be fun to try for a while. Or maybe installation art. The numbers games of the real world didn't stick in her head. But she loved Ben for sharing the process with her and overlooking her ignorance and utter inability to learn it well enough to be of any help.

On the day of the settlement, Lucy called in sick to work and she and Ben went to their new favorite place for breakfast.

They had been going to the neighborhood at all times of day to get a feel for daily life there. This was Lucy's idea, and she was proud of her contribution to Ben's house-buying process. They didn't want to be surprised to find out that his new neighbor was in a garage band, or the local softball team used the street for games, or it was the official location for a weekly mummers' fancy brigade practice.

So, back they went during commuter hour. Not bad. Their new favorite place was a corner-facing breakfast café. Since Ben had been staying with Lucy temporarily, they had both become early risers, not wanting to miss out on time together. They were also both breakfast eaters, which made a nearby breakfast place a selling point. Good coffee. A nice selection of newspapers. Lucy liked the homemade granola and Ben the frittatas.

When they arrived, their favorite table was open. "Ah-ha," Ben exclaimed, "the early bird gets the worm." He plopped himself into the maroon velvet wingback chair.

"And the early worm," Lucy said, "gets eaten." She settled into the navy blue wingback across from him.

Ben laughed. Too hard. She was sure she'd made that joke before. Ben fidgeted with the newspapers on his lap. Lucy wanted the arts section.

"Will you come with me today?" Ben asked, leaning forward.

Lucy started to answer but Ben interrupted.

"I know you probably had the afternoon planned, lunch with Kate or something. But I'd love the moral support."

"I didn't make any plans," Lucy said. "I called off work to be with you."

"I'm sorry. I didn't even wait for you to answer."

The waitress came to the table and poured their coffee.

"Maybe you'd better get decaf today," Lucy said, stirring in the cream.

"I am a little nervous," Ben said.

"Are you having second thoughts?"

"No, I'm completely sure. Positively sure. I love the place. Everything about it."

"Okay then. Let's think about this. You just sold your company, your whole livelihood, and negotiated well over the amount you're slapping down for this place. You've done all of the legwork for today. It's a no-brainer."

"See, that's why I need you there. You settle me when I'm being ridiculous. I just feel better . . . no, I feel great when I'm with you. I'm my best self with you."

"That's sweet," Lucy said, then took a sip of her coffee. "Perfect. I'm my best self with you too."

"I want you to put your name on the deed with me," Ben said quickly.

Lucy's head snapped up. Ben was leaning even closer. He reached out for her hand.

"Lucy, I want you to marry me." Ben stood and pushed his chair back. The newspaper fell to the floor. The other customers looked over. Ben got on one knee and opened a blue velvet box in Lucy's lap.

The moment reminded Lucy of when she got hit by a baseball at a Phillies game. She saw the foul ball coming toward her. It crested over her face, moving in slow motion. And then, right before impact, it came like a bullet and smacked her square in the face.

Everything was confusing. People were scuttling for the ball.

There was clapping from the customers and waitstaff.

Her friends were trying to help her up.

There was a ring, shiny, diamonds, platinum.

Blood was shooting from her nose.

They hugged. There was a tearful yes.

She was back up on her feet and ushered up the steps and to the first aid room.

There was a new house, a surprise weekend at his parents' and an impromptu engagement party at Kate's.

When things finally settled down, when Lucy actually felt her mind shift and catch up, she was in a furniture store mentally decorating Ben's, no, *their* new house. She had been driving a saleswoman crazy. She picked a sleigh bed, then a four-poster bed, then decided on the mission style. Then she canceled the order altogether.

She tried again at another store. She felt as if she were picking the only Chanel suit she'd ever own. Spare no expense. But will it match the shoes? Is there a blouse that goes? Will it be out of style next year? The year after that? Eventually?

"What if we fall out of love?" She was sitting in the parking lot of yet another furniture store, talking to Kate on her cell phone.

"That's what marriage is for. To keep you together during those times. Anyway, trust me, there are worse things than falling out of love," Kate said.

"Balzac said that marriage unites people who barely know each other for life. I feel like that. I don't know him well enough to live with him," Lucy said, "and now we're getting married?"

"Balzac was a maniac," Kate said. "I think he also said that no man should marry a woman until he'd studied anatomy and dissected one. Well," Kate added, "he may have had a point there."

"No one of note ever said anything good about marriage. With the possible exception of Socrates," Lucy said.

"What did he say?"

"Something like if your marriage is good, you'll be happy, and if it's bad, you'll be a philosopher."

"Well, that's encouraging," Kate said. "At least he said marriages could be happy."

Lucy's lease wasn't up until the end of the year, so instead of moving in, she concentrated on filling Ben's house with new furniture. He didn't bring anything from New York but his personal items. He wanted to keep the apartment there, just to have. His indifference to decorating was similar to her indifference to his business transactions. Active and agreeable indifference. He listened intently. He loved every idea. He went along with her to furniture stores to plop down on sofas and prop his feet up on hassocks. Lucy wanted pieces that they would have for the rest of their lives. Not rickety junk from their post-college apartments. After a month of shuttling between the house and her apartment, Ben pressed Lucy about her plans to officially move in.

"I figured I'd start moving in as soon as we had the whole place painted," Lucy said.

"Most of the rooms are done," he said.

"But the smell of latex paint makes me sick and I won't have anywhere to go if I move out of my place completely."

"Lucy, you've spent half of your life painting, suddenly the smell of paint makes you sick?"

"Yeah?" Lucy said meekly. "I used oil paints?" she added unconvincingly.

"Okay," Ben conceded, "we'll hire a mover for the end of the month then."

"I'll just bring things over bit by bit," Lucy said.

"You can't move all of that stuff yourself. What about your art?"

"Well, either way, we're going to have to move them in your car because I can't trust movers with them."

"Lucy," Ben said seriously, "some things have to be done in one big leap. Like jumping a gorge. It can't be done in a few small jumps."

"Good thing there's a road over the gorge between my apartment and here," Lucy said.

"That's not what I'm talking about."

Lucy knew it. She kissed him. Pulled back and looked at his face. "Okay, we'll hire movers."

Lucy met Kate for lunch at a new salad buffet near Kate's house. They joined the perpetually dieting housewives who had probably been at their health clubs in the morning and were heading to the salon in the afternoon. These were women who wore Lilly Pulitzer outfits and Louis Vuitton handbags. Lucy thought they were the fashion equivalent of a kitchen decorated in the "country style" with a light blue wooden duck paper towel holder and a matching wallpaper border.

Lucy and Kate bellied up to the salad bar and fumbled with the plastic tongs.

"What are you so scared of?" Kate asked, plopping mushrooms on her plate.

"Those mushrooms, to begin with. Other than that, I'm scared of packing. Packing and shopping. I've seen you pack Greg's bags for his business trips. Men's socks, belts, underwear. Shirts with neck and arm sizes. I don't want to pack for another adult human."

"Why don't women's shirts measure the arm?" Kate asked. "We mediums better all have the same arm length, damn it." Kate pulled her arm back and pretended she couldn't reach the bucket of baby corn.

"I want someone who will pack *my* bag," Lucy said, "and shop for *my* socks and underwear."

"Then marry a professional butler."

"Also, I don't want to send cards to his friends and family from the two of us."

"Maybe you could include it in your vows."

"And I don't want him to roll his eyes at my stories, or worse, wave his hand at me and say, 'Yes, I know, you've told me that.'"

"What if you have?"

"He's supposed to listen again. Focus on the telling, on my eyelashes, on the delivery, on my hand gestures," Lucy said, stabbing the cheese tongs into the air, flinging bits of Cheddar toward Kate. "Maybe work out his list of things to do while nodding thoughtfully. A story isn't a once and done thing. It's part of our personal mythology. It's oral tradition and our responsibility to keep it alive. If we don't remember, we're doomed to repeat."

"What was that last part?" Kate asked. "Oh, and remind me, I have to stop and buy Greg some new shirts."

"Make sure the neck size is right."

They sat at a table by the window. Lucy insisted that if they had to eat light in the village of clones, they should at least have a view of the parking lot.

"I feel like I'm living with a spy," Lucy continued. "He asks about everything. And I only stay there part-time."

"He'll get sick of you soon enough."

"My private grooming habits are now public."

"He just wants to know all of you. It's the Balzac thing. He's dissecting."

"I'm not dead yet," Lucy said, fiercely spearing a cherry tomato with her fork. "But this is killing me."

"Your trouble is that you're always wishing for something you haven't got," Kate told her.

"What else am I supposed to wish for?" Lucy asked.

When Lucy arrived at the house in the evening, Ben was cooking dinner for them. Lucy had settled on referring to it as "the house." It began as "Ben's house." She figured she was on the road to calling it "our house." There were red carnations on the table and asparagus in a pan ready to be steamed.

"I love this kitchen," Ben said, then kissed Lucy and took her briefcase. "Go change out of these bad, bad clothes." He tugged on her jacket pocket.

He handed her a glass of wine and shooed her up the stairs. He had been encouraging Lucy to quit her job, but only when she was ready. She hated it, so she had been seriously considering the idea.

Lucy quickly dressed in her cutest jeans, took her hair down, and joined Ben in the kitchen. "Tell me about this mysterious thing you're been doing in here," Lucy said, waving her hand toward the stove.

"I decided to cook." Ben kissed her and rubbed his palm on the flat of her back. "But," he continued, "it was only after I almost broke my neck getting the kitchen put together."

"Be careful," Lucy said, plopping herself on one of the bar stools she'd recently had delivered. She was still wondering whether they had been the best choice. "It would cost a fortune to make this place wheelchair accessible."

"We'd have to get a dumbwaiter," Ben said. "Or even a smart one."

"That's my line," Lucy scolded.

"Anyway, I didn't open the ladder all the way and it toppled," Ben said, stirring the sauce.

"It actually *toppled*?" Lucy asked.

"When I put the thing away I read the sticker on the side that said, 'Failure to read and follow instructions can lead to injury or death.' I would have thought that was funny before today."

"That kind of makes it funnier," Lucy said.

"I like that it says 'read and follow,' as if you could follow the instructions without reading them," Ben said.

"Oddly enough," Lucy said, "some people can manage it with ladders."

"My pop would die if I told him I fell off a ladder. His son, the klutz."

"Your pop?"

"You know," Ben said, leaning across the counter toward Lucy, "I've realized that I really care what he thinks. I consider his opinion before I make any big decisions."

"WWPD?" Lucy asked. "You know, What Would Pop Do?"

"He never worked for anyone but himself his whole life. That's saying something."

"You take after him then."

"I only started my company because I wanted to be like him. Actually, I wanted to be better. Make more. Have more employees. I just got lucky."

"You think your success is less admirable because of this thing you call luck?"

"My pop doesn't even care about money. He just wants to be his own man. You can't compete with that. By competing with that, I've already lost."

"I'm sure he's very proud of you," Lucy said. "I am." She reached for his hand and kissed it.

Lucy shuttled herself across the city in the morning in Ben's car. It was bigger than hers and he almost forced her to borrow it. Generous. She put it on the list of things she loved about him. She would fill it with some of her paintings, dress for work, then drive to the parking deck where Ben had gotten her a permit. He liked her to have a safe parking spot near work. Considerate. She added it to the list.

On the drive from Ben's, Lucy answered her cell phone to Kate singing out, "Only two more weeks until the big move. How are you feeling?"

"Ben's got some sort of father worship going on. It's always, 'my pop this, my pop that, my pop, my pop, my pop.'"

"You might not have noticed so soon if he'd called him dad."

"It would have helped."

"But you like hearing stories over and over, remember."

"He's in some imaginary competition with Pop. He makes more money than Pop. My engagement ring is bigger than what Pop gave Mom. He can bike farther, run faster, last longer."

"Last longer?"

"Okay, he didn't say that. But he may as well have."

"I think it's nice. Greg doesn't like his dad at all. All he ever says about him is 'selfish asshole.'"

"You've got a point," Lucy said. "Listen, I'm going dress shopping tonight after work. Are you meeting me?"

"Are you kidding? I've got a binder jammed with pictures of dresses that I want you to try on."

Lucy hated that she told Kate about Ben's "Pop thing." She should have had more discretion. And why did she care if he had a rivalry with his father? That was perfectly normal. And at least he admitted it to himself, and to her. He was great and she was a shit. Making up reasons not to move in. Sharing his secrets behind his back. She vowed not to talk about it ever again.

Lucy raced to the dress shop after work, where she and Kate met Nicole, their perky sales associate. They both instantly loved her.

"So, your dress should be a statement of who you are, Lucy," Nicole said, giving Lucy a once-over. "Let's look through the dresses, and we'll all pick out who we think you are." Nicole then held out a tea-length shift. "Nineteen twenties flapper?" She raised an eyebrow at Lucy and put it back on the rack.

"These curves," Lucy said, pulling at her bra strap, "don't do flapper. And my calves will not be making an appearance at my wedding."

"Wedding Dream Barbie?" Kate asked, holding a tulle cream puff toward Lucy. Nicole nodded yes. Kate agreed. Lucy said, "Only because you want me to."

In the dressing room, Nicole buttoned Lucy into lace and silk and chiffon.

"I don't want to be a wife slave," Lucy said. "Cook, clean, launder."

"Oh, you're career-minded?" Nicole asked. She sounded surprised. It was the kind of dress shop that catered to the baby-minded bride, Lucy suspected.

"No, not really," Lucy said, sucking in her gut. "I'd probably make a better mistress than a wife. I want to travel, dine out, have sex."

"It's a wonder marriage caught on at all," Nicole said.

"I do love Ben, though. And I love to gamble. If only to check and see if I'm still lucky."

After dress shopping, which made Lucy swear to get a personal trainer, Kate convinced her to go get drinks. Lucy reasoned that, since she would be working out as soon as tomorrow, drinks tonight wouldn't ruin her.

"Did I hear you tell Nicole you'd make a better mistress than a wife?" Kate asked as they clinked glasses.

"I shouldn't be saying those things, should I?" Lucy asked.

"I'm not advising you. You'll work it out," Kate said. "But I'm not sure if you should be *feeling* those things."

"Oh, thanks."

"I'll listen and volley my ideas over the net," Kate said, "but I can't be responsible for your future happiness or misery."

"Ben bought a mower and proceeded to destroy everything pretty in the yard. Baby trees. Queen Anne's lace. Lavender."

"Lucy, those are weeds," Kate said.

"I went grocery shopping for Ben's house yesterday and bought salt. You know, the big refill container. And it occurred to me that the next time I buy salt I'll be married."

"Unless you get slugs."

"*I'm* a slug. What's wrong with me?"

"And it's not Ben's house, Lucy," Kate said. "It's your house—the plural *you*."

Lucy began her workout with Steve the next day.

"Engage your abs," he told her as she lunged.

"But I'm already engaged," Lucy said through huffing breaths.

Steve didn't have much of a sense of humor from what she could tell. He reminded her of the kinds of guys she dated before Ben, the last man she'd ever date. Pretty men. Probably pleasant enough to be around in a let's-go-get-a-beer kind of way. Generally superior about some slice of the universe he knew something about—abs, Ford truck motors, astrophysics. Who knew? Okay, she was attracted to him, she wasn't proud of it.

"Concentrate on your white hot core," Steve said.

"I think it's just tepid," Lucy said.

"You're doing good. Five more."

"Lukewarm core," Lucy said as she exhaled. "Lukewarm,

I am your father." She inhaled like Darth Vader without even trying.

On the way home from the gym Lucy was going to stop at the mover's warehouse to pick up boxes. Instead, she stopped at the front desk and canceled her move. When she got to Ben's he was mowing their little lawn. He waved to her and shut off the mower.

"Doesn't the lawn look great," he said, and pointed to the spot where a baby oak used to be.

Lucy just waved and headed into the house. She went to the bedroom, stripped off her workout clothes, and stood in front of the mirror. Ben came in and sat on the bed.

"Beautiful," he said from behind her.

Lucy jumped and pulled her robe off the back of the door.

"Don't cover up for me," Ben said, hurt.

Lucy covered her face with both hands and started to cry. Big, heaving sobs that sucked her palms to her mouth. Ben jumped up from the bed and put his arms around her.

"I'm disgusting," she said.

"What are you talking about? You look great. You're perfect, Goosey."

"I don't know what I'm doing," Lucy said with her arms drawn against her body, shielding her from his embrace.

"Come here," Ben said, pulling her to the bed. "Talk to me."

Lucy sat, pulled a tissue from the box, and wiped at her nose. "I canceled the move today."

Ben was still.

"I don't know why," Lucy said, crying anew.

"Okay, you want to wait until after the wedding to move in, I understand."

"I don't think I'm ready to get married." Lucy hadn't known she was going to say that, but once she did, she felt relieved. That was, until Ben started crying.

"This is because of that painter, when you were a kid," Ben said.

Lucy didn't say anything.

"I'm going to find that guy and kill him," Ben said.

"Forget about that," Lucy said defensively. "I'm an adult, Ben, and I don't want to hurt you, but I feel like I'm being crushed by all of this."

"Don't you want to think it over?" he asked.

"How long would you wait?" she asked.

"Forever," Ben said, as if it were a matter of course.

Child Madonna
(Oil on Canvas, 1984)

The front porch step creaked under the fierce stomp of my sneaker. I was almost in the door of our Victorian. Away from *him*.

"Your mom told me you would come over tonight," Robert said from behind me.

I didn't break stride at his words. I bolted inside, up to my mother's room, grasped and twisted her precious crystal door-knob, and burst in. I was fourteen and it was the first time I raised my voice to her. "I'm going to the movies tonight."

She swung away from her dressing table mirror, eyes cut at me, hairbrush in hand. The rush I'd gotten from my anger was extinguished by that look.

"I won't sit for Robert tonight," I persisted. It sounded whiny. "You promised I could go to the movies."

My mother took a breath that said, "Ah, yes, now I know what this is about."

"I promised Robert you would sit for him," she said evenly. "Don't you think that's more important than a movie?" She turned back to her mirror and brushed her hair as if that were the last word in the conversation.

"Is a promise to Robert more important than a promise to

me?" I really wanted to know. I'd hoped the question would hang in the air, like big questions should. But it didn't.

"Lucille," my mother said archly, "you will call Samuel right now and tell him you're not going. Not another word about it."

I had my answer and she had the final word.

Robert was my parents' pretentious project—the one they undertook after my older sister, Nancy, went to college. Instead of giving money to a scholarship fund for an artist or something normal like that, they took in Robert and let him live in the carriage house behind their home. They rewired the barn, put in fluorescent lights, and fully stocked his art studio. Apparently all of that good-doing ignited their passion, and my mother at forty-one and my father at sixty had me a year after the Robert Project began. The first thing I remember about my childhood was trying to pinch Robert through his paint-crusted jeans. I loathed him.

After dinners with us he would joke that he was leaving the "big house" for the "servants' quarters." Sometimes my mother would give him a check for paintings of his she sold. But usually, she gave him a check because paintings of his hadn't sold in weeks. My father would ask if Robert was teaching tomorrow at the job my father got him at the university in the art department, of which my father was the head. And then Robert would stroll to his spacious, rent-free apartment, past the vehicle my parents bought him, wearing the black linen suit my mother ironed. He was breaking a sweat with all of those real-world pressures such as wondering if linen did or did not make him look continental.

With their generosity apparently knowing no bounds, they eventually gave him me as a model when I was old enough to sit still. That's my other vivid childhood memory. Sitting still. Very still, for Robert, frozen in orbit of him.

I suppose his sketches of me were good. He did them everywhere for pretty much as long as I could remember. I don't really have any childhood memories that don't include the echo of the "sit still" command.

"Make a pretty picture for Robert," my gin-soaked mother would say. Then she'd try to soften the blow by adding, "Aren't you so lucky?"

I was watched by Robert at my dance recitals, at the school plays, in the park, and at meals. He even sketched me sitting at my desk at parents' night at school. While the other children showed off the bulletin board on Pennsylvania wildlife or Porky the Guinea Pig, I sat still at my desk. Most of the kids in school as much as said they didn't know why anyone would sketch me. But I guess the answer was because he could, not because I was special.

I never looked at his paintings. After I started the formal sittings in his studio, when it would have been easy to glance at his easel, I'd just grab my book bag when the time was up and bolt out the door. I didn't want to look because I loved the art I'd seen in the museums my father took me to, and I didn't want to break the spell. I pretended that the women in the paintings I admired weren't miserable.

Robert met Carolyn at the university, proposed to her after a few months, and married her after my mother settled all of the details. Carolyn was as cool as a folksinger with her beads and hippie skirts that hung off her hips. She had silky straight blond hair and I had envy, with my frizzy brown hair and baby fat. Even more exotic was that she talked about things besides Robert and his career—greenhouse gases and recycling and the Peace Corps and Indonesia. Carolyn meant freedom for me, because she had replaced me in the studio. And for that, I worshiped her.

I started playing tennis at the park that summer. My best friend, Kate, was at tennis camp and we were going to try out for the team when school started. Every day I went to the courts alone and hit the ball against the practice wall for hours. It was difficult at first to shake the feeling of Robert watching me. I was spooked, thinking I saw a glimpse of black linen or smelled his cigar smoke, paint, and turpentine scent. I would hit the ball harder and try to make the thoughts dissolve. And sometimes it would work and it felt wonderful.

Samuel, a boy from school, moved into my neighborhood that summer and we started meeting at tennis courts to play champion-of-the-world matches until it was so dark we couldn't see the ball anymore. Sometimes I went to his house for dinner and ate SpaghettiO's with his three younger brothers in front of the TV. He would talk endlessly about boy stuff—Dungeons & Dragons and Atari. I was enthralled.

"I like him, like him," I wrote to Kate at camp. My mother, who thought I was still a baby, had no idea and was just happy I had stopped moping about Kate being gone. That was probably why she said I could go to the movies with Samuel and his older cousins—no parents.

Probably everyone, including Samuel, thought it was just a movie with friends. But to me, it was my first date. That Friday,

I was full of nervous excitement. I twirled in front of my mirror until I fell, dizzy-sick, onto my bed. I ran through the house getting ready to play tennis as if I were going to the Academy Awards. I got to the courts late and Samuel was hitting the ball against the practice wall. He didn't look at me. "Did you have to go with that creepy artist again?" he asked, looking at his watch, angry I was late.

During our warm-up I hit a lob over the high chain-link fence. Samuel told me to concentrate. Next, I sent a ball zipping across the other five courts to the far side of the play area. Samuel yelled at me and told me to get the ball myself. I laughed and ran across the courts full of silly energy.

"God, Lucy, you're worse than my little brother," Samuel said as we took turns at the water fountain.

"What are you complaining about? You won every game," I said, holding my hair back then leaning over the fountain.

"That's why it sucked. No competition."

"Well, then, I don't want to play anymore," I said. "I'll just see you tonight."

I had wanted to leave early anyway. I was going to take a long shower and make my hair look nice. I planned my outfit in my head as I walked home swinging my racket at the maple leaves, swatting them off their branches. I would wear my white denim shorts, my pink Izod shirt with the collar turned up, and my white shell necklace that made me look tan. I was wondering whether or not I could get away with wearing lipstick when a cold shock ran through me. I smelled *him*.

"Almost dinnertime," Robert said from behind me. "We're going to be late."

I didn't want to talk to him. I didn't even wonder what he

was doing there. He made me sick. I wanted to think about Samuel.

"I've been missing you," he said to my back.

I fought with my mother, I missed the movie, and I had to be with Robert. To make matters worse, when I arrived at the carriage house, Carolyn barely acknowledged me. She was talking on the olive green phone in the kitchen. Spider plants drooped above her head like suspended fireworks. No hug, not even a smile. She just jerked her angular chin toward the two slices of carrot cake on the orange countertop.

I carried the plates toward the studio. The acrid smell of turpentine came first. Then the oily roundness of the paint and the oak of the barn timbers. I balanced the plates and pushed at the slightly opened door with my hip. When I entered the studio, the smell of Robert's sweet tobacco and dirty hair overpowered the good smells, and I choked a little. A sepia glow from muted spotlights lit the corner of the room where an off-white tarp was suspended behind a daybed piled with bright yellow pillows. The high ceilings and wall-sized paintings stacked against the wall dwarfed Robert. There were paint tubes, jars of colored liquid, brushes, ashtrays, and sketchpads strewn everywhere. Smaller paintings were piled throughout. Symphonies of blue, red, and brown. Robert sat at his easel brushing gesso on a canvas.

I set his cake down in the middle of an empty palate and sat on the daybed to eat mine. As angry as I was, there was something comfortable about the studio. Calming. There was relief in its familiarity. It was what I knew. Some people were sent to their rooms. I was sent to Robert's studio. And once there, I escaped into my own mind. Once there, I went to movies with Samuel, played tennis on the team with Kate, and learned to paint so well that my parents kicked Robert out.

Robert ignored his cake, walked to a stack of paintings, and flipped through them. "How do you like these?" he asked.

I focused in on them. They were all nudes. Piles of nude men and women stacked on top of one another. He kept flipping. I only recognized Carolyn. My mouth was full and I just nodded and shrugged in response. He wasn't looking at me anyway.

"Do you think you'd like to?"

That was how he asked. "Do you think you'd like to?" Barely asking at all. I put another bite of cake in my mouth so I wouldn't have to answer. He kept flipping. He pulled one out, held it up, and smiled a practiced grin. I'd seen that smile. But I'd never seen the painting. It was of my mother and father. They were sitting outside at our pool playing chess. I tried to fathom it. Naked, my parents, outside and in front of Robert. It must have been from a long time ago, from before I was born, but that didn't occur to me then.

"It's just art, Lulu, nothing to be shy about."

I became aware of myself. My hair was messy from playing tennis. I tried to smoothe down the frizz.

"You look great. Don't fix a thing," he said, noticing me out of the corner of his eye. And that was when I realized that even when he wasn't looking, he always saw.

He stood silent with his eyes on his nudes then walked to the wall and dimmed the lights.

I took off my shoes and my feet were instantly cooled by

the cement floor. Then I took off my socks, peeling them inside out. Wet with sweat. It's only art, I told myself. Then I thought about my parents undressing in front of him.

Robert had his head down preparing his palette.

I pulled off my T-shirt and held it in front of my body as I unhooked the less-than-A-cup bra I had begged my mother to buy me.

I thought about the nudes in the museums. I wondered about the girls who were forever frozen in oil on canvas. Posing to become fairies or angels.

I dropped the shirt and stuffed my bra into my shoe. Still sitting, I wiggled out of my shorts and underwear at the same time, keeping my thighs pressed together.

"I'll stay one hour," I said firmly, the first time I was stern with Robert. I watched the clock and tried to keep my mind off the hair on my legs that my mother wouldn't let me shave, the new curve of my breasts that had just started developing, my chunky girl-body that was stretching out. My frizzy hair suddenly seemed to be the least of my troubles.

When the hour was up, I reached for my shirt, and Robert begged me to stay ten more minutes. I guess it was a mistake. I should have said no and left. I stayed, only nine more minutes. I thought I was taking a stand. Then I put my clothes on and tried to race past him.

He stepped in my path.

"Thanks," he said, looking straight at me. Then he thrust his plate of untouched carrot cake into my hand. "Could you take that into the kitchen for me?"

I walked up the gravel path at dusk and something dark moved in me. I felt jagged, loose, disjointed. Walking was difficult. My clothes were binding, suffocating me. They felt unfamiliar and too cool from the concrete studio floor.

I walked into the house and past the parlor.

"Lulu, you did a good thing tonight," my mother called out. It startled me and I flushed, then remembered I was supposed to have gone to the movies.

The phone rang after my parents went to bed. Half a ring before I snatched the receiver off the cradle of my coveted pink princess phone. It was the only thing in my room that my mother couldn't find in white. It was Samuel.

"You missed a great time," he said. "My cousin and her boyfriend made out during the whole movie. We threw popcorn at them. Some of it got stuck in her hair. It was hilarious."

After we hung up I imagined what it would be like to kiss Samuel. I practiced by kissing my hand. The phone rang again. *Samuel.* I picked it up with a quick hello.

"Lulu?" It was Robert. I hated it when he called me that. "I hope I didn't wake anyone," he said in a breathy whisper. "I need to see you again. Could you come over tomorrow? I can clear it with your parents if you'd like?"

That was a threat, I knew.

"I was going to play tennis." I was negotiating.

"If you play tennis in the morning you can come over in the afternoon. Okay? Great." He hung up before I could respond. But I knew that if I didn't show, he'd tell my parents I missed a sitting. "Is Lulu feeling okay?" he would say. Weasel.

Samuel tried to get me to play longer. He begged. So I stayed until four then walked slowly to Robert's studio. Carolyn opened the door before I reached it. "I saw you coming from a mile away," she said, smiling hugely.

It was one of those things adults said to kids. Pointless. Detached from anything important. It was the sort of thing bratty teens said "So what?" to. I smiled and smoothed my hair.

Carolyn led me to the studio, something she never did, as if I suddenly didn't know how to get there. She turned to smile at me. I half expected her to say, "And this is our lovely hallway." When she turned back, I watched her straight blond hair swing across the back of her tube top. She pushed the studio door open, tucked her chin down, and looked at Robert through her bangs. Robert wasn't watching. But the way she looked, her low-slung jeans tight across her swishy hips, made the envy-crush I had on her spike.

Robert posed me on the couch. He moved my brown-haired, naked leg. Bent it at the knee. He moved my elbow and cocked my head this way, that way. I stayed for an hour and twelve minutes, put my clothes on, and left.

Robert called every day for the rest of that summer and negotiated sitting times with me. He never asked while I was in the studio. The request always came as an insistent phone call. I made excuses and he plotted and begged. When I gave him too much resistance he issued veiled threats. "Your parents *are* pleased I'm getting so much done. Don't you agree?"

I was thankful when the school year came because I'd be out of the house for half the day. And I'd get to see Samuel every day. We went to the same private school. My father had picked it because it had a good arts program run by two former students of his. My mother agreed to it because the school had a prestigious college placement record, but I knew she only cared that it wasn't public school. Snob.

The best part about school was that I had an excuse not to see Robert. He still called, but my parents were strict about grades, so even when Robert made good on his threats and talked to my parents about our sitting schedule, they had to compromise.

That winter, my mother decided it was too dangerous to drive me to school in her precious new Mercedes. If she thought convertibles were so unsafe, I don't know why she bought one. She talked Robert into taking me in his beat-up Suburban, the one they bought him so he could cart his paintings around. It exhausted me to have to listen to him gab about his art for thirty minutes straight every morning. I realized that he had never really talked to me before. We talked "schedule" talk. In the studio, he didn't speak much at all. I preferred the scrape of hog's hair against canvas to this. I tried to tune him out and only responded when I was trying to steer the subject away from when I'd be free.

One morning some of the popular girls from school saw me get out of Robert's vehicle. They hurried over in as casual a way as they could affect.

"What's he like?"

"He is *so* cute."

"My mom said he uses you as his model, like a lot."

"Wouldn't you just love to kiss him?"

"He's all right," I said, not wanting to let on that I despised him.

"He's having a show here next month, my dad just told me," one of the girls said.

"Lucy, you have to introduce us."

I panicked. A show at my school? I called home and told my mother I was sick and to send Robert back to pick me up. I sat at the main gate to the school and waited.

When he arrived an hour later I hoisted myself up into the vehicle and plopped down on the bench seat. Robert pulled onto the main road and asked me what was wrong. I burst into tears. When I could finally speak, I begged him not to show the paintings of me at my school. "Why do you have to show at my school anyway?" I wailed.

"Lulu, relax. I won't. Whatever you want." He put his right hand on my knee to comfort me as he negotiated the winding roads back to my house with his left hand. "When we get home, come over to the studio and we'll pick the paintings *you* think I should show."

When I couldn't stop crying, Robert pulled the car into the parking lot of a closed ice cream stand and slid across the seat to hug me. I kept my arms crossed in front of my chest. He let me go, and when I looked up at him it was the first time I ever thought someone cared how I felt.

"I'm okay," I said. "Let's just go."

He gave me another hug and I hugged him back.

I walked into the studio and was confronted by my nude body. In plain view was a humiliatingly oversized painting. My nipple was as big as a dinner plate.

"Isn't it beautiful?" He gestured toward it. "But I won't show it if you don't want me to. It can be our secret," he said.

"Our secret," I said, thinking about the kids at school. "Then do you want me to look at your other paintings? For the show?" I reminded him, only vaguely aware of how silly it was for a fourteen-year-old girl to help him decide which paintings to display.

He shuffled through the canvases as I stood by his side, smelling the stench of stale tobacco on his breath.

"I love this one," he sighed over a painting of me. "I understand. Really, I do. It's just that the man who's sponsoring the show is a very important gallery owner from New York. He said he would probably be taking some of the best work to sell in one of his galleries."

Even I could see that his other paintings weren't quite as good. The ones of Carolyn were actually disturbing. She looked disproportionate; the colors were too bright. Something was off.

Then there were the paintings of me. Some were harshly realistic. Some softer, with a cottony glow. His best ones were like the paintings I'd seen in museums, with leafy backgrounds, animals, Madonnas, and wings and halos on the cherubs, which were all versions of me.

I saw myself in my crib, at the beach, at the playground, on the tennis courts, and sitting in the courtyard at grade school. The nudes showed that my development had been considerable since the beginning of the summer. They were my version of the pencil marks that marred the walls of my friends' homes that showed their latest height. My legs tucked self-consciously under me. My fingers and toes clenched. My hair frizzy and wild. Breasts, nipples, hips. Arms over my head. Eyes looking toward the clock—angry, sad, focused on nothing, or cast down possibly at a science book that time I had to study for an exam.

"The ones of you really are the best," he said in a final plea.

"I think it's because I've been drawing you since you were born. Since *I* was born as a painter." He looked at my dinner-plate nipple and I put my arm across my chest instinctively. Then he looked at the red and yellow scramble that was Carolyn. "The other paintings look flat. Something's wrong with the depth," he said, shaking his head.

I wouldn't give in. I sifted through all of his work, desperate to find paintings that were suitable to show. Meanwhile, Robert moved different versions of me from one pile to the next. He propped me up and admired the painted me. But I wouldn't give in.

"Lucy," Robert said looking at me, "let's forget all of this and have a session."

I agreed. There was something about how he loved those paintings that made me want to pose. So I kicked off my shoes and stripped. I knew he saw me, and I didn't fold my clothes carefully or squirm out of my underwear. I plugged in a space heater and turned it toward the futon and then plopped down. Robert approached to pose me. "I'm going to sit like this today," I said, and turned him away with a final tone. And then I watched him.

It was getting late and Carolyn wasn't home yet. Her Nova had yet to crunch down the driveway, and I asked where she was.

"She's gone," Robert said.

I took a detour on the way home, following the long loop through the woods, using the pinch light on my key chain to see. The path ended at the new development of homes where Samuel lived. His bedroom light was on, and I threw a rock at his window. It missed and hit his baby brother's, and I heard a cry. I crouched by the bushes and waited to see if Samuel would look out, but he didn't. Kate had told me that Marnie, a thin runner from my English class, had been bragging about how Samuel was joining the track team because of her.

My house was dark when I got there. My parents usually went to bed early. I was sure they just forgot to leave a light on. I was glad. I crept upstairs to my room with its lace curtains, white canopy, and white teddy bears piled on the white duvet. My mother liked everything in my room to be bright and clean. My empty canvas. I plopped down on the bed feeling frayed and dull. I thought about Carolyn leaving. Samuel. The girls at school. Robert hugging me in the car. The way he looked at me and the way he painted me.

I called him. "You can use the ones of me for the show."

"Thank you, Lucy."

I didn't really hate him. Not anymore. Not at all.

The show, it turned out, didn't ruin me socially. In fact, the serious art students, who were the only ones who ever went to the gallery shows, treated me like I was a celebrity. I got a couple invitations to a school dance from boys who thought it was cool that my parents didn't mind that I modeled "like that." But I barely noticed the attention. I'd always had a vague sense that everyone was watching me, so when they actually started to, I didn't register the shift.

Kate did, though, and she parlayed the attention into dates for us.

"We're going out tonight with my brother's friends." Kate pointed across the courtyard at school.

I squinted in that general direction, not much caring who she was pointing at.

"You see the tall one? That's Gage. And the guy in the blue is Trey. You're going with him, Lucy, he's sweet and cute." Kate always picked the nice boys who did well in school and talked about the things they learned rather than which teacher had spent the better part of the class burping his lunchtime indigestion into his hand. Kate called these boys "Mols" for Most Likely to Succeed.

"Yup, they look like moles to me," I said.

"They're both trying for early admission to the Ivys."

"I meant that they remind me of cancerous tumors that should be lanced," I said. Our ideas of cute were different.

But Kate didn't trust me to find my own dates since Samuel, who, she said, was "most likely to sell street drugs for a living." It didn't matter anyway. He was dating Marnie.

Since I didn't much care, I let Kate handle our social lives. I got calls from boys, but I didn't ever talk for long. I wanted to keep the line open. But Robert didn't call. He had disappeared. I was hitching rides to school with Kate and her brother, who, at seventeen, was finally allowed to drive us. I tried not to care about Robert. Kate and I were basking in fourteen-year-old glory with boys, notes, and approval. I was supposed to be thrilled. Having the time of my life.

I finally broke down and called him.

"Your show was a hit at school," I said.

"I know, I was there. Why didn't you come?"

"Did the New York bigwig take any of your stuff?"

"Yes," Robert said without enthusiasm.

"Have you been painting?" I asked.

"No." He made a loud, gulping swallow. Then I heard the distinct *ting* of ice cubes falling to the bottom of an empty glass.

"Would you like to?" I asked.

He was silent.

"Well, I'm coming over," I said.

"Don't . . ." he started.

"No arguments," I said, feeling very grown-up.

"Don't . . . tell your parents," he clarified.

His house smelled like booze. Robert was in the kitchen sitting in front of a glass of amber liquid. He looked wild. Tufts of his hair were sticking out from his head at all angles. Light brown was showing at the roots of his jet black hair, which was unbrushed and greasy. His clothes were rumpled and dirty with food stains. I didn't say a word. I took the hand that wasn't clutching a rocks glass and led him to the studio. He was silent.

I stood directly in front of him and slipped off my red cotton dress. I bent my head and blinked up at him. He took a gulp of his drink and stared toward me. His eyes focused and he saw me. I smoothed my hair down, turned, and walked toward the daybed. He followed. I sat and he pushed me into a reclining position. His hand was cold and my nipple went hard when it brushed against it. He grabbed my arm with his rough hands and placed it above my head. He held on to my knee and ankle and bent my leg. Then he turned and walked toward his canvas.

I stayed all afternoon. I didn't demand any breaks and only moved when he either moved me or told me to move. Finally, when evening fell, he came to me on the daybed. He lay down next to me. He rolled toward me and his odor was overpowering.

It made me take in a sharp breath and close my eyes. I waited. Nothing happened. I opened my eyes and looked at his face. He had passed out.

Robert called the next day. I was sure he would beg me to come over. I had been so good to him. Never complaining. Never breaking a pose.

"Lulu," he said, "I'm going on vacation. I'm going to stay with a friend in Hilton Head for a little while."

"The school play is this weekend," I said desperately. "You're going to miss it?"

"You're a good kid," he said. "Break a leg and a bunch of hearts."

Robert left. My parents never mentioned it. But once, after my mother heard me crying on the phone to Kate, she asked me if I wanted to talk to someone. "You know you can always talk to me or your father. But I was thinking about Dr. Pearlman." Our neighbor, the shrink.

Robert didn't return after a week. He didn't return after a month. He missed the holidays. He missed my fifteenth birthday.

Then, after I stopped wondering every day, he sent a letter. Inside there was a long note to my parents. My mother read it then silently passed it to my father. Then she opened another note, read it, and passed it to me.

"Happy Birthday, kiddo. Sorry I missed it. Those plants in the carriage house are going to need watering if they're not dead already."

My mother dropped the last piece of paper in the envelope,

a charcoal sketch, onto the kitchen table and left the room. It was of a dark-haired woman with crinkles around her eyes and mouth. She was laughing and had a ridiculously large flower in her hair. Robert had scrawled underneath, "This is Amy!"

I slammed the front door and stormed to the carriage house. Instead of watering the plants, I walked through the kitchen and into the studio. The smell of turpentine reminded me that I hated him. It made my skin flush with heat.

I opened the tubes of paint—the expensive cadmium reds and yellows—and squeezed them out onto my oversized nipple. Then I saw his prized Italian lead white he'd smuggled from Europe. He'd ranted about it for a full two years before he had the guts to even use the stuff. He started rambling about it when I was learning phonics, and was still talking about it the day my wisdom teeth were pulled. Like I cared.

I took his best ox-hair brushes, with the hand-packed bristles, and smeared the paint over my eyes and frizzy hair. I pulled thick hot blood, angry saffron tracks, across the surface. I stabbed at the canvas and globs of orange splattered my legs. Then I threw the brushes in the waste pail. As I did, an image caught my eye. It was a small oil painting of me playing tennis by myself. And I left the studio with it tucked under my arm.

Reflections
(Mirrors and Glass, 1996)

You break off your engagement, and you wonder how other women do it. How they forge ahead with broken hearts. Or with beat-up hearts. You decide to be a bitch. You spend a few months consciously preparing yourself for bitchhood. You've tried it before. Limited engagements, but bitchy nonetheless. To study, you watch Mae West movies. You fall in love with bitchiness. You determine that it only takes supreme self-involvement, something you've never been all that good at. But you're determined.

You decide that everything in your life shouts the wrong message about the you that you are to become. You're regretting the loss of a love, which is entirely your own fault. To compensate for your guilt, you're helpful to your colleagues at work, which only makes you late on your own deadlines. You try to be there for your friends, which is beginning to annoy you. So, you shed this old you. The one who is accommodating and sad. And you reinvent yourself. You will look out for you! It should be an easy transition.

You don't yet realize that the bitchiness you are soon to acquire will attract confrontation. But you do find yourself snapping at everyone you encounter. Convenience store employees are your archenemies. Coffee, groceries, lunch, dinner, all are easily accessed at the corner store on your city block of Philadelphia.

You wait at the checkout counter as the clerk counts cigarette packs above his head. You wonder why he isn't helping you. As you were pouring half-and-half into your twenty-four-ounce cup of dark roast, you watched him help a line of people. And now you, alone, stand at the counter. The other line dwindles and the portly female cashier reaches across for your items—gum, chips, coffee—and says, "I'll ring you up over here."

You move to accommodate her. You're not good at being bitchy yet.

"Two dollar scratch-offs, please," you ask. You like to gamble, even on bad bets. You might just like the thrill. You're not sure yet.

She gets them for you, rings you up, and then apologetically asks, "You're of age, right?"

You show her your ID and tell her you're twenty-six. "Don't you have to be eighteen to buy lottery tickets?"

The cashier who has been ignoring you all this time stops what he's doing and says, "I would have put you at twenty-three."

You giggle at how ludicrous that is. As if those three years would show a marked difference in your appearance. You are struck by the sound of your laughter. It's kindly. Flirty even. He probably thinks you're laughing at the "compliment." *Idiot,* you think. You want to say, "I thought you didn't see me since you let me stand at your counter without once acknowledging my presence." But you don't because you're not a bitch yet. Or maybe you are. You reason that a true bitch wouldn't take the time of day to insult this guy. This is going to be trickier than you thought.

The essence of bitchiness is not to insult people who have slighted you. All that does is show people that you are sensitive and easily hurt. Bitchiness is used to support selfishness. To bully.

Bitchiness is best used to your advantage when trying to get upgrades in hotels. This is something you've done before, but you wonder if it will work better when you're a bitch. You have been traveling a bit for work. They're grooming you for a new position. You like it. It helps with the invention of the new you. When they send you to London, the manager shows you to your room. You say, "Don't you have anything nicer?" And when he takes you to another room that is exactly the same, you nod as if you knew all along that he was holding out on you. You know when to stop pushing the envelope. You don't want him to spit in your room service order.

In domestic hotels, you have to employ this trick at the front desk. You snappishly ask if all of the suites are booked for the night. You then demand to be upgraded to one at no cost, of course. You act as if you deserve it. If you are met with resistance, you imply that you had a bad experience somewhere along the line—maybe someone at the hotel gave you bad directions, maybe your meal in their restaurant was undercooked the last time you stayed. Whatever the reason, you have to believe you deserve it or you'll never pull it off. The weary, exasperated princess needs some extra space for her ego.

You know that the bitchy girls get loyal boyfriends, doting husbands, and the best assignments at work. The trade-off, of course, is that you can't smile much. But the upside is that eventually you're not much inclined to smile. You are ever-vigilant, fiercely determined to make your life better. In the meantime it's making you miserable.

You only date men who will "do for you." It's an exhausting practice of seduction and rejection. An exuberant call after a first date and he's gone. The slightest implication that you pay for something and he's gone. The assumed Saturday-night date and he's gone. Sure, some redeem themselves. But eventually they tire. You stop asking your friends to fix you up because you don't want them to learn what you've become. To them, you're the same Lucy you've always been. You are now a double agent.

Your college roommate fixes you up with "Hello, my name is Todd," from her recovery group. Jayne went to New Orleans with you and saw your front desk trick. She thinks you're bitchy because you need to get laid. She also thinks you should date men who are recovering alcoholics. She says that everyone is an addict and the ones who haven't admitted it yet are trouble. She likes Todd for you because he doesn't go in for the God talk that gets flung around her little group, which isn't even AA, but is a rip-off of it. It has twenty-four steps. Jayne calls it group therapy, and she pays big bucks for it. It's made up of people who should just be going to AA.

By now you decide that bitchiness is not your forte, and the fact that you are hiding it from your friends tells you that you're not exactly proud of it. But some of it is sticky. It's in your hair and on the bottom of your shoe and you just have to wait until it grows out or gets covered over with street grime. You con-sciously cut Todd some slack. A feeble call two days later, that's okay. Todd remains.

On your first weekender together, you ride "down the shore" on the back of his motorcycle. Everyone in Philadelphia goes "down the shore" on summer weekends, and Todd is no exception, despite his aversion to booze. You have no idea why Todd likes the shore, since the shore culture is all about the party. The motorcycle ride is where you first notice his lean, muscular body. His street clothes hid the truth about his physique.

After you start having sex, you notice that his whole body is like an erect penis. Skin sliding over hardness. He becomes a massive dildo to you. Erect for your pleasure.

You decide that it's this quality you like best in him. But, as is the case with Todd, he matches any good quality with an appallingly bad one. He wants intensely for you to call him Daddy, especially in bed. You do it because he's nothing like your father, who is dead. Your daddy, whom you rarely called Daddy, was intelligent and funny.

You spend weekends at Todd's shore rental. Generally, shore house sex is indulged when the dozens of other housemates are out drinking. It's not hard to find a block of time, around happy hour, when the house is empty. But as the summer wears on, several of the housemates, low on cash, have happy hour on the deck.

So, the outside shower becomes a favorite rendezvous spot. He washes your hair. Lathers your body. Turns you this way and that under the hard stream of water. He may have been imagining himself in the daddy role. You try not to think about it. He kisses you as the water pours over your head, making it hard to breathe.

"Can I pee on you?" he asks matter-of-factly.

"No, thank you," you say.

You then feel the water on your thighs get slightly warmer. You look down, but it's impossible to tell. When you confront him about it, he denies it. You become convinced that you've not only been pissed on, but also lied to.

You try to get a handle on exactly who this person is that you're sleeping with. It seems important, because he wants to spend time together outside the shower. So, you dig in. Why not? Well, you don't ask yourself that, because you're pretty sure you would have more answers than you would like to acknowledge.

"What do you want most in life?"

Todd tells you he wants to belong to some ritzy country club in the suburbs that you've never heard of. He drops the name like it's a mutual friend or a celebrity you couldn't possibly not know. He is enamored of exclusive clubs and exorbitant membership dues.

"That's the big dream, the brass ring?" you ask.

"I'll get it."

"And then what?"

"Eye on the prize, Lucy. You see, that's your problem."

"I didn't know I had a problem."

"Well, you drive that piece-of-crap car."

"It runs and gets good gas mileage."

"When I got my new car, that was the focus. That was what I wanted. And I got it. Same with my motorcycle and the new car I bought my mom. Eye on the prize."

Mostly when you talk to Todd you say outwardly, "I see your point," and inwardly you add, *and it's ludicrous.* You're stunned that Todd thinks you have problems. Of course you do, but they have nothing to do with your car. You start to believe that you're both shackled by your nurture and your nature. They are not influences, they are heavy chains. And the prison is your geography. If you lived in some other time or place you would appreciate freakishly small feet or heavy lip plates. But for now it's cars and membership dues and good gas mileage and zero percent body fat.

You try to explain to Todd the reason for your so-called problems. You settle on telling him about Maslow's hierarchy of needs. He didn't go to college, but he's smart. Okay, you're not sure of that. He does think that the band Whitesnake speaks, or sings, the gospel truth. Either way, you know he'll like the tidy triangle. You mention it as something you're interested in. You're in advertising, so naturally you think about what motivates people. You talk about cars, and why someone would choose to drive a beat-up hatchback or a slick Lexus. He joins in, gets excited, when you talk about esteem needs. You linger over belonging needs. You hope your friends will like him.

They're all in relationships, so you're thrilled to have someone to cart around to dinners with the gang. But they don't warm to him. You don't know this right away, because they're friendly people. You suspect they sour on him when, at a dinner party, he reprimands you at the table. It's a big sit-down affair, quite raucous, so you're sure that only a couple of friends overhear it. But you're also sure that it'll come up in the "What do you think about Lucy's new man?" conversation. And then everyone will know. Your crowd isn't known for its discretion.

"If you're running late," he tells you sternly, "then call."

"That would have made me even later," you say. You don't

realize yet that he's truly angry. "Plus, what's the difference if you wait for me at my apartment or yours?" you ask.

"I don't want to have to wait at all," he says.

"Are you kidding me?" You won't be intimidated. "You were two hours late for a date last week because you were watching a *Leave It to Beaver* marathon."

"But I called," he says with righteous conviction.

"What grown man watches *Leave It to Beaver*? Postpones a date for it?"

"I can't tolerate lateness," he says with finality.

"I'm not talking about this," you say, trying to outdo his finality with your own.

Todd cuts people off in traffic with malice. You suspect that he has a lot of rage. The first time he does it, you're truly frightened. It's on the way to the grocery store, a chore you despise. But Todd says that if you do it together it'll be fun. Besides, he wants you to have the energy bars he likes in your cupboard. As he tells you this, he stops his car to let someone out in traffic. When he doesn't get the polite wave of thanks, he's appalled.

"Did you see that? She didn't thank me."

He tails the car. You ask him what he's doing. You brace yourself for the impact that's inevitable if the car in front of you stops short. He fumes that people are discourteous and just downright rude. He passes the supermarket. He races into the other lane and cuts the car off when he gets the chance. Your heart is pounding.

You begin to notice that he does this fairly often. It's worse when he gets slighted when he is not behind the wheel of the car. The threat of danger no longer has the protective metal shell. He holds the door open for a man at a restaurant who doesn't thank him. You have to talk Todd out of stalking over to the man's table and lecturing him, or pounding his head like a nail with his mallet-like fist. Instead, he's rude to the waitress. Hours later, after dinner, after television, after sex, he says, "Can you believe that guy didn't say thank you?" He laughs an angry laugh. He calls the guy stupid. A moron. A small-minded dink. Hmm, you think. Indeed.

Todd works as a landscaper and before he goes to move land and trim growth, he goes to the gym to train for triathlons. He likes the incentive of cheering crowds when he competes. He is a vegan. He says that consuming any animal products makes you sluggish. He asks you to try it. In an uncharacteristic show of solidarity, you do. It's a slight nuisance, but his reference to "animal flesh" whenever you eat meat turns you off of it anyway. You fully explore the wonderful world of the chickpea.

"You feel better, don't you?" he asks smugly.

He has a way of asking, a tone he uses, that gets your hackles up. You do feel good, but don't want to admit it to him. He is much too obsessed with his body. It's unhealthy, in your opinion.

"You are what you eat," he says, drinking a protein shake, which you call pseudo-foodo.

"Good," you say, "then I'll have something rich." You grumpily eat one of his energy bars. It has a chalky taste that the manufacturer optimistically calls "chocolate." You read the ingredients to see if chocolate is even on the list. You are an obsessive label reader now.

"This has whey in it," you say.

"So?"

"That's a milk product," you say, pointing to it as if it will jump off the wrapper and agree.

"No, it's not," he says.

That night you eat steak and cheese-smothered broccoli while he eats pasta in a sauce you're sure has meat in it. You feel better than you have all the days of your short-lived vegan life.

You have to give Todd credit, though. Although you might not agree with each goal in his step-by-step plan, you see that he manages to get what he sets his sights on. So, his philosophy, "You can't get anything if you want everything," seems to work for him.

The low point in Todd's life was when he was fourteen years old and his parents split up. His father took the tent out of the pop-up camper, moved to his brother's land in Louisiana, and never spoke to Todd again. Todd's mother couldn't afford the apartment and refused to get help from the government. She made these bad decisions and she had to live with the consequences. So, she and Todd hooked the tiny, half-moon camper up to their El Camino and pulled it to different RV sites on a rotating basis. They did this for five years while he finished school.

The first summer they lived in the camper, Todd started his business mowing acres and acres at the RV parks. By the time he was twenty, he and his mother moved into a two-bedroom apartment. Five years later, they bought a house. By the time Todd was thirty-five they both drove nice cars and took a Caribbean cruise together each winter.

You know that you're part of Todd's plan. You see that everything is. Plus, you're sure that there's no possible way he can like you for who you are. You have nothing in common except, possibly, that you both hate yourselves deeply. Aside from that, you have no interest in club memberships or nice cars. You don't exercise. Your goals are vague at best. So, you conclude that he must have checked you against some list of things that are important to him. "Date a girl who grew up in a house," check, "who has a college education," check, "and something to say about politics." Check.

Todd doesn't have much to say about politics, except that he hates the pin you have on your jacket. The hated pin has a picture of a stuffed animal sitting inside a hanger. It's from a performance-art piece a friend did. Todd thinks it's a pro state-ment on abortion, which never occurred to you. But you don't mind that he thinks that. Or that anyone might think that. No one asks and you now suspect they aren't thinking, A hanger and a stuffed animal? Must be from that obscure performance artist who did a show in an art gallery last year.

"I fucking hate that thing," he tells you and flicks it.

"Since hate is really fear, maybe we should explore this hate of my pin," you say, not really interested in exploring his fear. You're already too bogged down exploring your own well-spring of damaged notions. "And then we can look at why I hate that you just flicked my lapel."

"I'm afraid of people who make up their minds about something because of a pin," he says in what you think is un-characteristic insight.

"Did you know that Marie Antoinette wore a hairpiece that had a snake strangling what was supposed to be smallpox disease to support inoculation?"

"I hate the French," he counters.

"Because you heard what they said about you?" you ask.

"Where would they be without us?" he continues. "Part of the Nazi empire. That's where."

"You know, I'm a quarter French," you say.

"They like Jerry Lewis and David Hasselhoff."

"That's the Germans who like Hasselhoff," you say, surprised you're having this conversation. "And I like Jerry Lewis."

"Name one Frenchman who has ever done anything important." He believes this will stump you.

"We could be here all night talking about important French people," you say. "But if you want one, I personally like the newspaper columnist DeBlowitz. In the late eighteen hundreds he memorized a speech by the premier, all three thousand words, and scooped his colleagues." You learned about him in journalism class and you're glad you can finally use this tidbit.

"He probably wrote it," Todd says.

"Not a bad theory." When Todd makes a good point you try not to show your utter surprise.

Todd's godlessness interests you. Mostly you find that atheists are just militant for another sort of god—the anti-god. Todd is that variety atheist, the kind who tries to convince you to believe what he believes. You don't mind so much, but come to hate the little rituals of his belief.

"You know, just because you're an atheist doesn't mean you can't say 'bless you' when I sneeze," you tell him.

"No, that's exactly what it means," he says. "How can anyone believe in that crap? It's just a sign of stupidity."

"Couldn't you find something else to say?"

"Something generic that I could use when people fart or burp too?"

"You say that when someone sneezes because you are wishing them good health." You realize that although you hate it when Todd is imprisoned by his culture, you also hate it when he breaks free.

When Todd asks you what your religion is, you know it's a trick question. You try to be honest while not provoking his inner missionary. You tell him that you've lost your faith in religion.

"If I had to nail it down," you say, "I'd classify myself as a non-Christian, part-Jewish Buddhist with a smattering of pagan rituals and a touch of Santeria." You want to tell him his religion is jingoism and then sing, "J-I-N-G-O and Jingo was his name-oh." And you might as well. Todd doesn't know what jingoism is, despite his apparent adherence to its tenets. You fear that he might look it up and explore new lows in close-mindedness.

You can't really joke with Todd, unless you're quoting a movie. These are the jokes he likes, and you're terrible at quoting. In fact, since you started dating Todd, you have almost no memory of anything anymore. Your quotes go something like this: "You know, that thing that guy said about hot dogs in that movie about golf." You reason that he's trying to help you get along better in his world when he buys an obscenely huge TV and puts it in your apartment. You wonder if he's done this because he prefers television to your company. You suspect he does.

You too are beginning to prefer television to your company. You watch the big TV. You're a slave to it. You begin to hate your ordinariness. Your obliviousness. Your jokes that you have to explain. Your tendency to want to nap in the afternoon. Your desire, like everyone else, to lose a couple pounds.

You call your best friend. You're glad to have one. She makes you remember a time when you didn't hate yourself. She tells you what you need to hear when you don't know you need to hear it.

"He is much too common for you," Kate says.

"I'm common," you say.

"Yes, you really should align your life more closely with your station," she says. "Could you get a job at one of those megastores?"

"I tried," you say, taking the bait, "but I let slip that I'd never spanked my kids in public. I was escorted out of the store."

"Not to mention that these imaginary kids aren't by several imaginary baby-daddies," she counters.

"You see how common I am? I mock people who aren't like me."

"Better to mock than to become."

"I *could* have several baby-daddies."

"But you believe in birth control." Kate sighs. "Listen, I know there's something about Todd's sincerity that you're attracted to, but you can find sincerity in both a prince and a dunce."

"He's the kind of guy you wish would lie a little to make himself look better."

"And, Lucy," Kate says, "you can get satisfaction from a

vibrator. Trust me, I'm married. So break up with him before he pisses on you again."

You wish you hadn't told her that story.

You go to Jamaica instead. You're of the philosophy that any relationship can be salvaged or broken by a vacation. You wonder what it is you think you're salvaging. You cut in line at the airport then demand to get upgraded to first class. Your bitchy travel behavior snaps you to attention. You thought you'd abandoned the inner bitch, but your feelings of entitlement seem natural. You're shocked. Then you suspect that a Todd is exactly what this bitch deserves. You are more and more convinced that you've forgotten how to be nice.

You spend most of your four days and three nights getting spa treatments and reading Chomsky, which you can't talk to Todd about. The instant you settle yourself in the hammock, he starts.

"Do you want to take a walk on the beach?"

You refuse.

"You want to go inside and roll around on the big bed?"

You refuse.

"Take a swim?"

"I'm reading."

"Lucy," he says, pouting, "I'm trying."

"Yes, you are," you say, "very trying."

When you return, you develop heartburn that no antacid will quell. You're convinced it's because you're an erupting volcano of seething hate. You don't blame him. It's your fault. You take full responsibility. You tried something new and it was a mistake. You break up with him. It's not a big scene. You tell him on the phone. You've seen what he's done to strangers from behind the wheel, so you figure a quick conversation is the best way out.

Then, it turns out that the thing that attracted Todd to you becomes the very thing that keeps him advancing on you. You had never considered how you would get rid of someone who was attracted to bitchiness. He calls as if you're still together. He sends you cards and gifts. He shows up at the bar you go to even though it's nowhere near his house and he doesn't drink. He brings dates and tries to have casual chats. You get very drunk and stumble by him, pushing him out of the way. You're sure that this enrages him and that he seethes about it later with his decoy girlfriend. And you're secretly terrified.

You ignore all of his overtures. After three months you give away his TV. You change your phone number. You want to move. Or get a different car, at least, so he'll think you've moved. And after you wreck it, that decision is made for you.

The accident happens on your drive to the suburbs to have dinner with Kate. Your brakes feel a little soft, but you don't give it too much attention. Then, when you take that turn too fast, you prove exactly how soft the brakes really are. You hit a tree, and although you manage to limp the car to your mechanic's, you're pretty sure it's not going to pull through. You're okay, and that's all that matters.

It's an adventure to take public transportation in Philadelphia. Subways, trolleys, buses, cabs, trains. It's a city with variety. It's exhausting.

You do love having a car, and you hope it can be fixed. Your mechanic, a jovial man, calls you and asks you to come to the shop. He's serious when he hands you your back brake line and shows you that it had been cut.

"Couldn't this have happened in the accident?" you ask.

"Not unless that tree got up under your rear bumper with bolt cutters."

You're not surprised.

Enchanted Cottage
(Ceramic and Latex Paint, 1998)

When I changed jobs, I took a vacation to mark the transition. There were reporters who said that American workers made too much money and took off whenever they wanted. I wanted to make too much money. They also said that even people who loved their jobs took inordinate amounts of time off from them. I wanted to love my job.

I went to my mother's cabin on the Delaware River to mull over my old life and prepare for the new person I needed to be. I had always been a still person, so solitude was a necessity at times. Plus, it was a mental exercise to adopt a persona. And I was all persona. I was quite sure that if I didn't affect a persona, I'd be a social deviant. I'd talk to strangers and forget family. I'd forget to bathe and remember Arbor Day. Sure, the personas I'd picked had brought me attention from men. Even love. A fat mess I made of that. My new goal was money. How could that go wrong? If it fell apart, at least I'd have some nice shoes out of the bargain.

The cabin, in all truth, probably wasn't the best place to embrace the new, corporate Lucy I was planning to be. I had been working in the creative end of advertising until a work friend, a sales account manager, helped me see the twinkling jackpot lights of the corporate slot machine. He had been grooming me for a new position in sales by giving me an account or two to manage on my own.

I was pretty good at it. All it took was confidence, and I could do bravado. In fact, I could convince anyone of anything. All I had to do was believe it myself. It hadn't worked yet with love (I deserve love . . . nope, don't believe it yet). But I could convince myself that if others joined our team, they would be better for it. Okay, I could convince myself that they wouldn't be worse for it. And that was good enough. Before the promotion was to take effect, my mentor recommended I take time off to integrate this belief. Maybe I wasn't as good at it as I thought.

My problem was that I had the temperament for creative work. Brooding. Silent. Determined. Furthermore, the cabin was filled with reminders of this temperament. I began work on it as a teen, and over the course of time had turned a simple summer house in the woods into an enchanted cottage.

Ceramic gingerbread adorned the borders. The pièce de résistance was the mural I painted inside. It was a mosaic-style Venus de Milo, which was in honor of my father's lineage, the Veniers. They were an old clan from Venice—the one in Italy. The story goes like this. My grandmother was from a small town in Italy. It had a hitching post and all of the families had a ring designated for their house. This system was put in place to prevent townwide fights over who got to entertain the next stranger who visited. That was a big deal. When my grandfather passed through the town, he hitched his horse to the ring of my grandmother's house. They fell in love and hitched their next horse in Manhattan. In the mosaic, I put a hitching post in the background with a golden ring.

My dad loved it. He got to see the Venus before he died. What he didn't get to see was the nighttime garden. I did that when I was into installations. I constructed two white rock-based benches that faced each other. I lined the path to them with white rocks. The blooms of the trees in the garden were gallon and half-gallon milk jugs pocked, melted, and stretched with a heat gun. Some hung weeping-willow style. Some grew skyward. I made an entrance of white chiffon and man-made shrubs of aluminum poles with twist ties and white screw-on bottle caps. He would have loved it.

Inside, the house was crammed with paintings, pottery, tile work, scarves, jewels, and bright colors—my mother thought it was an explosion. She preferred interior design to be simple, white and clean. But she let me do what I wanted, so it was my own personal nest from the age of sixteen, when I started painting seriously. That was before I knew I couldn't spend my life making my own dishes or inlaying crushed glass into a coffee table in the design of a bass. Back then I was unstoppable. I thought the world began and ended in my cottage.

I propped my feet up on the inlaid coffee table and searched the range of my personal reserves. I had the desire for the account management work. The finessing and selling, I could do that. I'd stopped reading women's magazines, so I felt less and less trivial every day. I chose a goal, one goal—to make more money. Just this once. I had learned a thing or two, and one thing was that you could achieve your goals if only you chose one, the same one each and every day until you got it. It was the secret of all masters. Of course, the bigger secret was in the choice.

It wasn't true that money could lead to no good. First of all, they weren't talking about the pittance I made when they said that. Besides, for me it meant that I was going to be a people person and convince others to love me. I generally worked to convince others to hate me, despite their protestations. I figured that this transition might help in other areas of my life as an added bonus.

I knew that I would have to dig deep to find the superficial cheerleader who could convincingly tell the makers of Brand X's industrial epoxy that if they went with my firm they'd be gluing the whole city of Philadelphia together. Nothing to it. Nothing a week in the woods, in silence, wouldn't sort out.

First, I needed to fall in love with myself. Remember who I could be. Tap into the wellspring that told me I deserved to achieve this new goal. *How would I do this?*

I was asking this question when I heard them for the first time. My surprise neighbors. My loud, drunk, music-loving neighbors. I immediately embraced a seething hatred for them. If it was true that love and hate sprung from the same well, I was in luck because I'd successfully tapped into the dark side of that hole. I despised these people. I churned and roiled and doubted their value in the world—except, of course, for the mirror they inevitably held up to my intolerance. I was a people person, damn it!

Okay, so I might not have been yet. But I knew that people could change. I knew this because I myself hadn't always been so uncharitable. I did still wonder if people could also change for the better. That mystery remained, but I was hopeful.

The time when I felt I was most charitable was when I was required to write an essay about noblesse oblige for admittance into a leadership camp. I was so damned charitable to the people the nobles were supposedly obligated to help that I took offense on their behalf. At least I acknowledged that the caste system was a superficial crock of elitism. But I was naive. I was claiming superiority to elitists.

The truth was that I knew someone who was truly noble. And true nobility comes from generosity and humility. Consider Ellen. She was my neighbor while I was growing up. Her real house was a short hike down a woodsy path from our real house, and her cabin on the river was next to our cabin on the river.

The summer Ellen and I became friends, she was staying in her cabin while she got work done on her house. When I was a kid, we always stayed in our cabin for the summer, even though it was just down the way from our real house. That small stretch of beach was my whole world for three months. My father had his boat, my mother had her books, Robert had his painting, and I had Ellen. She was twenty years my senior and a busy sort who liked having a little sister around. She played cards with me and taught me how to bow paddle in a canoe and avoid poison ivy. We've been close ever since.

Her nobility was vast as far as I could tell. Unfortunately, it was inspired by a certain kind of man. We all had our weaknesses.

"I'm in love again," she told me one summer when I was on break from college. She had been reading on her porch and marked the book and set it down the minute she saw me walking up the path.

"Tell me everything." I plunked myself down on her wicker porch chair and dropped the bag of rhubarb I'd picked for her.

"He's a Christian."

"There's one temple and no mosques in this town," I said. "His *not* being a Christian would be newsworthy."

Ellen didn't mind a little ribbing about her religion. Some people might refer to her tolerance and good nature as "Christian," but I never did, lest any realist get the wrong idea.

"I mean," she continued, pretending to be exasperated, "he's taken Jesus into his heart."

"I think that's pronounced Hay-Zeus," I said. "I know him, good guy."

Ellen rolled her eyes. She didn't mind the jokes when they were funny.

It wasn't that I didn't believe in something bigger than myself, I just didn't believe anyone else's ideas. And I didn't believe that my ideas would suit anyone else. As far as I was concerned, I had a deal with my own personal god. Part of that deal was to keep it to myself. I also agreed to try not to wreck other people's images of their own private gods. Joking was allowed in this deal.

My first meeting with the God-fearing Tim made me grateful that Ellen's god was not my god. The first word that came to mind was *hobo*. I wanted to start a boxcar sing-along when I met him: "She'll be comin' round the mountain when she comes." I'd stomp my foot and swing my fist. *Beer from a can in a paper bag, anyone? Tim's holding.*

But I knew when to draw the line on joking, and I didn't let on to Ellen that her high faith might have been the cause of some of her bad decisions. What I told her was that often what happened to people who were Ellen-variety-good was that they projected their own good traits onto others. And so it was with Tim. I'd seen it before. She nursed these guppies only to watch them get gulped down by a fish the second she let them loose. Her full-bore effort to help the Tims of the world by loving them never helped anyone.

She saw Tim's goodness fade the first time he called her a fucking bitch. He was extremely drunk, so she said, as if she were reasoning it away with that old excuse. By then she was entangled. Tim needed a car, so she was loaning him hers. He needed a place to stay, so she let him use her cabin. He needed some equipment so he could start his own painting business, and she was in debt for that.

"Jesus will help him," Ellen said. "I've been praying."

"Okay, then," I told her, "you pray for him and I'll pray for you."

So, with faith in Jesus, Ellen married Tim. Four miserable years later, with faith in her own potential to be happy, she divorced him.

In her last supremely humanitarian gesture—and by last, I mean latest—Ellen had let her bum of an ex-husband and his rough-around-the-edges girlfriend—also known as his "old lady"—live in her cabin again for a "short spell."

This happened to coincide with my short spell at my cabin. Now, the Walden experience I enjoyed involved a lot of quiet and solitude. With Tim and the Old Lady nearby, I endured nightly noise pollution of the foulest kind. My silent tolerance of them was simply the survival instinct that told me to avoid conflicts with drunken lunatics. The meek might inherit the earth, but I wanted it now. *Please? Sorry to sound pushy.*

Tim and the Old Lady would get in late from work and immediately start hollering to each other. It began with a general whooping. Now, I'm not judging this behavior, I have no feelings one way or another about this kind of stupidity. But I was lost to classify it. I was raised in a quiet family devoted to arts and letters. We worked crossword puzzles to let loose. We never whooped. Well, there were a few limited engagements when I was learning how to play craps. We didn't live at the library. I knew something about whooping. But it always struck me as being very specific. Whoops were for sports teams. Whoops on the dance floor. Whoops as a mating call to other whoopers. This could have been the case with Tim and the Old Lady.

Or maybe they were just rootin', tootin' happy to be in their rent-free cabin on the river. Whoop! Or maybe they'd just bought sum' more beers and were happy to be on the brink of many more. Whoop!

When the whooping died down, there was a sustained loudness. Conversation was done at a shout. Then, merely at high volume. Finally, just an ebb and flow of audible phrases, insincere laughter, and deathbed coughing attacks that broke through my cabin windows.

The second night of my stay some pals from the boxcar jamboree joined them and I heard how whoopers socialized. At one point one of them asked, "You win the lottery yet?" *If he did, I'd suspect he wouldn't tell you. Just a guess.* "Yeah, I won the lottery. I'm squatting in this sweet cabin in the woods for free."

Heavy metal music blasted. Oh, my favorite. It was followed by a new R & B tune that was apparently a favorite of the Old Lady's. She sang along at the top of her voice. I marveled at this. She wasn't even close to the melody. She wasn't even trying to get the tune right. Although she did nuance her performance by modulating her volume.

I disliked them with abandon. I sent black magic curses to them. By the third day, I'd constructed rudimentary voodoo dolls of them out of potatoes and stabbed the dolls so many times they turned to pulp. I willed a skunk to spray them. I sent a colony of ants to their tape deck and cassettes. I floated hate messages from my nighttime fire. I ordered the smoke that twisted out of my chimney to choke them. It was dark, dark magic. But this, in my personal religion, fell under the "don't tell" category, so the details of my curses will have to remain sketchy.

In my bed at night, breathing the woodsy cedar of the land and the mushroomy cool of the rushing water, I pretended I was Ellen. I explored my own boundaries of charity. I spent a good deal of time thinking about hatred and decided that it wasn't about anyone but me. Some people cycled through stages of hating their parents or their lovers. But that was just misplaced blame. Sometimes other people got in the line of fire, sure.

Ellen's charity, not just to Tim, led me to see that I truly was not noble. I didn't even know what it meant. Since that was the case, I figured I was eligible for Ellen's charity. But I wondered if it would be right to petition her to change causes. To persuade her from helping Tim to helping me. And that was when I saw that my mission was clear. Sure, I was nearing the middle of the week and I could stick it out. Maybe get used to it. Learn to live with it.

But I was at the cabin for a reason. I was about to begin a career in which I would confidently ask people to do what I wanted them to do. I was going to be convincing, damn it. Everyone was supposed to join my team. I had to ask them to, though. *Come to my side. See my point of view and take action!* Ultimately, I had to believe that I was entitled to ask. And whatever I asked, it was best for all of us.

Was it right to test out my new persona on Ellen? A friend? Hell, I was doing Ellen a favor telling her what kind of rabble-rousing was going on at her cabin. She needed to have those freeloaders out of her life. Tim and the Old Lady needed to find someone new to take advantage of.

I took a deep breath and said my own private prayer to Ellen's god.

Then I picked up the phone and dialed Ellen's number.

Roadside Diner
(Gold Leaf on Masonite, 1999)

When Lucy met Keith she had been celibate for over a year. She had purposely taken time off from men to sort out a thing or two. Naturally, in that time the whole world fell in love. Spending the holiday season with her urban clan in Philadelphia seemed unbearable. Everyone was in a couple, and they tended to talk endlessly about weddings and rings and house costs and whose insurance was better. So, Lucy took some vacation days and went to visit her mother, just a short two-hour drive, but a world away.

When she met Keith, she'd been working too much to notice if she'd sorted out any of her issues with men. So, without too much thought to the original reasons for her celibacy, she considered Keith's advances while sipping eggnog at a neighbor's party.

Keith seemed exotic to Lucy because he spoke his very own language—a mix of old slang, new jargon, and invented words. It was fun. Like pig Latin was for kids—forget that Lucy never actually thought pig Latin was all that much fun.

She and Keith stood in the corner of the room and he "gummed" about who was who at the "clambake." To be honest, Lucy didn't understand a lot of what Keith was saying. She caught up when he launched into a game where he described all of the guests in the room. The Voluptuous Ignoramus and the Yuppicus Domesticus were cooing over the dog. There was the already drunk Lushus Debatus on the sofa smoking a cigarette. There was the Snootus Elitus who waved away the smoke then dragged her Victimus Lemmingus friend into the kitchen. Maybe it was a not-too-clever way to be clever, but Lucy thought it was hilarious.

Her mother disapproved. "I know his family, and they're not good people."

Lucy restrained herself from pointing out that her mother was openly dating a married man. It was too low a blow. Or not. "Well, I suppose they could say the same of us to him."

"Well, they'd be wrong."

Her mother was un-insultable.

On their first date, Keith took Lucy hiking. Sure, it was winter, but Keith explained that he needed to find a suitable resting place for his pet hamster, who had "punted it" that very afternoon. This said that Keith was spontaneous enough to change whatever plans he'd previously made for their date. He was open enough to include her in the memorial service of his beloved pet, Mr. Marizecki. He was weird enough to name his pet Mr. Marizecki. And, he wanted to bury his old pal in a charmingly childlike way. Lucy liked him.

"My little hairy brother loved this pile of fluff."

"Who?" Lucy asked, tripping on a root and sliding on some slick leaves. Lucy wasn't much of a hiker.

"My parents' dog K. K-10, actually, because he's that much better than a canine. He's my hairy brother. Dig it?"

Lucy liked that he explained the oddities of his vernacular to her. And she liked that he didn't see her slip. She wanted to be hearty, or at least appear to be.

The ground was frozen, so Keith buried Mr. Marizecki under some old snow. Then he bowed his head and said, "Yo, cheese, this hepped-up mini-pup is dream dust now. But he's the cat's, all right. So, clap one on him for me. Peace out."

Lucy figured that was the end of the prayer since Keith was blessing himself elaborately. Lucy followed suit.

Keith led Lucy to a scenic spot up the trail so they could "set their seats." When they settled on a big rock with a view of the valley, Keith pulled out a joint and offered it to her. Lucy hadn't smoked since college, but was game.

"Hip chick," Keith said in approval. "I'm not trying to be sly, but I want to knock you some sugar before we spark this."

Before Lucy could interpret, Keith kissed her.

Keith led the way out. Lucy stumbled on a rock. She swiped at the imaginary spiderwebs on her face. Paranoia gripped her. Her breath got shallow and labored. Adding just the slightest physical exertion to her mounting pot-induced anxiety seemed like a bad idea. Could her heart explode? She convinced herself that a bear was going to come strolling along and maul her. Go downhill to outrun a bear, right? Don't climb a tree. Her panic had reached its peak when Keith turned and asked her if she wanted to "toke more before we pound out." She could only shake her head no because she wasn't sure if her mouth would work without any saliva in it. When they got back into his car, she grabbed the bottle of water from the front seat and gulped it. Keith said it was copacetic. He dug a duchess who felt free to reign.

It's like thinking a man with a British accent is smart," Kate warned, as only a best friend could. "You need an interpreter to understand him."

"He's a very patient translator." Lucy firmly defended him. "So, see, there is substance behind the accent."

"A better trait would be if he were understandable in the first place. He's doing double work."

"And he's a hard worker."

"I'll bet this self-imposed language barrier makes for a fascinating career. What does he do?" Kate asked.

"His lingo indicates a way of thinking that's outside the norm."

"Lucy, I'm trying to steer you toward the norm. It's norm for a reason. You need a degree in psychology for the men you've dated, except for Ben, of course."

Ben was the only man Kate, Lucy's mother, and pretty much all of Lucy's friends ever truly liked. Lucy was sick of hearing about him. She already compared all of the men she dated to him. She didn't need any help, thank you very much.

"Keith is really sweet to me," Lucy said.

"Of course he is, Lucy. You're a shining star, and he's a slacker."

"If I'm so good," Lucy asked, "then why distrust my ability to discern?"

"Experience," Kate deadpanned. "Now, come on, you know I judge people by their jobs. Tell me what he does for a living."

"You really don't trust me at all," Lucy said.

"No," Kate answered without hesitation.

In a way, Lucy was proud to be the only one she knew who appreciated Keith. Eventually everyone would see that he was worthwhile, and then they'd have to apologize. Lucy's problem was that she inadvertently poisoned her friends' opinions by revealing the awkward things men did on early dates. Lucy knew, the second it came out of her mouth, that she shouldn't have told Kate about Keith's interesting dialect.

Lucy vowed to keep a low profile with Keith. For example, she would not tell her friends about Keith's grandest dream. And oh, how Lucy wanted to tell everyone. It was classic. But she kept this gem all to herself. Keith's lifelong obsession was to produce a line of bookmarks that were pictures of dogs' ears.

"Like a German shepherd ear, a poodle ear, a Chihuahua ear."

"For the bookish dog owner?" Lucy ventured.

"For everyone," Keith answered, puzzled that she was not fully on board with the genius of the idea. "Dog ears," he said. "Get it?"

Lucy supported Keith's fantasy by allowing him to think that a bookmark could earn someone millions. She figured it was the least she could do since he was tolerating her "no sex for three months" policy.

"Whatever I gotta do to get you to round-trip to me," Keith said, "it's right on."

Lucy was pretty sure that meant Keith was okay with the arrangement.

"But Bob the Knob's a horny corncob."

He may have been a little frustrated by it as well.

After they had sex, Lucy broke her vow of silence and

picked all of the best stories to tell Kate. She loaded her down with how sweet he was and how he made her laugh. She also told her about Bob the Knob. It was only a small piggyback on a bigger story about his tendency to name things.

"Ugh, Lucy," Kate said, "don't mistake crude manners for verve or wit."

"Verve or wit?" Lucy laughed. "Are you talking about my old neighbor? Irv Everitt?"

"Talking about spunk does not mean he's spunky," Kate said. "You know what I mean?"

"I think I do," Lucy said, "but I'm trying not to mistake it for genuine concern."

Lucy was poisoning public opinion again. Although it was probably too late with Kate. Nevertheless, Lucy recommitted herself. She told her friends that Keith was fine, they were great, nothing to report, all's well. Then Lucy told work stories. She finally realized that work was what people talked about when they didn't want to expose their goofy boyfriends.

Lucy's work was in advertising sales. She brought boxes of original Philly soft pretzels to meetings and tried to carbo-load midlevel employees into indifference. However, she found that once her standard approach bombed, she was drained. Empty. She felt like she'd just looked at an ugly baby and the only thing she knew to say about babies—"how cute"—was taken away from her. After these meetings, Lucy fantasized about buying some clay and making plates for a living. She wasn't so sure she was cut out for corporate America.

Her problem was that she believed just about any other firm could do as good a job as hers. It was advertising. Really, how hard was it? Lucy's other problem was that she didn't have any business role models. Her father had been an academic. And although her mother was a savvy art broker, all she really did was flirt with old, rich men who bought art from her for as long as they thought they had a chance. Hence, Lucy mishandled lots of meetings, which made for a few half-decent work stories.

Despite her plans, as Lucy and Keith rounded the corner of the first year, Lucy felt antsy. It started with the job. No, it started with Keith. She wasn't sure. She was traveling too much, entertaining clients, finding herself attracted to other men, using her mother's business tactics. This was cause for concern.

And Keith's job embarrassed her. Okay, so he managed a Dollar Store. Lucy valued the retail industry. She valued low-priced bric-a-brac. And yet when someone asked Lucy what Keith did, she heard herself say brightly, "He's a store manager for a local chain." What was that, a local chain? It reminded her of the guy she went on a date with who told her he worked for the International House. All night she thought he was an interpreter. What he left out of the employer's name was "of Pancakes." Now, that was a business name you just couldn't shorten.

Her prejudice about Keith's job brought her unbearable shame. She wanted to blame other people for it. Her classist mother, her elitist private school peers, her haughty professors. She couldn't possibly be that shallow all on her own.

On business trips, Lucy drank too much in hotel bars. At a convention in Chicago she ran into an old college friend, Alex. So relieved to see a familiar face, she unloaded on him in a messy display in the corner of a rowdy hotel bar.

She remembered little about the night. Evidently, she drank the contents of the minibar in her room because the next morning she woke amid accusing little empty bottles. Alex was in her bed—in his underwear. And she had a headache that might have killed a smaller woman. She shooed the poor guy out of her room, puked, showered, and plopped down on an easy chair in the corner of the room. She had booked her ticket for later the next day so she could see some of Chicago. And she saw it all from the window of her hotel room.

People like to say that all hotel rooms look the same. But Lucy disagreed. It was the little differences that mattered. And if she could get upgraded, which was something she was good at finagling, then the differences were even greater. The upgraded room she had in Chicago boasted a reclining easy chair, whirlpool jets in the bathtub, and prompt room service. Sitting in the recliner in her complimentary robe and slippers, Lucy decided that she needed to make a change. She picked up the little empty Kahlua bottle and spun it on the end table. Toward her chair was "yes," away from it was "no."

Lucy closed her eyes. Concentrated. *Will Keith and I get along better soon?*

Chair. Yes.

Should I quit my job?

Chair. Yes.

Should I go back to school?

Chair. Yes.

Art school?

No.

Lucy concentrated harder. *Oh, great and wise Kahlua bottle, should I go to art school?*

No.

Okay, okay, how about I go for . . . philosophy?

No.

Sociology?

No.

Law school?

Yes.

Really? Lucy straightened in her chair. *Law school?*

Yes.

Should I go to law school?

Yes.

She never admitted it to anyone, but that was the first stone that started the avalanche. She figured other important decisions had probably been decided by an empty mini-bottle of Kahlua. Why not? Plus, she wouldn't have asked if she didn't really want to do it. Right? She'd be a good lawyer.

She called Keith when she got back from Chicago and told him she was going to go to law school.

"Saccharine, baby! You make big skins and I'll be minivan man for BamBam and Pebbles."

"And don't forget about the bookmarks," Lucy said, then pulled her birth control dial pack out of her bedside drawer where it sat, without any sense of the irony, next to her vibrator.

Lucy focused. She studied for the LSATs. She researched law schools. She filled out applications. She wrote essays. Through all of it, Keith got on her nerves. She attributed it to stress. A change in their routine.

"Roger the codger's been doping out the store. Pouncing on us," Keith told Lucy over dinner.

Lucy nodded, pretending to be engrossed in her sea bass, which was easier than feigning interest in Keith's story.

"I said, if he's the heavy, that's crackerjack. But we're raking in skins. So, go be a creaky monkey at the south-side store."

"Isn't that 'cheeky monkey'?" Lucy said vaguely, thinking it was ugly of Keith to implicate the other manager. Keith gabbed on, and Lucy silently interpreted, getting more annoyed with each story he told. All week at work she listened to people bitch about office politics. Now, on the weekends, she had to hear about the troubles in Dollar-world?

And Keith's vernacular was annoying Lucy. Proving again that the things she initially liked about someone would eventually become the very things she grew to loathe. Take the poop talk, for example. Keith found it necessary to inform Lucy of his bowel functions on a regular basis. Now, this was never exactly pleasant for Lucy. Size, texture, scent, length, duration, endurance. Not a fan. But in the early stages, she truly appreciated that Keith was comfortable enough with her to reveal such private news.

Over time, she suspected that his obsession with his feces was the reason for the twinges of disgust she felt when she was with him. But Lucy knew parents who were obsessed with their children's excrement. And that kind of attention was probably as close as anyone ever came to being loved unconditionally. Spoken or unspoken, wasn't this need to experience unconditional love the real reason people coupled?

And just when she thought she'd had enough of Keith, he emerged with a new charm. He told Lucy that when they weren't together on weekends, he spent his Sunday mornings at his local soup kitchen.

"Eating?" Lucy asked.

"You're doofin' me, right?"

She hadn't been kidding. She was truly stunned. She was still in bed nursing a hangover and berating herself for calling Alex, her Chicago hookup. He knew about Keith. He had a girlfriend. It wasn't a big deal. But it wasn't exactly earning her any good-citizen awards. Meanwhile, Keith had been serving whatever it was soup kitchens served on Sunday mornings.

Lucy believed that people with no personal connection to childhood illness manned soup kitchens, fought for the environment, and supported the arts. Lucy didn't know any children with leukemia, so the next weekend she visited Keith, Lucy suggested they volunteer together. As they walked up to the community center, Lucy tried to let Keith take the lead. But he lagged behind. They stutter-stepped to the door until a stout volunteer marched toward them, announced her name, "Felice," then herded them into the kitchen to outfit them with hairnets and aprons.

"First-timers?" she asked. Lucy was puzzled. Keith mumbled something about helping out before. Felice thrust a tray of juice at Lucy. "Just one box each," she told her firmly. Lucy looked helplessly at Keith but he was already happily stirring scrambled eggs and chatting with another cook.

Lucy had imagined a different version of the day. Keith, the old vet, would introduce Lucy to the other volunteers and to his favorite customers, regular folks down on their luck. They would all tell Lucy how much they loved Keith. And he sure did tell them nice things about her.

But no one seemed to know Keith. The regular folks down on their luck took their juice and said thank you. However, it was the deranged customers Lucy got a bellyful of. They yelled at her, demanding two or three juice boxes. Given strict marching orders, Lucy just smiled and wished them a good morning. But they would not be brushed off. So Lucy reasoned with them and said that there were just enough juice boxes to go around. But she was unconvincing, because she didn't believe it. Loaves and fishes, anyone? She *wanted* to give the thirsty more juice. Finally, Lucy passed the buck. "You want more juice? Take it up with Keith. He's in the back." What did it matter? No one knew who he was anyway.

Keith told Lucy that if she was accepted to law school they should quit their jobs and take a cross-country road trip. They could both give up their apartments and move their stuff into a storage unit he had a key to. That would net them over a thousand bucks right there. When they got back, he would find a job, they'd move in together, and he'd help put her through school. "Supportus Sugardaddyus." Swept away by his enthusiasm, Lucy agreed.

Privately, she admitted to Alex that she was terrified of this plan. She had been calling him more often. It was easy to have a little phone flirtation here and there since she and Keith saw each other only one or two weekends a month. This arrangement with Keith suited her. Drinks, dinner, sex, snacks, sex, jokes, movies, more food, and off you go. Things really were going well with him. That lump in her throat could have been from anything. Job stress. Law school rejections. A goiter. Throat cancer. Anything.

A deal being a deal, after Lucy got her acceptance letter she gave up her apartment, moved her stuff into storage, and packed her bags for the "junket" with Keith. He had told Roger the codger from Dollar-world that he was "hitting bricks." Lucy wondered if Roger knew what Keith was talking about. In the surprise move of the century, Keith had already lined up a job in Philadelphia for when they got back. He was going to be managing a head shop. He said the owner was "right on" with Keith starting in a month, since the owner himself would be taking three months off to go boarding in Tahoe. It was a mystery how those birds of a feather found each other.

Keith loaded his 1982 Plymouth Reliant with "the essentials," which included a tent, sleeping bags, a grill, a coffeepot, a gallon bottle of rum, a big bag of pot, and a carton of cigarettes. Keith said the rum was because "camping is dry enough." Lucy stopped asking him what he meant. The weed was for "scenic enhancement," and the cigarettes were to pass the time. Keith had quit smoking when he started dating Lucy, but said "tobacco goes with the open road like TP goes with the butt butter." Lucy doubted her decision.

She armed herself with travel guides, an atlas, a flashlight, and a first aid kit. She was set for lean living. No fancy hotels. No executive suites. Lucy wasn't a fan of the motel. She'd stayed in them, sure, she wasn't Catherine de Médici or anything. But she disagreed with them as a general concept. Lucy liked that there were hotel/restaurant management experts. Both food and lodging were best left to trained professionals. Lucy didn't know why the guy who clapped up a few rooms on the side of the road and attached a steak and grog chain was still trusted. But she could rough it. She *was* hearty.

In the driver's seat, Keith was wearing his lucky tie-dyed T-shirt and his too tight cargo shorts. Lucy desperately wanted him to wear clothes that fit. But she didn't feel right telling him this. She felt like a 1950s man of the house who told his wife to wear a dress to the dinner she'd spent all day preparing for him. Who was she to tell Keith to wear looser clothing? That a T-shirt from high school, while soft and *possibly* lucky, made him look like Gulliver on wash day when he had to make due with Lilliputian duds. But Keith was an adult, chronologically. He could make his very own dressing decisions. Lucy would stay out of it.

Keith wanted to drive the first leg of the trip, which was fine with Lucy since she liked it when he drove. Neither of them was a particularly good driver. Keith had so many small accidents that he joked about painting his car different colors on each side so witnesses would give conflicting reports. But Lucy felt safe with him. Sure, the car swerved slightly every time he ashed his cigarette out the window. And when they hit construction an hour into the drive, Lucy privately hoped he'd be a little more careful.

"Aliens put those concrete barriers up," Lucy said, passing the joint back to Keith. "They come down and freeze the world and drop those things into place."

Keith laughed. He once told her that sometimes the things she said weren't so funny, but he laughed because she said them as if they were. Lucy suspected that the alien comment was one of those not-so-funny instances. The pot made her stupid and sleepy, but it seemed to make Keith sharp and energized.

"Driver picks the music," Keith said. He reached into the backseat, where the boom box sat, and the car swayed as he put in his N.W.A. tape. *Straight Outta Compton* blared from the boom box, and Lucy dug two cans of root beer out of the cooler. Keith sang along, lit a cigarette, drank his soda, and squeezed Lucy's knee to the beat. He was possibly the most distracted driver she'd ever seen. It didn't bother Lucy, but Keith was doing all of this in the passing lane, and it bothered the guy in the white sports car who flew by them in the right lane.

"He gave us the finger," Lucy said jovially.

"Jerkus Tyrannuosaurus." Keith was not amused. "I hope the asphalt sheriffs clink him."

Keith told Lucy his own story about the "asphalt sheriffs," or highway patrol. The din of N.W.A. complicated Lucy's translation job, however she determined that Keith was pulled over with a hitchhiker ("ride snaker"). Naturally, Keith had pot in the car ("stash in the dash"). He made the poor, unsuspecting ride snaker dig it out of the glove box and hide it under the seat ("they'll peep a box, but don't usually harass your ass"). Lucy had just deciphered the whole story when she noticed that they were about to overtake the little white car.

"There he is," Lucy shouted, pointing to the right lane.

Keith perked up at this news.

"You should throw your soda can at him," Lucy said in a moment of poor judgment.

"Roll your glass down all the way," Keith commanded as he stepped on the accelerator.

"You can't throw that at him." It was an absurd idea. "I was just kidding." Lucy rolled her window up.

As they passed the white car, Keith leaned forward and looked over at the driver.

Lucy watched Keith, wondering if he'd give the driver the

finger or if he'd make some other ridiculous hand gesture that would be too elaborate for anyone to understand.

Keith gunned the gas and the car lurched forward. Lucy watched as Keith looked back and forth between the road and the white car. They were neck and neck. Lucy looked at the guy in the white car. He wasn't looking at them. She looked at Keith. He was still looking back and forth between the white car and the road. Back and forth. Back and forth.

"What are you doing?" Lucy asked.

Keith told Lucy to lean back. He looked over at the white car one more time then whipped the can of root beer past Lucy's perplexed face. It collided into her closed window. In an instant, soda erupted over Lucy and the can ricocheted into the side of her head.

"What happened?" Keith was stunned. He looked over at Lucy, who was rubbing her head. "Your window's up?" Keith yelled.

"Are you insane?" Lucy yelled back. "I said you *couldn't* throw your soda at him. I rolled the window *up.*" Lucy didn't even know how to begin cleaning herself up. "You can't throw stuff at cars on the road. It's dangerous and illegal."

And that was when Lucy began imparting the basic rules of civilized life to Keith. They included things like, "No, it wouldn't be great to be homeless. Working and paying bills is *not* more burdensome than pushing a cart around and living on the beach." And "It it not acceptable to curse loudly in front of children in public."

By Ohio, Lucy was officially tired of Keith's smoking. She probably wouldn't have minded so much if she consumed something, anything, in mass quantities. She might have understood. She almost admired it, in a way. She wanted a consuming passion. But for tobacco? She didn't get it. She didn't have the stamina for addiction. Keith's constant smoking was exhausting her. And the stories Keith was telling her, they were bringing her down.

"Me and Sam and Joey," Keith said, "we laid down some crazy town-chase riots. Tore it up on our bikes. We was loco cads."

Keith started a running monologue about his preadolescent years that lasted for most of the Bible Belt.

"We'd take a flash of Joey's mom getting tarted up for her dates. Cop a squat at the peephole where he kept his duds."

"You mean his *closet*?" Lucy was translating in an exhausted tone whenever she could get a word in.

Keith started talking about eleven-year-old Joey and Sam at dawn and had only reached age twelve by the time they stopped for a late breakfast at a Waffle House.

"We'd push his geegaws out of the way and pull up fisticuffs over who would get the first gander."

"Okay, gotcha, you fought over who got to look through the peephole first."

"That honey hole pointed right at her baby shooter where she'd sit to slap on the war paint."

"Her makeup?"

"She'd be in the same old yellow bathrobe."

"I'm sorry, did you say 'baby shooter'?"

"Right at the pecker kisser."

Lucy looked around the restaurant, hoping no one was listening to them. "There are so many things that are gross about what you said, I don't know where to begin. What were you, like, twelve?"

"*We* thought it was the bee's knees. Maternus Fullbushicus. Joey'd knock us aside and hog the hole."

"'Fullbushicus'? Keith, you know, if you spoke English, you'd get kicked out of biker bars with the disgusting shit you say." Lucy pushed aside the ashtray when her country-fried steak, smothered in white gravy, came. "Sick."

"Sam and I hit bricks when the babysitter came." Keith doused his grits in syrup and dug in, holding his spoon in his fist.

"Joey was spying at his own mother's . . ." Lucy stopped herself from saying "fullbushicus." She suddenly had a picture of herself, with country-fried-steak hips, waddling into court to post bail again for her head-shop-working boyfriend. Busted again for possession. Then and there Lucy vowed to lay off the white sausage gravy and the pot. She was going to law school, for crissake.

Miles away from the stench of "golden brown home fries and skirt steak done to your liking," Keith picked up the strand of his earlier monologue. He told Lucy that Joey and the babysitter would have sex on the couch while he and Sam watched through the porch window.

"Joey told me she'd have a go with us once," Keith said, "but I was too scared."

"Maybe because you were twelve?" Sometimes Lucy felt bad for him although she wasn't always exactly sure why.

Suddenly, Keith burst into convulsive laughter. He couldn't speak. Instead, he pointed. Lucy saw a sign hanging from an old roadside restaurant. The daily special had been vandalized to read "hot poop." Keith had a fit of the giggles for miles. Sometimes she felt bad for herself and she was exactly sure why.

By Wyoming, Lucy was sick of cheap motels, so they decided to camp out. The boulders were mammoth and otherworldly. Lucy felt like she was in a Dr. Seuss book.

At the campsite, Lucy pitched the tent while Keith went for a hike to "secure the perimeter." When he returned, she had camp set up and a fire going.

"Didn't you hear me?" Keith asked.

"Speak into my good ear," Lucy joked.

"My foot got stuck."

Lucy turned to see Keith limping. His leg was smeared with blood.

"I yelled for you. I finally got my foot out, but when it came unstuck, I knocked myself down this super-sized boulder."

Lucy noticed that Keith's language was much clearer in the face of a personal emergency. "Let's have a look," Lucy said, suppressing a laugh. She thought that falling was hilarious.

Keith sulked over to a rock and lit a cigarette.

"Let me start dinner, then we'll get you fixed up." Lucy threw chicken on the fire and swatted a bee away. The bee buzzed around her angrily then flew straight at Keith and stung him. By the time Lucy got the first aid kit out of the car, Keith's arm had swelled to twice its size.

"First, a little pain reliever," Lucy said and gave him his flask of rum.

Then Lucy played nurse. She cleaned up his blood and put ointment on his sting. She gave him two aspirin and retrieved his weed from the car for him.

Keith smoked and sulked. Lucy poked feebly at the chicken. She hadn't wanted chicken, but Keith had vetoed her choice of veggie burgers. They were disagreeing often over food, but for once Lucy opted not to fight about it. It was part of her new plan—she didn't smoke pot, eat sausage gravy, or fight in the supermarket.

The sun had set and it was getting dark. Keith was uncomfortable, and where was the rum, and he needed another pack of smokes from the car, and was there any more salve? Lucy thought he seemed quite comfortable—playing the victim, that was. She got him settled, but then he was starving. Unable to wait any longer, Keith pulled a chicken leg out of the fire and took a big bite. Lucy trained her flashlight onto the drumstick.

"Let me see," she commanded.

As the light hit the bite mark in the chicken leg, Lucy saw that the flesh was still raw and pink. "Great," Lucy said, with as much sympathy as she could muster, "now you have a bum leg, a bee sting, and salmonella." At that thought, Lucy ate trail mix for dinner.

In the morning Keith came out of the woods holding his stomach. "I think that chicken mixed me up."

"Isn't discomfort so very troublesome," Lucy muttered. She was rubbing the kink in her neck she'd got from sleeping on the ground with a T-shirt for a pillow. She'd lent hers to Keith, who forgot to bring one.

"I just had green diarrhea," Keith said, oblivious to Lucy's pain.

"Green?" Lucy sighed inwardly. She did not want to discuss

his bowels. Whenever he did, which was every day, Lucy's version of The Police song played in her head. *Every shit he takes, every mess he makes, every turd he takes, every fart he fakes, I'll be hearing it.* She started to think of his crap as "endangered feces" and they were the scientists. The "head" scientists. She would not mention that thought to Keith. It would only encourage him.

The Florence Nightingale treatment threw Keith into a tailspin of laziness. He stopped driving altogether and spent eighteen hours sleeping in the passenger seat, slack-jawed, snoring. At about midnight, Lucy looked at his face illuminated by the highway lights and thought about punching him. A straight punch to the side of his head. Or maybe just a casual backhand. But then he'd jolt awake and ask what happened. Maybe she'd just slam on the brakes and let him hit the dashboard. He never wore his seat belt. The highway was deserted. It would work. She slammed on the brakes.

"There was something in the road," she said through shotgun bursts of laughter. "Are you all right?"

Keith rubbed his head and mumbled. He struggled to dig into his pocket, and he eventually pulled out his pipe.

"Maybe you should get some bigger shorts so you could get into your pockets easier." She went and did it. She gave wardrobe advice. "Not that I'm trying to make it easier for you to smoke or anything." And followed it up with some nagging. *Nice job.*

"Are we making good time?" Keith asked, taking a hit off his bowl.

"Oh sure," Lucy said mock cheerfully, "we're lost, but we're making great time."

Keith exhaled. "Rock on," he said. "Vegas or bust." Then he closed his eyes and was out.

Good lot of help he was. Lucy decided that she liked her men manlier than Keith. Men were supposed to want to drive. It was one of the modern ways to prove stamina. Men drove for eighteen hours straight without stopping. Men worked out the fastest route and bragged about time and gas mileage. Lucy didn't make these rules. It was fine if he wanted to prove his manhood in other ways—blind ambition, shrewd money management, all-night-long sex sessions, heavy-equipment operation, map folding. But driving seemed to be the only thing within Keith's reach.

Lucy thought about slamming on the brakes again, but then he'd be awake.

They arrived in Las Vegas at three in the morning, and Lucy went straight to bed in their twenty-dollar-a-night room. Keith, however, came alive. Sure he did. Why not? He'd been sleeping for the better part of the past twenty-four hours. He went gambling.

Well into Lucy's REM sleep, the phone woke her.

"I shit a huge turd in the casino bathroom." Keith giggled. "The attendant." Keith giggled. "Was in there." Keith giggled. "I was like, 'Sorry, dude. Daily special—hot poop.'" Keith laughed and laughed.

Lucy held the phone away from her ear, looked at it, then hung up.

Keith slammed into the motel room and woke Lucy. She watched him stumble into the bathroom and puke. Then he lurched into the room and belly flopped on the bed. "I lost eight big skins," he said into the pillow.

"I'm not sure I caught that," Lucy said. "Do you mean eight hundred dollars?"

She sat up in bed. "Hello," she said, poking his prone form. She shook him. She bounced his skull up and down like a basketball. It was no use. He had passed out.

Eight hundred dollars was all of their budget for the rest of the trip. They'd have to turn around and drive night and day to get home. Forget California. Vegas or bust, indeed.

Would he really have gambled away all of the cash they had? If he did, then they were going home in the morning. He couldn't have lost *all* of their cash. But why would he say it? Lucy couldn't sleep. She took a shower. She watched TV. She stepped out of the motel, saw the hookers and a couple junkies, then stepped back in. When Keith stirred about six hours later, she bounced his head like a basketball again. He swatted blindly in her direction then rose and stumbled into the bathroom. When he came out he was apparently too hungover to give his typical full report. All he said was, "Bad medicine. Bad. Let's get out of Dodge," and left the room.

Lucy gathered her things and met him in the car. Keith was waiting in the passenger seat with his sunglasses on.

Lucy pulled the Reliant onto the strip and broke the silence. "So, are we going home?"

Keith looked over his sunglasses at her. "No way, Doris Day, we're going to L.A."

"What about the eight hundred bucks?" she asked.

"That freakin' Flamingo," Keith groaned. "I didn't know I told you that."

"Right before you puked and passed out."

"I just used the plastic," he said. "We're still in bills, so we're riding shady, baby."

"You used my credit card?" She'd given it to him to pay for gas and when he put it in his wallet, she thought, What the heck, he always pumps the gas anyway, it makes more sense for him to hold it. "So, *my card*, which we were only using for gas." Lucy was livid. "Wait, how does that even happen? It has my name on it."

"ATMs take credit cards as long as you have the PIN number," Keith said to Lucy as if she were an idiot. "Man, that pink pelican pecked my purse."

"*Your* purse?" Lucy yelled. "And how the fuck do you know my PIN?"

"Dame Luce, they tell you not to use your birthday for your PIN."

Lucy rolled down the window and screamed.

"Don't chafe your brain, baby, I got a job."

Then Lucy turned toward Keith and screamed again.

Keith sat up straight but didn't say a word.

"We're going to have a deposit. First and last months' rent. Tuition. Books. Food." Lucy ticked off the expenses on her fingers. "Apparently you'll be needing rum, and I don't see you kicking the cigarette habit too quickly."

"You got my marker. I'm not worried about it." Keith pushed his sunglasses back and closed his eyes. "I got my ways."

Lucy didn't know what that meant. She wasn't happy. But she had to believe him. He wasn't going to steal from her and then lie about paying her back. "Give me the card," she said, and held her palm out. "And, next bathroom break, you're driving."

"Right on," Keith said. "Let's stop now. I've got the rum runs."

Lucy winced. She knew she'd have to hear all about it after the pit stop.

She braced herself for the full report as she settled into the passenger seat. She kicked off her sandals and put her feet up on the dashboard. "I feel like I'm watching my leg hair grow," she said, rubbing the stubble on her calf.

"Yeah, me too," Keith said, glancing over at her legs. "Your toe hair too." He shuddered.

In L.A., Lucy convinced Keith to go to some boutique art galleries. Well, she didn't necessarily convince him.

She did scream at him. "I didn't do anything in Las Vegas except sleep in a crappy motel room and get eight hundred of *my* big fucking skins thrown to your solo party. So, we're going to do whatever I want to do."

They went to an artsy square in town with brick streets and dreadlocked vendors selling overpriced candlesticks and dream catchers. While Lucy wandered from gallery to gallery, Keith sat on a bench, smoked, and sipped from his flask.

The art invigorated Lucy and she felt magnanimous when she joined Keith on the bench. She wasn't a grudge holder. Keith put his arm around Lucy then summoned a roving musician to play for them. Keith really was quite sweet when he wanted to be.

Keith's cigarette smoke wafted into Lucy's face. When she tried to move, her hair was caught in the crook of his arm and it pulled, hard. Keith goaded the banjo player to "give us another for free." Lucy's muscles tightened. Keith continued.

"Hey, man, how long you been picking? How much money've you made tonight? Is that how you pay the rent? How much cash can you stash on a Saturday night?" Keith barraged the banjo player until Lucy dragged him away.

"Why do you have to do that?" Lucy demanded.

"Ask questions?"

"You don't even listen to the answers." Lucy was sure that Keith wanted her to pick a fight with him. So she did.

They were arguing in the street about eight hundred dollars, leg hair, raw chicken, driving, smoking, and dirty motels when a gentleman in his late sixties with gray hair and ash-dark skin approached and introduced himself as Nasser.

"Don't fight, children," he said in a gentle voice with a heavy Middle Eastern accent.

Keith and Lucy just looked at him.

"You need a place to stay?" he asked.

"No, we're fine," Lucy said.

"You're hungry?" the man asked.

"With all this food around?" Lucy made a sweeping gesture toward the snack vendors.

"Starvin' marvin'," Keith said, then glared at Lucy.

It was true they hadn't eaten all day. Once again, they couldn't agree on where to eat. Keith liked bars that had menus with "award-winning nachos" and "famous hot wings." Lucy liked local spots that started with the owner's name and ended in *café*. Fine dining to Keith meant a restaurant attached to a motor lodge or bowling alley. To Lucy it meant a restaurant with leather menu holders and a bill they couldn't afford.

"A drink," Nasser said. "You both need drink."

At this, Keith's eyes lit up. He liked nothing more than a free drink.

"You come to my place and I give to you."

Lucy was leery. She wanted to politely tell this nice man that she was in the middle of berating her boyfriend, so buzz off.

"In my country," Nasser said, "we offer hospitality." He gave a little bow.

"Righteous," Keith said.

Lucy felt like a jerk. *In my country, we fight in the street then get drunk and sleep in seedy motels.* A drink with a Nasser-type was the kind of adventure she really would have liked—before she had turned into the shrieking shrew that she was. What was she doing fighting in the street with Keith? It was ridiculous.

Lucy assessed the situation. Nasser seemed harmless. And if he turned out to be crazy, well, he wasn't very robust. They could overtake him. They were hungry. Keith wanted a drink.

"Why not?" Lucy said. "I mean, thank you very much." She bowed a little bow to Nasser.

So they walked away from the busy square and Nasser told them he had moved from Iran in the 1980s. "I am living in an International House." Lucy hoped it wasn't "of Pancakes."

"Diplomatic immunity," he said.

The International House was a large brick building in a darkly lit section of the neighborhood. It had heavy iron bars on the first-floor windows. Lucy wondered if it looked like a place where people with diplomatic immunity would live. What did he mean by that anyway?

They walked up two floors to Nasser's small studio apartment, which smelled like wet cigarette butts and chicken. The kitchen was big enough for one. The dining area had room enough for the small round table surrounded by three folding chairs. The bedroom and living room were one and the same and about a half step from the table. There was a full bed, which took up most of the room, and a small straight-back chair in the corner with a white button-up shirt draped over the back.

Nasser had a big stain on his T-shirt, which Lucy could see since he had unbuttoned his overshirt when they got in the room. His stomach was hanging over his belt, and his gray hair, which had looked distinguished on the street, now looked as if it needed a cut.

"Brother, I try very hard to learn English so I get along easier here," he told Keith, who lit a cigarette. "I promised food," Nasser said, turning to Lucy.

"Thank you," she said, smiling.

"You are woman, so you serve," Nasser said to her. "The chicken is on stove and bowls over sink."

Keith didn't even try to suppress his laugh at Nasser's suggestion. Lucy glared at him. She considered telling them both that in her country, men who wanted women to serve them would most likely only ever get served divorce papers. But she decided against it. It was one of those stupid jokes that made only her laugh. She recognized them since Keith had taken to pointing them out.

In the kitchen, Lucy pulled the lid off the large, dented pot on the stove and saw vegetables, bones, and chunks of bloated chicken skin stewing in a watery sludge under a layer of yellow oil. She cheerfully ladled three bowls of it. For Keith she filled the bowl to the brim with a generous helping of pimply chicken skin. She made sure she ladled a bone into Nasser's bowl. Then she served herself a tiny portion of cooked carrots, hold the grease.

Nasser poured them each a tumbler of Jack Daniel's, straight up, and they toasted to new friends. Lucy looked at the big thumbprint on the side of her glass and tried to assess where the lips to that thumb might have been. She turned the glass to what she figured was the safest spot and took a big gulp of it.

"I think it very important to learn English. Yes?" Nasser asked Keith. Keith nodded with his head bent over the bowl and his spoon in his fist, a gesture that maddened Lucy.

Nasser took out his portable cassette player. "These are my tapes, how I learn. Listen, please." He put the headphones on Keith. Lucy was pretty sure the tape could help.

Keith took the headphones off. "I speaka the language, brutha," he said.

Lucy rolled her eyes, silently disagreeing.

"Yes. You listen and tell me if they are good," Nasser said as he replaced the headphones.

"It might be a good idea to learn the cultural differences too," Lucy said. She just couldn't help herself.

Nasser smiled and nodded, then slipped his hand on Lucy's knee.

Lucy leaped out of her seat. "Excuse me. Bathroom?" she asked as she rushed toward the only other door in the room. Before Nasser could answer, she was safely in the bathroom with the door closed.

Lucy panicked. She wondered if Nasser would have a gun pointed at Keith when she came out. She looked around for a weapon. Soap, soap dish, electric razor, cotton balls. Nothing. Well, the soap was a hard, sharp sliver. That would hurt. She tucked it into her hand so the tip poked through the crack between her fingers. Then she felt guilty taking his last sliver of soap.

She peeked out the door. Nasser was sitting on the bed. He caught her eye and patted the spot next to him. Lucy threw the bathroom door open and bolted for the front door, grabbing Keith on the way.

"Thanks for having us, but we have to go," she called out.

"We could all sleep in my bed," she heard Nasser say meekly, in perfect English, as she slammed the door and hustled Keith out of the International House.

"What was that all about?" he asked. "I had half a drink left."

Lucy explained that while Keith was "learning English," she was learning why a sixty-something Iranian with "diplomatic immunity" invited a fighting couple in off the street.

"I should have known."

"He didn't *do* anything," Lucy said.

But Keith was inconsolable.

When they got back to the car, the trunk was wide open. Lucy's bags were gone. Naturally, Keith's things were still there. Even his boom box was left untouched in the backseat, in plain sight.

Then Lucy was inconsolable.

The trip was over. They'd had it. They both agreed—Chicago, then home.

As they headed east, Lucy felt miserable. She was wearing

Keith's underwear, his old shorts, his stupid lucky T-shirts. But the shirts really were soft. Actually, she'd never been quite so comfortable. Eventually, Lucy's vagabond condition gave her a renewed sense of freedom. She had nothing. No money. No job. No clothes. No apartment. The car was Keith's. The tent was Keith's. And she was already used to it. She convinced herself that she was now prepared for her future. She had passed her vision quest. She could take the plunge and go to law school and live with a man who supported her by working at a head shop. It would be fun.

Lucy was at the wheel a few hours outside Chicago. On her last stay in Chi-Town she had gotten too drunk to see anything she'd wanted to see. She was excited to check it out. She asked Keith to put in her Madonna tape, and she reached back and did it herself when he refused.

"Don't be a baby. You'll like it."

Keith was silent.

"This tape reminds me of when Kate and I were in high school. We were in art class with this kid, John Callahan. Kate used to say that his mother was his sister. I'd call him her secret boyfriend. She'd say, 'I love the way his eyes look in different directions. It makes me feel safe and loved at the same time. He's looking *out* for me and he's looking *at* me.' "

"You told me that already," Keith said.

"Well, I listened to your perverted stories about Joey's mother's crotch."

"But I only told that once."

"It seemed like you told it twice, it went on for so long," Lucy said then laughed. She wasn't going to let Keith bring her down. She figured he was in a bad mood because of the

Madonna tape and because she'd accidentally scooped his bag of weed into the garbage during her one feeble attempt to clean the car. She didn't care. Stupid pothead. Incomprehensible stoner.

"I wanna drive," Keith said.

Lucy was elated. In the passenger seat she looked at a guidebook. She told Keith that she was sick of all of the driving and eating. Driving and eating. In Chicago, she wanted to see sights, listen to good music, and dance. She was asleep when they arrived at the last crappy motel they'd be staying in. Keith checked them in, then gently woke Lucy and helped her to bed. He really had his moments.

When Lucy woke, Keith was already up and had planned the day using brochures from the motel lobby. They went to the Museum of Science and Industry. They drove through the city looking at the Art Deco architecture. They pretended they were mobsters from the 1920s and called each other Mugsy and Bugsy all day. And they ended the night at Buddy Guy's blues club. Lucy was happy and exhausted.

"Thanks for today," she said to Keith as they drove back to the motel.

"I don't remember where the motel is," Keith said, speaking quickly.

"Good ear," Lucy said, tapping the side of her head. She couldn't have heard him correctly.

"I . . . don't . . . remember," Keith said, drawing it out, "where the fucking motel is."

"Well, I was sleeping when we got in last night," Lucy said.

"Look on the key. Does it say on the key?"

Lucy pulled it out. It was a metal key with a green plastic

key chain. "Well, that wouldn't make much sense anyway," Lucy said. "If someone lost the key then any lunatic could rob you blind. Oh, wait, that already happened," Lucy said then laughed.

"Why are you laughing? Nothing is funny right now. Not this situation and not your stupid jokes." Keith was actually stern.

"Just pull over," Lucy said. "We'll figure something out." She didn't know why he was so mad. She was the one who'd had all of her stuff stolen.

They stopped at a neighborhood bar. Lucy got the phone book from the bartender, and Keith paged through it looking at the names of the motels. To give the rum some time to soak in, Lucy ducked into the bathroom. She took her time and was relatively sure that Keith would have the mess figured out when she joined him. He would salvage the perfect day. She just knew it. They were both wearing lucky shirts.

Keith was using the old-school pay phone that was mounted on top of the bar when Lucy came out of the bathroom. He looked at her as she hopped up on the stool next to him.

"Did you take a shit?" he asked.

Lucy glared at him.

"The deep dish pizza," Keith said, "it'll scramble the innards."

"Did you find the motel yet, Captain Caca?"

"Have a drink," Keith said. "I'm getting close."

At two in the morning, just before they gave up and took the bartender up on her offer to use her sofa bed, Keith found the motel's address stamped on one of the brochures he had taken from the front desk. He had dug it out of Lucy's purse as reading material for the bathroom. "Gotta go to the library and do a little research," he said, slapping the brochure as he walked toward the men's room. The bartender had laughed and Lucy cut her eyes at him, trying not to wish him death by colitis.

In the car, Lucy begged Keith not to talk about his bowels, or anyone else's, for that matter, for a day. Just one day. "Nothing about yours or mine or anyone's," Lucy pleaded. "I don't need to know about the inner workings of your body. That's what's so great about inner workings, they happen without a lot of fanfare."

Keith giggled. He couldn't help himself. But he agreed.

Since excrement was off the list of acceptable topics, the car was quiet. The silence cursed Lucy. She couldn't stop thinking about his poop talk. Was it symbolic of his need for parental love? He did always seem to be looking for her either to scold or protect him. He turned his body inside out for her to see. It was cruel of her to cringe. Or maybe he just wanted her to laugh with him.

But Lucy had long stopped laughing at potty humor. That wasn't exactly true. She and Kate, on their annual Christmas-time window-shopping trip to Manhattan, had stopped in front of a Times Square electronics store packed with toys and junk. Kate pointed to the plastic battery-operated man who pulled down his pants and farted. They were just guessing that he farted. However, it was a pretty good assumption as the dominant feature on the toy was a brown, puckered hole on his butt that flapped open when the pants were pulled down.

"That is demented," Lucy said.

"You know," Kate said, "if we were kids, that would be cracking us up right now."

"Childhood," Lucy reflected. "The reason for the potty humor industry."

"It's an enormous market," Kate said. "Think of it. Absolutely everyone goes through a stage where farting is at the top of the humor scale."

"Revision to the guarantees in life. Death, taxes, and finding fart jokes funny," Lucy said, thinking how Keith probably would have bought this knickknack.

"Honestly," Kate said, "just imagine how that would have cracked us up. It almost makes it funny now."

"Whadya call the Cambodian custodian who let all of the toilets back up?" Lucy asked.

"What?"

"Poop Pot."

"Proof," Kate said, "that some of us don't outgrow scatological humor."

"More proof," Lucy added, "a scientific name for it."

Keith was sullen the next day.

"What's up, buddy?" Lucy asked from the driver's seat.

"My stomach's raging. My poop was really smelly this morning. It was like an ana-condo. It had floors. Coils of crap."

"Jesus, Keith, I asked for just one day without poop talk."

Keith tried to suppress a smile. "Okay, sorry. Only it was so—"

"No, no, no." Lucy blocked her right ear and steered with her left hand. "I'm not listening to you, lalalala."

"I'm sorry. I forgot."

They drove in silence and Lucy tried to reset her internal barometer. She was going to have a good day.

"Did *you* poop this morning?" Keith blurted.

"Keith, do you think you have a serious mental illness? I've heard that some mental disorders come with an obsession with feces."

"I'm just trying to figure out if it was something we both ate."

Lucy really wanted to be able to give Keith what he needed. Laughter. Diagnosis. Sympathy. Now. Because this was the last chance she'd ever get to help him. In that moment, she was sure. She had never been more positive about anything. She was Breakupicus Soloist and he was Poopicus Alonicus, Ancienticus Historicus, Nevermoreicus. She'd get a cheap apartment, maybe campus housing, loans, a job. She could probably go back to her old job part-time. She'd be fine.

She glanced at Keith, an arm's length away, and felt as if she'd stumbled upon a fire-walking ceremony. She'd better walk the stretch right now, because she had no idea how she'd happened upon this place and she was sure she'd never get another opportunity.

She looked over at Keith again and tried to think of something to say. Anything.

He looked back at her. "And all the gas. I felt like I was blowing an air horn into the can."

And Lucy pictured the toy doll in the midtown store window and her five-year-old self with Kate at her side. And she laughed until tears came to her eyes.

Snowflakes

(Notebook Paper and Thread, 1999)

Lucy moved into her sister Nancy's apartment in Philadelphia, sight unseen, with two suitcases. She was a refugee and her belongings were simply about survival. Later, Nancy would joke that Lucy moved in with a toothbrush and a hat. But when Lucy arrived, Nancy wasn't in a joking mood and Lucy was too tired to try to make it better.

Lucy had just finished her first day of law school. She didn't have a car, so she had stashed her bags in the law library then wheeled them to the subway and then two blocks to Nancy's at ten at night. Lucy knew what she was in for with Nancy. So she planned just to be polite then scoot off to bed. Nancy was doing her a big favor, and she wasn't going to do anything but show gratitude.

Nancy wasn't aware of much of anything but her own misery. She was in the midst of a separation from Bob and on the brink of clinical depression when their mom called saying Lucy needed a place to stay. Nancy was trying to enjoy her solitude and hadn't admitted yet that she was failing miserably. She was secretly glad for some company.

Even though they were sisters, Lucy and Nancy were virtually strangers. They'd spent some birthdays together and most holidays. But being nineteen years apart in age, they were essentially both only children born of the same parents. Nancy's husband used to say that they shared genes and a collective past, but not jeans and a specific past. Nancy laughed at it the first time he said it. Lucy thought Bob was a dork. Nevertheless, he was right. Essentially, Lucy and Nancy would both be living with an acquaintance that they'd heard rumors about from their mother and neither one had any say in the matter.

Nancy's place had that gentrified-warehouse feel. It wasn't ever a warehouse; it was just designed to look like it had been. Two bedrooms, private garage, huge open living room-kitchen-office space. Exposed brick, big picture windows, high ceilings with painted pipes and ductwork. All that and a very posh Society Hill address. At forty-eight, Nancy had the yuppie-bachelorette pad she'd dreamed of in the eighties when she was living Bob's upwardly-mobile-suburbanite dream.

Lucy was glad for the exhaustion. Otherwise, she might have been nervous to move in with Nancy, who had always seemed to have something negative to say about Lucy. She plopped herself on the new sage green Pottery Barn sofa and put her water bottle on the oak coffee table from Ethan Allen and waited for an opening to dash off to bed.

Lucy was chunkier than Nancy was used to seeing her, but as beautiful as ever. It occurred to Nancy that this was the reason for her jealousy of Lucy. She had gotten the good looks and the good curves.

"Thanks for letting me move in," Lucy said.

"So, what kind of law are you studying?" Nancy asked to make conversation. She sat perched on the edge of the over-stuffed chair. Lucy had never struck Nancy as much of a student, nor a lawyer. Nancy thought of lawyers as desperate approval seekers who wanted to one-up the people they were in imaginary competition with. Or so sexually insecure they could only attract the opposite sex with a shallow attempt at social status.

As far as Nancy could tell, Lucy was never overly concerned with appearances. Nor was she ever particularly interested in a grand ideal of justice for all—but neither were any of the lawyers she knew. Nancy worked for a big pharmaceuticals company, and all the lawyers she knew did too. She had long ago sold her corporate soul and reaped the financial benefits. She just couldn't see Lucy doing it.

Lucy couldn't see it either. But Lucy didn't believe in the selling of souls. She had gotten so far as to decide that people did what they were. It wasn't good or bad. Still, Lucy didn't know why she was in law school. She had convinced the admissions committee, her mother, and herself with a few flimsy regurgitated ideals and killer LSATs.

Nancy thought that maybe Lucy didn't hear her question, but she waited to see if Lucy would speak. It annoyed Nancy that it took Lucy a couple beats longer to answer questions than it took the general population. It was as if Lucy had grown up in a different culture.

This quirk annoyed Nancy particularly because it mucked up the rhythm conversation was supposed to have. "How are you / fine / great / so I heard you changed jobs / yeah / how's that going / I can walk to work now / that's excellent / no more parking tickets / ha ha / good to see you / yep, you too / take care." And that was conversation in Nancy's world.

Lucy considered small talk to be a necessary survival tactic of the modern jungle. Maintaining loose relationships through banal social interactions was what everyone did. But it was not conversation. Lucy didn't realize that she forced conversation out of that mold whenever possible. She thought her interactions with the world were perfectly normal. She noticed that people were often impatient with her, but she thought that was *their* issue, and it had nothing to do with her.

Nancy watched Lucy blink and Lucy watched Nancy squirm.

"I guess," Lucy started then paused again, for an overly long time, "I guess that I want to do sort of what Mom does. Work with artists and buyers. Broker deals. Sotheby's—that would be a dream job."

"Not litigation?"

"Hell no. Can you picture me arguing with people?"

"Sure. Arguing can be fun." Nancy couldn't picture it. Lucy seemed to be a classic avoider. The type who said all was well and forged ahead.

"I suppose if I end up working with Mom I'll be able to enjoy that kind of fun." This was typical sister-bonding stuff. Joking about Mom. But Lucy and their mom didn't fight and they both knew it.

"You and Mom argue?" Nancy asked, just to check.

"I don't know why I said that. I can't win an argument with her." Lucy tipped her head to the side and her neck cracked.

Nancy winced.

Then Lucy cracked her neck the other way. "I guess I always wanted to be a painter. But there's significance in law that I like. Importance in each day. Seriousness in the details."

"So, you're not joking?" Nancy said.

That made Lucy laugh, a quick burst. A joke from Nancy came as a complete surprise. On that high note, Lucy got up, refilled her water bottle, kissed Nancy on the cheek, and went to bed.

Nancy entertained the idea that it might not be so bad living with Lucy. Even at twenty-nine years old, she was still her adorable kid sister.

Lucy went to Nancy's spare room and collapsed. She wasn't going to think about Nancy or law school or the reasons she was here now doing this. She resolved to stay the course and trust her choices for once.

Nancy put her feet up and held the stereo remote in her hand. Would it bother Lucy if she turned the music on? She wasn't going to tiptoe around anyone in her own place, which was beautiful, even if Lucy didn't notice it. When Nancy first moved in she spent weeks playing CDs that Bob wouldn't listen to. After twenty-six years of marriage she could finally listen to her favorite Broadway musical scores somewhere else besides her car. She also kept the TV off all day Sunday and never again had to listen to the inane chatter of football commentary.

Nancy put on the score to *The Mikado,* which was Bob's most hated CD of hers. She turned up the music and kicked her feet up.

Lucy was lulled to sleep by the music from the hall. She wasn't sure if any of this was a good idea. Law school. Living with Nancy. She tried to determine when she had started to doubt herself so deeply. And then she drifted off thinking about a trip she had taken with Ben. Ben in a hotel room pulling at the remote attached to the bedside table then laughing on the bed after realizing it was attached. What if she'd married him? Where would she be now? What would he think of her going to law school?

Nancy had bought her apartment in Philadelphia when she'd landed a top executive position in pharmaceuticals. She was thinking that Bob would eventually move in and they'd sell their house in the suburbs. But he never did. So Nancy got a therapist and stopped worrying about what made him happy. Sometimes people mistakenly thought that they would be missed when they went away. And some probably didn't go away because they suspected they wouldn't be. Nancy hadn't expected her life with Bob would pan out the way it had.

Nancy had always felt somewhat snarky around her sister. According to Nancy, Lucy had grown up in a bohemian household with parents who could afford to send her to private school and have her portrait done by a hotshot painter. They bought Lucy everything she ever wanted and occasionally supported her during her arrested adolescence, which looked like it was going to last well into her thirties.

Lucy had always felt somewhat defensive around her sister. But she resolved to make the best of it, not only because Nancy was doing her a huge favor, but also because she'd have to be in top form to compete in law school. Plus, she felt a softening toward her sister, whom she'd only ever known with Bob. Nancy without Bob had only existed in family pictures and lore. She'd been an excellent student who grew up happy with parents who wanted a child. Her mom had made her Halloween costumes and her father had toted her around on his shoulders. They'd given her haircuts at home and taken her to the neighbors' farm to ride their pony.

How's she doing?" Their mother called Nancy to check up on Lucy.

Nancy turned the music down and asked her mother why she was so worried.

"Lucy's a poor, lost soul." She sighed. "I never could get anything right with her." Her mother's spoon clinked against her ubiquitous teacup. She had replaced gin with tea when she turned seventy, which looked more like fifty-five on her. "Your father told you how Robert—"

"The painter?"

"Yes, the one who lived with us when you went to college, how he'd painted Lucy in the nude?" Her mother whispered "the nude" as if someone could overhear them.

"What do you mean Daddy told me? *You* showed them to me years ago. And you bragged about them all the time. You said that nude paintings were very fashionable." Nancy kept her voice even. But she really didn't want to hear about Lucy's charmed life as a model and an artistic prodigy. And she hated it when their mother rewrote history, like Lucy's nudes weren't top on the list of conversation for years. "What do you mean you couldn't get anything right?"

"Well, we had no idea."

"About what?" Nancy asked. "Because if it was about raising kids, I turned out fine."

"We found out about the nudes," she whispered again, "after

Robert had a show at Lucy's school. I can't imagine. That poor girl. Well, of course we forbade him from ever seeing her again. And when he did, we kicked him out."

"I thought he fell in love and moved?" Nancy wasn't expecting this.

"I did everything wrong with her." Their mother sighed.

Nancy wondered if Lucy might have been sexually molested. A nude fourteen-year-old and a young eccentric painter? It was suspicious. Suddenly Nancy felt unimaginable sorrow. She was lost in her own tightly constructed world. Her paradigm had shifted. Her own family wasn't how she'd imagined it. Her marriage wasn't how she'd imagined it. What else was askew?

Their mother told Nancy that after Robert left, Lucy had painted angry abstracts over some of Robert's nudes that he'd left in the studio. When she saw what Lucy had done, she removed his paintings, stashed them in the attic, and replaced them with blank canvasses. "I didn't approve," their mother said, "but if he was going to be famous one day, I'd have a clean conscience that I didn't allow his work to be ruined."

Nancy's heart sank. She knew what her mother meant about doing things all wrong with Lucy. She should have joined Lucy in her rage and had a bonfire with those paintings and then put a curse on Robert. Instead, she'd meekly supported Lucy's artistic leanings by stocking the studio with canvasses.

Before this bleak news, that was how Nancy had known Lucy. As the artist that her parents praised and rewarded. But now Nancy had a dark feeling—short, sharp shock.

Nancy's newfound sympathy toward Lucy aside, she still wasn't sure if she was going to like living with her. But her jealousy had instantly been eradicated. It was replaced by pity. She wasn't sure if that was any better.

Lucy had dismissed her dread of living with Nancy almost instantly. If she was good at one thing, it was living fully in her current reality. She knew that she'd made stupid choices, and she suspected that her current situation was the result of a series of them, but it was all she had. Every morning she popped out of bed, splashed water on her face, and ran out the door with her backpack over both shoulders. Lucy forged ahead.

Nancy worried. She fantasized about the loss of her fetter-free life. Nights before she had to go into the office, she imagined that in the morning Lucy would be showering during her shower time. On her way home, she assumed Lucy would have slopped into the house with dirty sneakers on her Persian throw rugs and refinished hardwood floors and would be watching TV during Nancy's TV time. On days Nancy worked from home, she made coffee and expected to find that Lucy had used Nancy's favorite coffee mug. Sometimes Nancy called Bob to complain, but he was never home.

But Lucy never did any of those things. In fact, she rarely did what Nancy expected. When Nancy split the bills at the end of the first month, she figured Lucy would go over them and obsess about an unknown phone number or an unexpected charge. Maybe she'd hem and haw about the money until Nancy eventually just paid it. Instead, she wrote Nancy a check and thanked her profusely for taking care of it. For making her life easier. Lucy called Nancy a goddess and hugged her.

Lucy was grateful for any help she could get with the

minutiae of her life. The thought of tallying bills or grocery shopping was daunting. She ate on the go from the carts at school and rarely showered. She got up early, went to class, stayed at the library until late, and arrived home with the same bottle of water that she'd refilled so many times that the label was peeling off and the plastic was puckering. On the weekends Lucy studied in her room or on campus. Essentially, Lucy was Nancy's silent squatter.

Eventually, Nancy found herself complaining to her secretary that she wanted to get to know Lucy better.

"It's easiest to get to know someone if you open up to them," her secretary told Nancy.

Nancy thanked her profusely for the advice and called her a goddess, which surprised both of them a little.

Of the two, Lucy was the wild child and Nancy was the superstar. Lucy went on family vacations and drank until she was practically poisoned. Nancy rarely drank, and never touched sugary tropical drinks. Lucy slept all day on the beach, only to wake in time to party all night again. Nancy sat under a hat covered in sunblock and wished she'd taken her vacation without her family. Lucy drank about a gallon of coffee every day for breakfast, ate spring rolls from one of the carts on campus for lunch, and shoveled in fast food for dinner. Nancy watched her fat, cholesterol, protein, and vitamin intake so she wouldn't end up taking the products her company sold. Lucy had tons of ex-jobs, ex-boyfriends, and an ex-fiancé. Before she moved in with Nancy she quit her job to take a cross-country trip with a boyfriend who, as she told it, talked about his shit too much so she broke up with him. Nancy only ever dated Bob, and she married him. The day before school started Lucy was sleeping on a friend's couch and had no idea where she was going to live or how she was going to pay for it. Nancy had a nice apartment and an extra room. And that was how the by-the-book types got saddled with the fly-by-night types.

Whenever Lucy was in a financial bind, their mother, who was terrified of losing her wealth, grudgingly helped out. Lucy didn't expect anyone to help her, least of all her mother, but when help was offered, she wasn't the type to turn it down.

Nancy didn't expect anyone to help her, and her life was such that no one ever had to offer. Nancy never struggled. After college she got a good job and a husband with a good job.

"It makes Mom happy to help me," Lucy told Nancy's raised eyebrow. Nancy had convinced Lucy to skip studying and have a Sunday brunch of steak Benedict and Bloody Marys on South Street—it was a yearly indulgence she allowed herself, and she was sure Lucy would love it.

"Do you think it's because of that painter?" Nancy asked, feeling warm and bold from alcohol in the afternoon.

Lucy thought about it. *That painter?* She wondered what Nancy's version of "that painter" was.

Nancy waited her out. It wasn't easy, but Nancy was determined, if not hopeful. Once, over lunch, Nancy had asked Lucy what she was thinking and Lucy looked at her ham and cheese on rye and said, "I was wondering which part of the sandwich to bite. You know, which would be the best bite." Ever since, Nancy had been skeptical of Lucy's silences.

"Do you think I'm holding Mom hostage because I had a weird childhood?" Lucy finally asked.

"Did you?"

"In some ways." Lucy shrugged. "I guess."

"What ever happened with that?"

"With that or with him?"

"Either." Nancy was glad the subject had been opened. She was willing to hear whatever Lucy was ready to divulge. She signaled the waiter for two more.

"Last I heard he was in love and living with her in North Carolina. Or South."

"Wasn't that where he went after he left Mom and Dad's?"

"We never talked about him again."

"You know it's because they found out he was painting you in the nude when you were like twelve, right?"

"Fourteen," Lucy said. "I think that might have been what stopped me from painting seriously."

"And what stopped you from treating men seriously?"

Lucy was surprised by this idea. "Maybe." It had never occurred to her. "No," she said, "nothing ever happened with him like that." But when Lucy answered quickly, when she gave a knee-jerk response, it showed who she really was. Instinct was always more honest than intelligence.

"Lucy, being nude and fourteen in secret with a man scrutinizing you has to have some lingering effects."

"Was Mom upset?" Lucy asked, churning this new idea in her head.

"She still is," Nancy said.

"It's funny how you really can't know how people feel unless they tell you," Lucy said matter-of-factly. "You could misinterpret actions for years and years."

"And unfortunately," Nancy said, "you can't retrospectively rewrite history."

"Actually, that's the very definition of history. It's written from a distance. Like Mom did, making all of that Robert stuff seem normal. I mean, you don't think it was normal, right?" Lucy dug into her steak and eggs and felt a gloom fall over her. It was the way she always felt when she thought about Robert and those days. Eating helped.

"What's normal?" Nancy asked.

"Actually, I was in love with him," Lucy said. "I hated him, too."

"Do you think Robert loved you?" Nancy asked. "Because, you know, if you'd been in some other culture, there wouldn't have been anything wrong with your age difference."

"Ben's the only one who ever loved me." Lucy rarely talked about her ex-fiancé. But everyone else in the family did.

"Where's that waiter with our drinks," Nancy said, annoyed.

Lucy believed that Ben was perfect and she was the complete moron who left him. She came dangerously close to making the connection between the love she had for Robert and the love she had for Ben. But she wasn't ready for that yet.

"Don't rewrite history and beat yourself up," Nancy told her. "If anything, make yourself out to look good."

"You make a valid point," Lucy said. "Plus, I hate to blame anyone for anything, including myself."

Nancy tended to lay blame, so she liked the bits of "Lucy logic" that were beginning to invade her thoughts. However, it was all she could do not to blame herself for Lucy's downfall. Lucy started with a bang, but quickly became the worst law school student ever. Their quick nightly chats that had long since turned into marathon gab sessions on the sofa may have had something to do with it.

There were also the drawn-out grocery shopping trips at the trendy market where they drank coffee, sampled summer sausage on toothpicks, and chatted with the single city men dressed in their wrinkle-free casuals. Technically, Lucy had sworn off men, but she was what Nancy called "Y Wild," named for the Y chromosome. So, on these trips, Lucy taught Nancy how to flirt. This was a skill set Nancy didn't possess; she had never even batted her eyes at Bob. And Nancy taught Lucy to live a little and buy brand names and organic veggies. Lucy only shopped when she was hungry and ate the least expensive thing she could find.

What surprised Lucy and Nancy was that they were both having fun. Lucy was prone to burst into song, or rather, song *parody,* at pretty much any moment. And Nancy found out that she could make Lucy laugh. It was gratifying to make someone weepy with laughter even if the humorous bit was that she'd acted out of character.

Lucy's favorite song parody was created the day she determined that she would study more if she bought a bedside lamp. So Nancy took her to a funky South Street furniture store and told her it was her treat. They walked into the shop and were assaulted by loud, chingy Moroccan music.

Lucy shook her hips in a belly dance move. "Pretty hot, huh?" she asked Nancy.

"Actually, yes," Nancy said.

"Quite." Surprise. A beautiful, dark-skinned, dreadlocked, British-accented god was standing right next to them.

Lucy's face turned red and she, never one to miss a chance to flirt, recovered and thanked him.

"What can I do for you today?" he asked regally.

Lucy straightened and pulled down her shirt. "I'm looking for a lamp table. I mean, uh, a table lamp?" She was looking less composed as she nervously smoothed her hair. "You know what I mean," Lucy continued with a shaky smile, "a lamp you put a table on. No," she shook her head and blinked her eyes hard, "a bedside lamp, you know, one you would put *on* a table." She let out an audible breath, then turned and walked out of the store.

And after Nancy repeated "lamp table" through tears of laughter for about a block, Lucy broke into her version of the Flintstones TV theme song: "Law school, failing law school, it's amazing just how easily. Law school, failing law school, it's for sure when you just don't study. Let's walk, with your sister to the store. Tongue-tied, because talking is a chore. When you're failing law school, have a boutique shopping good time, won't cost a thin dime, I'll be a tongue-tied mime.'"

Shortly after Lucy claimed the title of worst law school student ever, her friends appeared. She *knew* people. It was as if she'd managed to get herself listed on some hip-class social register. Lucy knew tons of characters, but had been lying low because of law school. Once her gang knew where to find her, she was on the call rotation. Lucy would drag Nancy with her to see a friend's band, or to an art show, or to an experimental theater performance.

Nancy had never been much for socializing. And even though she looked like she was in her thirties, she felt her age. She had no room in her life for loud music, cigarette smoke, and obnoxious drunks.

Lucy had always been one for socializing. And even though she was supposed to be learning that Roe versus Wade were not choices for summertime activities on the Delaware, she began to think that it was more important to hang out with Nancy.

Nancy considered that she was having a midlife crisis, but then settled on just enjoying herself. She remembered, or maybe discovered, what it was like to have a good time.

Lucy felt vindicated. She remembered, or maybe realized, that helping, and not just by letting someone help her, felt pretty damn good. Okay, maybe she was just looking for a co-conspirator. But she felt as if Nancy needed some lightening up. She was separated from her husband in a way that was probably the most insidiously demoralizing. He was neglecting her. Disregarding her. Ignoring her. It was as if she and their marriage had never mattered.

So every Friday night they would dress up, put on makeup and cute shoes, and grab a cab to meet Lucy's friends, including her old shore-friend Trina. Nancy would balk at the cover and Lucy would pay for both of them before Nancy had the words "no way" out of her mouth. Lucy thought this was perfectly normal. Her priorities were solid. She bought generic brands to save a few cents and paid her sister's cover charge. Why not?

One night, after they both drank way more than they meant to, they poured themselves into a cab and Lucy eventually passed out, listing sideways onto Nancy's lap. Nancy, who was considerably less drunk, stroked Lucy's hair and watched the row houses whiz by, thinking how she was probably going through a midlife thing and she was dragging her kid sister down with her. Her kid sister. A girl she'd hated for most of her life, for what? She never even bothered to get to know her, and she truly was a kind, fun, interesting person who never deserved such harsh treatment. Nancy thought of all the times that she'd treated Lucy with indifference or disrespect. It was unfair and she vowed never to take her sister for granted again.

Lucy was awakened by Nancy shaking her gently and the cabdriver yelling, "She better not puke back there. Bunch of lunatics in my cab tonight."

Nancy told him to hold his horses, which made Lucy laugh.

"Yeah, and cool your jets," Lucy said to tease Nancy.

The second Nancy slammed the cab door, the taxi squealed around the corner. Laughing, they staggered toward their apartment building, Lucy holding on to Nancy and calling out, "Fancy Nancy, Fancy Nancy."

Out of the corner of her eye, Nancy noticed two men were walking briskly toward them. Lucy didn't notice. The mood in the neighborhood changed significantly when the streetlights came on, and Nancy felt uneasy with the night people who weren't her neighbors. She felt like an injured antelope. As the men walked toward them, Nancy's adrenaline surged through her limbs and she tightened her grip on Lucy's arm.

"Fancy Nancy, cool your jets," Lucy sang to no particular tune.

Nancy kept an eye on the men as she pulled Lucy up the steps toward the door. The men were still moving quickly. Nancy fumbled for her keys.

Lucy leaned against the railing, waiting limply on the top step, singing softly, "Fancy Nancy, this chick is sick."

The men were at the bottom of the steps.

"Fancy Nancy . . ."

Nancy jammed the key in the lock.

". . . sick, sick chick."

Then, suddenly, the men backed away. They looked surprised, as if someone had pulled a gun on them or flashed a knife.

Nancy pushed Lucy into the front foyer of the building and slammed the door.

"Ow, ow," Lucy whined.

Nancy peered out the window and watched the men walk away just as quickly as they'd approached.

"My tongue," Lucy said, holding her hand to her mouth. "I bit my tongue."

"You'll be all right, sweetie." Nancy was shaking. "We're all right." She unlocked the apartment door and considered calling the police.

"To bed," Lucy mumbled and headed down the hall toward her bedroom.

Nancy flicked on the hallway light for her and that was when she saw the blood. Lucy's whole backside, from her shoulders to her knees, was covered in it.

"What the heck? Lucy, go to the bathroom," Nancy commanded. Then she hurried behind Lucy and gently guided her away from her bedroom door. That was when Nancy saw the blood on her own hands. In the harsh light of the bathroom, Nancy was accosted by their reflection. Both were smeared with red. Their hair, Lucy's face, their arms, elbows, shirts, pants.

"Is that from my tongue?" Lucy slurred.

Nancy patted Lucy down looking for stab wounds or an open artery. Then she searched herself as Lucy plopped down on the open toilet, closed her eyes, and lolled her head back, leaving smears of blood on the white tiles of the bathroom wall.

"Someone must have gotten stabbed in that cab," Nancy said.

"Are you sure it's not my tongue?" Lucy asked. "It really hurts."

If either had been sober they probably would have retched. Instead, with a very level head, Nancy got a step stool from the closet and put it in the tub. "Sweetie, we're going to have to get in the shower."

"Bed," Lucy said.

"Yes, to bed, this way," Nancy said and guided Lucy into the shower and plopped her onto the step stool.

Then she got in and stripped off both of their clothes. "You owe me for this one," she said.

"Why? "Lucy asked. "Did I puke on myself?"

"I wish," Nancy said.

The next day they agreed that being soaked in the bodily fluid of a stranger was definitely the most disgusting thing that had ever happened to them, and the luckiest, since it probably saved them from being attacked. At three in the afternoon they convened on the sofa for takeout and a movie, and the requisite swearing off of alcohol.

Lucy cited reasons to quit drinking. She was failing school, they could have gotten killed, they ended the night bloody, and she felt like death. She sang, "Green sofa is the place for me. Pain and whiskey is no life, you see. Almost killed, but saved by being bloody. Keep your Tully, and give me beef and broccoli."

Lucy didn't mean it, though. Swearing off alcohol, or swearing to stick to a sensible diet, or swearing to study, was a flexible agreement for her. She exaggerated for the fun of it. She wasn't accountable to herself. But she could always be counted on to change her mind.

For Nancy, after a night of drinking, she felt maudlin about Bob. That was what made her swear off late nights and booze.

"Bob would purposely try to make me mad," Nancy said. "He wanted my mood to be dependent on his."

"He'd push your buttons?"

"I guess I had a lot of them to push."

"Please, you're perfect," Lucy said.

"In what universe?"

"You're always helping me. You're funny. Everyone loves you."

"Like who?"

"Well, those guys last night at the bar."

"Until they found out how old I am."

"They liked you even more then. They were like *coo-coo-ca-choo, Mrs. Robinson.* Plus, with that body and your perfect skin, no one believes you when you say you're forty-eight."

"My body is like a twelve-year-old boy's," Nancy said. "You, with the curves and the hair, that's what guys go for."

Lucy smoothed down her hair and pulled her sweatshirt over her knees. "Fat and frizzy. It's every guy's dream." Lucy thought of how nice it would be to be fit and trim like Nancy. But she had what she had. And she didn't want to talk about it.

Nancy was shocked. Lucy didn't see what everyone else saw. Since they'd been living together, sometimes Nancy thought

Lucy was so beautiful she couldn't stop staring at her. Nancy rewound her memory and thought of all of the times she and her mother told Lucy how to lose weight, because that was what *they* cared about. Or they'd try to tame her hair, which really looked best when it was in a bouncy Afro.

"You're beautiful in every way," Nancy said.

"Things you appreciate in others, you often possess," Lucy replied in a terrible Dalai Lama imitation.

"And faults you imagine in others," Nancy said in an excellent Indian accent, "are only reflections of things you don't like about yourself."

"Are you thinking about Bob?" Lucy asked.

"The thing about Bob," Nancy said, "is that he's good on paper, but the moment-to-moment living actually matters more. Who cares what his career is or what his politics are or whether or not he reads?" Nancy was really talking about Lucy, who was terrible on paper—drinker, freeloader, bad student—but good in reality. "You scratch my back. And you leave the section of the newspaper I like for me at my spot."

"Yes," Lucy said, taking her knees out from under her sweatshirt, "and you wash a stranger's blood off of me when I'm smashed. And you make excellent coffee." She raised her mug into the air.

Lucy wanted Nancy to like herself, to see her own good qualities. And her campaign was working. Some days Nancy completely forgot to hate herself.

"I like making coffee," Nancy said. "That was what went wrong with Bob. I took responsibility for things I didn't like to do to make him happy."

"You mean you took the garbage out?" Lucy nodded her head toward the overfilled kitchen garbage that they'd both forgotten for the second week.

"And I embarrassed him."

"How?"

"You know, just with the dorky things I do."

"The dorky things *you* do?" Lucy snorted. "At least you didn't ask if you could have a look at 'a lamp you put a table on.'"

"No," Nancy said, "but last night I asked some guy if he'd been smoking *grass.*"

Lucy snorked her coffee out of her nose and tried to suppress her laughter until she swallowed.

"Trina told me that the term grass went out with disco. Excuse me," Nancy said, mocking herself, "but are you on the marijuana?"

"You potting it?" Lucy added, glad Nancy could finally make fun of herself.

Lucy taught Nancy how to turn her self-loathing into humorous self-deprecation. There was a difference, as far as Lucy was concerned. Lucy and Nancy mostly agreed on what was funny. Spewing a beverage while laughing was hilarious. Nancy was partial to getting bonked on the top of the head—by an acorn, a ball, a piece of candy thrown from a parade float—it didn't matter as long as it was on the very top of the head. Lucy preferred one getting shat upon by a bird. Mistakenly eating bad food? Usually funny, but only if it wasn't life threatening. Couples arguing in public? Not usually funny unless it involved a loud statement like, "Damn, girl, why we always gotta go to KFC?" And then there was tripping, slipping, and falling. They both loved slapstick. Those were guaranteed sidesplitters.

One Friday night a guy they met at a bar did a spontaneous karate kick and fell onto his back on the dance floor. They both burst out laughing. They helped him up, since they were already bent over. Neither wanted him to feel bad, but they just couldn't help themselves. Trina asked him if he was hurt while Lucy and Nancy excused themselves to run to the back of the bar so they could laugh with abandon.

Lucy assured Nancy that her verbal faux pas about "grass" wasn't as embarrassing as she thought. Nancy was way too hard on herself. "No one will even remember," Lucy assured her.

"You will."

"That's what sisters are for, to take the sting out of public humiliation."

"Speaking of sting," Nancy said, "this happened years ago, but I've never told this story to anyone."

"Are you sure you're ready?" Lucy asked.

"Well, it humiliated Bob so much that he wouldn't ever let me talk about it," Nancy continued. "We were at a dinner party with his work colleagues. At the time Bob and I had just finished writing out our living wills. I had a do-not-resuscitate clause in mine and was discussing it. I said that I had read a statistic on how few people were actually saved by CPR and I didn't want to die with someone pounding on my chest. I smugly announced that I wanted to die with dignity. Anyway, the woman across from us got up and ran out of the room. Her husband had just died of a heart attack and it pretty much ended with someone pounding on his chest."

"Well, how were you supposed to know?" Lucy asked through staccato bursts of laughter.

"The thing is, I did know. I'd just forgotten."

"Oh, Nancy." Lucy put her head in her hands and laughed some more. "Die with dignity."

Finally, Nancy joined her, which was what she'd wanted to do all along. It was the only way to diffuse humiliation, and she'd never gotten to do it with Bob. She was finally unraveling the knot of anxiety she'd become. She was also seeing that she just needed a little permission to relax. She wondered what Lucy needed permission to do.

"Marriage changes your fights," Nancy told Lucy. "You'd think that after the wedding you'd be more inclined to keep peace. To pick your battles, like everyone says. But with us, our moods dictated what we fought about. And everything was fair game. We poked each other's bruises."

Lucy wondered if she and Ben had gotten married if they would have done the same thing. Would they have resorted to cruel fighting tactics? Would they have made compromises and then resented each other?

Nancy was happier than she thought she would ever be without Bob. She had to admit it was because of Lucy. She felt guilty that she'd prejudged her. That she'd prejudged anyone. As far as Nancy could tell, Lucy didn't, and because of this, she negotiated her life better than Nancy ever could.

But Lucy had prejudged people. In fact, she felt as if she'd spent her whole life passing judgments. She did it with her last boyfriend. She'd let his personality flaws, or what she perceived as such, gnaw at her. She obsessed. She judged and judged until she had to run away. Who was she, torturing these men because they weren't Ben? But she'd done it to Ben too. She didn't know where it came from or how to stop it, but living with Nancy was helping her become a better person. In their relationship, Lucy was the one who didn't care what people thought. Lucy didn't let the judgments of others bother her. Lucy was the free spirit. And nurturing these qualities helped give them power.

She had exaggerated this tendency at first to show Nancy there was another way to live her life. But she soon realized that she really was sick of trying to decide what people could handle and what they couldn't. She was done with the disappointments her expectations brought her. And gradually other people's judgments and actions ceased to bother her. Nancy was no longer her critical sister who as much as told her she wasn't good enough whenever they were together. She was a woman who didn't like herself, and sometimes unwittingly took it out on others. She was a woman whose husband had left her without a reason or a decent conversation. She was a woman who opened her home to her sister and loved her despite their rocky past. She was a great woman who was getting better every day.

Nancy saw that she was softening. She realized that Lucy's pregnant pauses weren't for effect or because she was "out there." It was because she was really listening to what people said. She wasn't filling in the blanks, hearing what she wanted to hear while she thought of what she was going to say next. She just listened. It was respectful in the most unexpected way. And eventually Nancy stopped seeing herself as a persnickety, childless wife-slave. She wasn't Bob's anymore. She wasn't her job anymore. She wasn't what she had or hadn't done, what she'd bought or hadn't bought. She wasn't Lucy's angry sister or the good daughter. She wasn't sure what she was, but she wasn't any of those things anymore. She was thankful, she was sure of that.

The end of the semester was nearing and Lucy was sitting on the sofa, with her law book opened in front of her. Handel's "Messiah" was playing softly. She was intently cutting a snowflake out of a piece of notebook paper. She had about ten or so already taped up around the house.

When Nancy walked into the room, Lucy unfolded the snowflake and gave her a big smile. "Do you have any thread?" she asked excitedly. She attached the thread to her pen and threw it like a shuttlecock over the exposed piping on the ceiling. She hung snowflake after snowflake from the threaded pipes, making the apartment a winter wonderland.

Nancy hoped, for Lucy's sake, that law school wasn't as much work as everyone made it out to be.

Lucy hoped that she hadn't hung the snowflakes too low.

On Lucy's first day of winter break, Nancy took off from work and they went skiing. They'd planned on visiting their mother to do some of her chores and maybe ski a little. But Lucy was driving, Nancy's car, of course. That was never good. First off, she wasn't a good driver. But Nancy never much liked driving and Lucy loved Nancy's car. "You've got a fast car, I've got a lead foot to get us outta here," Lucy sang to an old Tracy Chapman song whenever she drove.

"Mom, I'm so sorry, we can't make it," Lucy shouted into her cell phone while negotiating the Conshohocken curve.

Nancy gripped the armrest.

"Yes, we're fine. Yes. Another time. I hope it's not too much trouble. I love you too."

Lucy flipped her phone shut and changed lanes without looking in her mirrors.

Nancy was baffled. She would have gotten the second degree. "How can you just cancel without giving a reason?" Nancy asked.

"I watched movies to see how people got out of things," Lucy said. "Say you're at a party and you get cornered by someone crazy, or someone who just can't end a conversation, or someone who's too drunk to know she's told you the same story twice, right? So, here's what people in movies do. They smile and say, 'Could you excuse me?' Very polite. And they walk away. There's no, 'I see someone I know over there,' or 'I have to get a drink,' or go to the bathroom. So, I don't give awkward excuses anymore. People can think what they want. It works like a charm." Lucy loved this move and she was proud to be able to give it to Nancy.

Lucy lurched and braked and cut cars off all the way to the nearest ski resort. In the cold, muddy rental shop that smelled like funky feet and fake snow, they filled out forms and were handed boots then skis and poles. They sat and clipped on their clunky footwear, which was fatal for Lucy. While Nancy was compact and had control of her muscles at all times, Lucy had one of those organic bodies. She was the type who tripped over phantom sidewalk cracks. In ski boots, Lucy walked like the Bumble from Rudolph the Red Nosed Reindeer. Nancy marched along, using her muscles, and Lucy waddled, using momentum.

They had to walk over a little bridge from the rental shop to the base of the mountain. It was possibly thirty yards. In that distance, Lucy dropped her skis once. Dropped her poles twice. And in a fascinating feat of balance, or lack thereof, she got her boot toe stuck in the bridge grating, stumbled, spun one complete turn, and somehow catapulted her mitten over the railing and down onto the frozen pond below. As Nancy stood at her side laughing, Lucy leaned against the railing and eulogized, "What a shame, it was such a young glove. So warm, so protective."

Always prepared, Nancy gave her an extra pair.

They strung their wickets through their zipper holes and put on their lift tickets. Nancy folded her ticket carefully and made sure it faced the right direction so the lift operators could see it. Lucy slapped hers on the wrong side of her coat and folded it crooked so she had to bend one edge over again.

"Lucy, you're supposed to put it on so the lift guys can see it," Nancy told her.

"Yeah, but if you do that then they don't have an easy reason to talk to you. And it's fun to make friends with the lift guys. They're usually cute."

"God, Luce, what do you want with some slacker ski-lift operator?"

"I told you," she said with sparkly eyes that meant trouble, "I want someone cute to flirt with."

And flirt they did. Lucy didn't have the hip snowboarder look. She wore her ancient fitted white ski jacket and snow pants that were taut across her butt. Men nearly popped out of their skis turning to look at her.

"Oh, I'm sorry, I put the ticket on the wrong side," Lucy

said to the lift attendant, and she twisted to show it to him, giving him a close and personal view of her chest. "I wasn't thinking."

When he smiled at her, he looked like he could be a Calvin Klein model. "What's your name?" he asked.

Lucy giggled and mumbled her name as they swayed up the lift away from him.

"I can't believe that worked," Nancy said, pulling the safety bar down.

"You've got to give men a reason to talk to you," Lucy said. "A conversation piece. Something nonthreatening. See how I said my name quietly?" She pointed a finger in the air. "He'll have to ask again."

"Bob started talking to me because I stole his parking spot. The first thing he ever said to me was, 'What the hell do you think you're doing?' "

"What's the answer?" Lucy asked with a raised eyebrow.

"I'm watching Miss Y Wild flirt with boys who work at a dinky Pennsylvania ski resort."

They bombed down the hill without any finesse whatsoever. In fact, it was a wonder they could manage to stop themselves at all. Nancy felt completely out of control. She was cold, but sweaty.

Lucy was exuberant. "That was great," she yelled triumphantly at the end of the run. She flung her poles into the air, throwing off her balance and pitching herself, quite indelicately, onto her ass.

Nancy felt like she was going to have a heart attack *before* she started laughing.

"You're fine," Lucy said. "It's me you should worry about. I could have broken my butt bone! Thank God it's got so much padding." She shook and slapped her butt like the girls on the MTV shows they passed while channel surfing.

Lucy told the Calvin Klein model her name again and they swayed back up the mountain. Nancy pulled the safety bar down and asked Lucy what she thought of her first semester of law school.

"I think it'll be a miracle if I stick it out."

"You don't like it?"

"I like some things about it."

"Such as?"

"The idea of it. The reality? Not so much."

"Is it as hard as everyone says?"

"Not for me. But I'm older than the typical student, which means that I don't care if I'm humiliated in class and I'm not panicked about failing, which I probably am."

"What do you think Mom will say?" Nancy asked.

Lucy made a little question-mark noise in her throat. A lilting "hmm," and said, "I hadn't thought of it."

She truly hadn't thought what their mother would say. When Nancy mentioned it, Lucy suddenly thought that maybe she should have considered this. Her mother *was* paying for it.

Nancy had considered it. That was because their mother would call Nancy and ask her what went wrong. She would ask her if Lucy needed help, if she was suicidal, if she was on drugs. She would bitch about the money, about Lucy's irresponsible behavior.

"I guess she'll be disappointed," Lucy said, then shrugged

and hopped off the chairlift. "I'm a bad investment," she added when Nancy caught up.

And then Lucy took a hard left and popped over a mogul and down a slope that Nancy wasn't sure she was ready to attempt. She followed anyway. Nancy always skied behind Lucy, who was much more daring. Nancy watched her to read which moguls were out of her league. Lucy took as many big jumps as she could, and almost always bungled them. After a spectacularly bad attempt at a back-scratcher, Lucy hit the ice, a trademark of snow skiing in Pennsylvania. They said you could ski anywhere if you learned to ski in PA.

Lucy slid sideways and jerked her poles into the air at odd angles, which instantly gave Nancy the giggles. Then Lucy did a dance of high comedy that Goofy would have been proud of. Her right ski twisted and she managed to plant a pole still keeping her balance. Then she reeled sideways and caught an edge. She was instantly a jumble of clattering equipment surrounded by a halo of snow. Head over skis, she rolled into the uncombed glen. It was *Wide World of Sports*—the agony of defeat.

Nancy was laughing as she approached Lucy, propped against a tree with her legs akimbo. But as Nancy got closer, she saw that Lucy was bloody. Lucy opened one eye, looked at Nancy and said, "Did I go big?" Then she passed out. Her head was swelling like a rotten tomato. Nancy screamed to the skiers going by, "Get ski patrol." She yelled it over and over as tears stung her eyes. Finally, a fellow skier stopped. He pulled out his cell phone and called 911. Nancy was grateful to have someone with her, especially because she felt compelled to pound on Lucy's chest and yell dramatically, "Don't you die on me." But she didn't want to touch her. Instead, she took off her coat and covered her body for extra warmth. Jim, the skier who had stopped, kneeled beside Nancy, took off his coat, and covered her.

In the hospital, Lucy got her jaw wired shut. When the nurse let Nancy in to see her, Lucy opened her one good eye and said through swollen lips, "I 'hink I'n 'ucked up."

"Oh yeah, sweetie, you've got a fractured jaw and a broken collarbone for sure." Nancy didn't want to tell her about her face, which looked like an uncooked meatball. Or about her ribs or the concussion. Lucy had gauze over her right eye and they weren't sure how long it would take to heal. Her clavicle was so smashed the doctor said she might have permanent nerve damage.

The day they released her, every bump in the road made Lucy catch her breath sharply.

"Nom knows?" she asked Nancy through the wires.

"Yeah, I called Mom," Nancy said, "and she was pissed."

Lucy wrinkled her swollen, pumpkin face. "Non't nake ne naff."

"I don't know why that would make you laugh."

"'Ecause," she said, then interrupted herself with a wince. Her puffy lips were slicked with grease so they wouldn't crack any more than they already had.

"You mean you know that I caught hell because you bailed on her without giving an excuse? And because I was with you when you ended up in the hospital? Mom said, 'Is that what you girls were doing? Skiing instead of coming to see me?'" Nancy did her best imitation of their mother and exaggerated her outrage to amuse her poor, broken sister. "She said, 'I placed an order for Antonio's takeout and had Jean come in and clean.'"

"Non't nake ne naff." Lucy winced again with her one good eye.

Nancy helped Lucy into the house and onto the sofa. She gave her the remote and hot tea with a straw. Nancy put a fresh bottle of water on the coffee table and lined up her meds. "Are you in pain?" Nancy asked as she covered Lucy with her favorite down blanket.

"Only 'ecause I'm awake," Lucy said. Then she squirted a syringe full of narcotics into her mouth and fell asleep.

And that was how it went. Lucy took medicine and Nancy refilled her water and tea. Lucy slept and Nancy worked from home so she could stay within five feet of her just in case. Lucy moaned in pain, and Nancy made her broth with pureed vegetables and milkshakes.

Jim, Nancy's slopeside savior, had been calling every night since the accident. He had followed the ambulance to the hospital and met Nancy there. She thought it was to get his coat back, but when she gave it to him, he told her that he hadn't come for his coat but for her number and to see how her sister was, of course. Nancy burst into tears when he asked, and he stayed with her.

Nancy had replaced Lucy's white gauze eye covering with a black patch with a strap that cut into her nappy hair. When Lucy felt better she greeted Nancy with a hearty, "Ahoy, matey." Lucy thought the eye patch was hilarious. "They couldn't come up with anything better than a black eye patch? Come on. Look at me. As if I don't look ridiculous enough with this hairdo. I have dreadlocks. I should be smoking grass," she joked. She had been camped out on the sofa for weeks, afraid to sleep in her bed without the cocoon-like protection of the sofa's backrest. Since the swelling in her lips had gone down, Lucy's speech had improved. Nancy still called her "the Godfather," though.

She and Nancy started watching movies together in the middle of the afternoon. Nancy had been working from home exclusively, which was something her position allowed her to do. During the climax of *Terms of Endearment,* the phone rang. It was her secretary connecting her with the conference call she'd forgotten she'd scheduled. Nancy, the consummate pro, blew her nose, told them she had a cold, and fumbled through it beautifully.

"I know you have to work," Lucy said when Nancy finished with her meeting. "I'm so sorry. I'm not used to needing help."

"What kind of thing is that to say? You're being ridiculous." Plus, it seemed to Nancy that Lucy was always getting help. "Who took care of you when you got sick?" she asked. Nancy had memories of her father reading to her and giving her medicine. Of her mother giving her soup and rubbing mentholated ointment on her chest.

"No one." Lucy shrugged. "The first time I got sick with Ben and he tried to take care of me, I screamed at him to get away."

"What about Mom and Dad?"

"When I got the chicken pox they hired a nurse," she said. "They didn't like sick people. Dad was worried that he would get infected and die. And Mom said my room smelled like disease. She couldn't stand it."

Nancy was horrified. She couldn't imagine. But it was likely, since their mother had yet to come to visit. She called often, but her exact words were, "I'll come when her face heals, I can't bear to see it battered and swollen." It hadn't struck Nancy as odd at the time.

The truth was that Nancy didn't really want anyone visiting. There was an element of caretaking that she was enjoying. She'd never been needed. Certainly not by Bob. When he got sick, he'd holed up in the bedroom and told her to go away. And Nancy didn't have children or pets. So this was all new. Lucy needed prescriptions filled, needed food pureed, needed hot tea, needed laxatives.

"I don't want to talk about it," Lucy said, "but get me something strong and get bran."

"Those pain pills will bind you up."

"I don't want to talk about it."

"I'm your sister," Nancy said. "I'm not going to break up with you because you're talking about shit."

"Or the lack thereof?"

"I'll get prune juice."

On the big day, Lucy called Nancy into her room and asked her to help her out of her bandages. She was finally going to shower. They took their time and got her undressed. Then Nancy put the step stool in the shower and Lucy started to cry. "It hurts."

Nancy stripped off her clothes and got into the shower with Lucy.

"Last time we did this we were drunk and covered in someone else's blood," Nancy said.

"Don't make me laugh." Lucy had her arms wrapped around her midsection.

"That's your battle cry these days." Nancy had never made anyone laugh consistently. But the absurdity of their lives together was in such sharp contrast to her life with Bob that she couldn't be serious anymore. Lucy lifted her good arm and Nancy soaped and shaved her.

"Just think," Lucy said, "if it weren't for me, you might have lived your life without ever having shaved another person's armpit."

With her arm lifted, Nancy could see Lucy's ribs. She was horrified. "I'm making you drink bacon grease. A bacon grease milkshake."

"You're always trying to get me to diet."

"No, I'm not."

"You and Mom have a thing about my weight."

"That's just because we don't see things as they are, we see things as *we* are," Nancy said, feeling very clever. "Anaïs Nin said that, I think."

"I don't even get it. You and Mom are both tiny and thin. You look like you're teenagers."

"Yeah, but we're like Grandma, who looked like a brick when she gained weight. You're a Renaissance Venus. A Thomas Eakins nude."

"Not anymore. Now I'm a dirty heroin addict," she said, looking down at herself.

"Nah, it's heroin chic," Nancy told her. She was still going to make her a milkshake.

Lucy started physical therapy and Nancy went back to the office. When Nancy couldn't drive Lucy to appointments, she reserved the company car service for her. Lucy felt like a princess and Nancy was her knight in shining armor.

After weeks of physical therapy, Nancy opened the apartment door not to her sleeping sister on the sofa but to a bright-eyed Lucy sitting at the kitchen table with canvas board in front of her and a paintbrush in hand.

"I was in PT today and asked my therapist if she thought painting would help my rehab."

"How do you feel?"

"The painting takes my mind off of the pain for brief moments. And all of the drugs make me feel like doing psychedelic Dada crap."

Lucy was purging her demons. Painting had always helped with that. She painted her body wrapped in a sling. She was swinging over a cubist background that looked like blood, snow, and tree bark. Her one-eyed perspective gave a surreal quality to the depth. In another painting, she sketched herself as a pirate on a ship; the mast was attached to a ski-lift cable, and it had a border made of broken crossbones. Another was an exaggerated rendering of her collarbone X-rays in bright reds and oranges. Another day Lucy filled the kitchen table with brightly painted papier-mâché masks with exaggerated lips.

"Classes started," Lucy told Nancy over a cup of tea.

"You could go. All you'd have to do is sit there and take notes."

"I'd have to think. And I'm not sure I can do that just yet."

"Painting takes thought," Nancy said.

"Not as much as you'd think."

"Do what you need to do to get well," Nancy said.

So Lucy stayed at home and Nancy called the bursar's office. She asked them if they would apply Lucy's tuition payment to next year. Then she called the program secretary and explained to him what had happened. He said Lucy would have to send a formal request to the program director, but usually they would extend the program of study. Then she wrote a letter to the program director and read it to Lucy, who cried at the end of it and thanked her.

"Are you crying because you're afraid they won't extend your program?"

"I don't think so."

"Is it because you think they will?"

"No." Lucy snorted a bit.

Nancy suspected that she'd guessed correctly.

"It's because you're so nice to me." Lucy had realized that failing law school didn't matter. She was fighting a bigger battle and Nancy was helping her. In fact, it was because Nancy was helping her that she was winning the internal battle over what she felt she deserved in life.

"Anyone would do it for you," Nancy said, a little shocked. "It was just the luck of the draw that I got you when you broke your body." Nancy sat down and pulled out the lotion to massage Lucy's arm, which had started to give her trouble because of the broken collarbone.

"See," Lucy said, "who else would do this for me? Rub my arm? Write letters? Take off work? Screen my calls? Make me soup?"

"Everyone who's ever known you?"

"No, just you. And I'm really grateful."

"Well, I guess you got lucky you weren't out skiing with someone who would have left you for dead."

"Like Mom? Or any of my boyfriends?" Lucy joked.

"Ben would have helped."

"And I would have poked him away with my ski pole."

"That's the tricky part. Actually letting people help you," Nancy said. "So," she ventured, "is that why you broke your engagement? You were afraid of what? Trusting men? Ben?"

Nancy pressed on the taut tendons of Lucy's forearm. She figured Lucy was about to drift off, when she finally spoke. "I think I used to reject help when it was offered and demand it when it wasn't. It was a bad cycle of desire and guilt instead of real need and gratitude. I thought no one would ever help me when I needed it, so I demanded that people help me to test them."

"Tests aren't a good idea. Look how well it worked out with Bob."

"Were you testing him when you moved out?"

"I don't know if I was testing or if I was just testy."

"I also back myself into corners. I did it with Ben and now I'm doing it with law school. It's not likely that I'll do well, but I'll probably never do what I really want to do. I put myself in either-or situations and then I always pick the wrong thing." Lucy closed her eyes and Nancy rubbed her arm until she could tell from her breathing that she had fallen asleep.

Lucy got her jaw released and her eye patch off, and their mother decided she could finally visit. She and Bob came on the same day. Nancy half suspected that Bob was making an appearance because he wanted to trick her mother into thinking they were fine. Nancy had no idea why he cared what she thought. And her mother didn't think a thing. Nancy hadn't told her about their problems. She had sort of stopped caring. First there was the new job, and then Lucy moved in, then the accident, then Jim. Plus, there was all of Lucy's art in the house. It was hard to be miserable watching someone with pretty much everything going against her just ignore it all to make beautiful paintings.

Lucy was looking forward to seeing her mother. When Bob walked in, Lucy shot Nancy a look, but Nancy didn't seem to care; she hugged them both and told them to help themselves to drinks. Lucy was proud of her.

Their mother gasped. "Lucy, you look fantastic. You're so thin."

"Mother!" Nancy scolded. She wanted to defend Lucy, but when she looked her way, Lucy winked at her.

Then their mother gasped again. This time she was looking at the walls. Canvasses were everywhere. Nancy had bought a drill and masonry bit and covered the brick walls with Lucy's work. "Oh, Nancy, you've become an art lover," she said. She looked like she was about to burst.

"Do you like them?" Nancy asked, instantly wishing she hadn't, just in case their mother said something to hurt Lucy's feelings.

"Tell me what you paid for them and I'll tell you if they were worth it." When she hit the section of Lucy's self-portraits, she stopped. "Lucy?"

Then their mother excitedly appraised each piece, saying things like, "I have a buyer for this," and "what the market

will bear," and, "We've got to get you a gallery show immediately."

Nancy was expecting Lucy either to ignore her or shrug and
say, "Sure, whatever," like she usually did to their mother. But
Lucy smiled and thanked her. "I'd love that," she said. "Plus, if
you can sell some of them, then I could pay you back for law
school, which I'm failing, by the way."

"You don't have to pay me back," her mother said, waving
her hand in an uncharacteristically dismissive way.

"Well, it's not the greatest deal," Lucy said. "I mean, you'll
be doing the work trying to sell this crap."

"That's one thing I don't allow," her mother said sternly.
"My artists are not allowed to bad-mouth themselves. No arguments."

"Deal," Lucy said. "I can't win an argument with you anyway."

"Then you'll be a pleasure to work with," her mother
joked.

"I still need lots of practice," Lucy said.

Her mother disagreed but told Lucy that she had to be
happy with her work. "I'll send someone to pick up the paintings next week," she said, then gently shook Lucy's hand.

Their mother and Bob left at the same time, and Nancy noticed an envelope on the kitchen table with her name typed on
it. Inside were divorce papers and Nancy thought how she
wouldn't miss him. Not even a little bit.

When Lucy got well enough to take care of herself, she moved
into her own apartment outside the city. She'd saved the checks
her mother had sent her and hired movers. Lucy took Nancy's

car and led the movers on an excursion from the apartment to a storage unit that she'd shared with the shitting boyfriend, and then to her mother's house to sort through her childhood belongings. She had rented a cheap place on the Delaware River, an hour north of Nancy and an hour south of her mother. She needed to be on her own, but not too far away.

Jim and Nancy wrapped and packed her paintings. They arrived at the new place before Lucy and the movers got there, and Nancy made Jim practically run all of the paintings inside so she could surprise Lucy by hanging them before she arrived. Nancy didn't want her to be depressed by the bare walls.

Lucy was thrilled. But mostly she was beside herself because the new place had a separate studio with great natural light. That was all she cared about. She was going to buy an inexpensive car and commute to law school for another semester. See how it went. Maybe tape the lectures and listen to them on the ride. "What the hell, I can't get a refund; I might as well go."

Nancy gave it a month.

Jim kissed Lucy on the cheek and told Nancy to take her time. He was going to move the truck because it was double-parked. After he left, Lucy told Nancy to get out of her apartment. "I'm a busy student and I need to avoid work by painting something new."

They hugged. "Jim's staying over tonight," Nancy said.

"You little hussy."

"I know, I'm a little tramp," Nancy said.

"I've been cramping your style this whole time."

"Nah, it's just that I'd be lonely without you in the house," Nancy said.

"I know you love him," Lucy said. "But if you get sick of him, you can always escape to my place. I'll let you shave my armpits."

"You know, Lucy," Nancy said, "Jonas Salk wanted to become a lawyer."

"Really? What made him change his mind?"

"His mother."

Lucy brightened at this.

"Yeah, she told him she didn't think he'd be any good because he couldn't win an argument with her."

Lucy laughed. "Sounds like someone I know."

As Lucy stood in the doorway of her new place and watched Nancy and Jim drive away, she thought of William Wordsworth, who said that the best portion of a good man's life were his little, nameless, unremembered acts of kindness and love.

But both of them were sure they would always remember each and every one of those moments.

The Hard Way
(Charcoal on Paper, 2000)

I should have been squinting over minuscule print on the onionskin pages of my law books. Instead, I was buying two pumpkins, one Laurel, the other Hardy, for Halloween, the only holiday worth celebrating. It was a day when you could be anyone you wanted to be, and I sincerely needed a break from who I had become and from who I was trying to become.

At one point, I thought if I were a lawyer I'd make enough money to subsidize my artistic leanings. My most impressive artistic claim to fame so far was that one of my paintings had sold for three thousand dollars to a lawyer from Manhattan. It was a fluke. My mother, who was hawking my art, convinced a friend that it was a steal at twice the price.

I wondered how long the money would last and looked for the courage to quit law school—to do the art thing the hard way, struggling like most everyone else. Sure, even now some artists had sponsors, but I suspected that nobody liked them. Horrible people, all of them.

I thought that being a lawyer was the way to "be someone," which was something I thought mattered not so long ago. I grew up right outside my county's seat and a lot of lawyers lived near us. They tried to outdo each other with Alfa

Romeos and expensive vacations. You grow up seeing that all of your life, you start to think it's the only road to prosperity. Even my father, who generally cared only about art and education, admired the lawyers. Especially the ones that dealt with estates and saw that my parents got their share when my mother's moneyed relatives died.

Turned out that the glut of attorneys graduating from law school each year had made the profession as competitive as the NFL, only with less money and talent. But I wasn't afraid of a little competition. What I didn't fully think out was my utter distaste for conflict. If a fellow motorist angrily honked at me or gave me the finger, I usually waved or gave a hands-up shrug of apology. The "oops, sorry" of hand gestures. When I was finally honest with myself, I figured that I'd be better making ends meet by showing kids the wonders of construction paper and soup-can pencil holders at summer camp. It came to me while my eyes glazed over as I stared at the details of the malpractice case of Ms. Ida Hypochondriac. I really didn't need that much money, just time and peace of mind.

I was pondering my poor career choice and the cost of law school thus far—LSATs, applications, books, gas for the hour commute I'd been making since August—when I saw *him* at the farm stand. He was carrying pumpkins from the back of a truck to the display bench by the side of the road. The woman who rang me up yelled to him, "James, give a hand, could you?"

He had to take both Laurel and Hardy for me since I'd smashed my clavicle and various other body parts skiing less than a year before. By the time we reached the hatchback of my fourth-hand hatchback, I found out he was trying to make enough money to buy tires for his truck. I couldn't imagine why he wasn't dancing at the all-male revue for extra cash, except that the small town I lived in didn't have an all-male revue. As casually as possible I gave James my phone number and told him I needed some work done if he needed extra cash. Okay, I lied. I didn't have any extra cash. I had stopped borrowing money from my mother at the ripe old age of twenty-nine and at a most inopportune time. I'd already moved to the cheapest town within a hundred-mile radius of school to save on rent. But I'd worry about that later. I made a note to call Mom and see if she'd had any luck selling anything else. I hadn't stopped accepting her professional services.

I was painting burnt-umber treetops, the ones outside my second-story apartment window, when he called. I almost didn't answer the phone. I usually didn't when I was painting. But burnt-umber treetops hardly counted as inventive, and I hadn't forgotten that I'd recently given my number to the strapping pumpkin guy.

"I hope I'm not calling too late," he said. He reminded me who he was. I knew, but I played it cool. "I just got back from a football scrimmage," he said, as if to explain his breathlessness. I suspected he was nervous. I was feeling a little breathless myself.

"You said you needed some help?" His voice went up at the end and cracked a little.

He was nervous. That was good because I was smoothing down my overly poofy hair and wiggling my foot as I sat on the stool at the island between my kitchen and living room. I had never dated a football player, but I had to remind myself that he wasn't calling for a date. He was calling for a job I hadn't yet invented.

"Could you hold on a minute?" I asked then put my hand over the receiver. I listened to him breathing. I heard country music playing in the background. A football-playing good ole boy. I could do worse.

"Sorry about that. I had to cover my paints or they'd dry out," I said.

"Paints?"

"I'm an artist. That's what I need help with. I have a show and need someone to help me move my things." I mentioned the healing clavicle again. "The show's not for a couple weeks. More immediately," I ventured, "I need models. I've been doing a lot of figures lately and my neighbor is getting sick of sitting for me." I was talking too much. Running it all together. I tried to make that last part sound light.

"Oh, cool," he got in edgewise.

"I usually pay her in paintings," I said, "but in your case I could arrange a contribution to the tire fund."

He fell for it, and on Saturday night James arrived smelling like a mixture of soapy cologne and beer, which was unsuccessfully covered up with cinnamon chewing gum. I imagined he'd spit it out right before he knocked on the door, which I opened to his grinning face—a big toothy smile, his front two with a slight space between them. He wore a navy blue flannel shirt and khaki pants. He stepped inside and looked wide-eyed at my paintings, which covered every bit of wall space in my small apartment.

"The walls weren't anything special to look at anyway," I explained, looking at the way James's black hair hugged his head in one big wave. "It's just old brown paneling under there."

James scanned the wall and his eyes stopped at a self-portrait—"Nude in Bathtub." I had painted my dark, wet hair clinging to my crooked collarbone. My nipples were an unnatural cadmium red with canary yellow.

"That's not my best work," I said, embarrassed.

When he turned and looked at me, he was blushing too.

"I like them," he said. "All of them," he continued, the red in his face deepening.

"Most are of friends and I can't bear to part with them," I said.

I gestured toward a picture of a hotel in New Orleans with swirling wrought iron, pink blooms peeking into the frame from the latticework on the side, and my friend Jayne on the porch.

"It's not easy to make a living this way. I was going to be a lawyer. But then I realized compared to that lifestyle, poverty didn't look so bad." It was the first time I had spoken the thought out loud and I liked the way it felt.

"Well, you sell stuff, right?" James asked.

"Yeah, but you need an angle," I said.

"Like that elephant that paints," James said.

"Or, there was this artist in the sixteen hundreds in Rome, Salvator Rosa," I said, "who pretended he was a doctor. Dr. Formica, he called himself, and he told patients that looking at Salvator Rosa paintings would cure depression."

"Too bad there are drugs for that now."

"He was really popular."

"Maybe you could tell people that your paintings raise the dead."

"Or they'll bring you luck."

"Or love."

James looked at me and then down at my beat-up hard-wood floor that I wished I'd swept. His jaw was square and his skin as smooth as if he had just stepped out of a barbershop in Nepal. I wondered if he'd ever been there and gotten his baby face shaved in style. Probably not. It wasn't a favorite vacation spot for football-playing, country-music-listening Americans.

I pointed to Jayne in the painting. "She killed herself. My college roommate. It wasn't long after that trip." I had no idea why I told him that. Maybe to fill the silence. To deflect attention away from the fact that I was staring at him. Maybe as a litmus test for his suitability as a sympathetic lover—I hadn't had one of those in a while. All of the above, probably.

His brow was wrinkled and his mouth curled down at the ends. "I'm so sorry." An appropriate response. I was touched. I had revealed tragedy to other men and was met with disappointing responses. David, who was in my communications law class, had told me about his dog getting hit by a truck. Apparently Fluffy pulled through after considerable expense, only to choke on a rawhide treat given by a well-wisher. David wanted to sue. In the end, the disposal of the body was paid for by said well-wisher at the request of David's lawyer. Actually, that was why David decided to go to law school. And David was why I decided not to date law students.

When I'd told Mark, a mental-health-care caseworker, about Jayne, he'd asked, "Were you in New Orleans for Mardi Gras?" He then told me about his spring break adventures on Bourbon Street. He did whippets on a side street and fell backward. His head cracked on the curb while the echo in his head rang, *"whaa, whaa, whaa, near, near, near."* That was the sound effect he made. I guess it would have made sense if I'd ever done whippets.

"You miss those good old college days, huh?" I'd asked, trying to mask my sarcasm. Indeed he did. He reminisced about all of them that long, long night.

But James's response showed he had some experience. Something more than partying or threatening to sue someone for a hundred bucks. If the story was a litmus test for maturity, then James passed.

"Do you want a beer?" I asked, heading toward the kitchen and waving my hand in the air to erase the negative memory I'd evoked. I wanted this to go well. I'd hate to be known as the morbid artist who talked about death all night. I'm sure I've been memorialized as "the bad date to top all" by several men in the tri-state area. But I was trying to transcend my past and the stereotypes of my future profession as an artist. That was a heavy current to fight.

The longer hair on the top of James's head fell in curls over his forehead as he shook his head yes to the beer. "Please," he said.

"Music?" I asked, gesturing toward the CD collection as I popped the tops off the pony Rolling Rocks.

He studied the label on the beer I gave him.

"Pick whatever you like," I said as I retrieved my charcoal and paper from a cupboard in the kitchen where I stored some of my supplies. James had the sort of solid frame charcoal drawing was invented for.

He filled the five-disc changer and put it on shuffle without asking how to work any of it. Two Tom Pettys, two James Taylors, and a John Denver. He was competent. I often fantasized about having a boyfriend who wouldn't stand with the refrigerator door open and call out to me, "Where's the lunch meat?"

We settled in the living room and I began sketching.

"So, you play football at the university?" I asked. He could have played for the farm team, but I doubted it. "The team's doing pretty well this year." The little nearby university was not known for its football, but they were getting better, which was a nice scenic bonus at the bars in town. I didn't go out to check out the young meat, I mean men. It was just that there was only one place that supplied free bar food for happy hour on Fridays, and it happened to be right across from my apartment. So the lawyers, college students, married men, and single women rubbed elbows over chafing trays of hot wings and nachos. Free food united the masses. Anyway, I was only twenty-nine, so I figured I could still check out the college boys, or have them up to my apartment, as it were.

James shifted on the green faux-leather couch, which came with the apartment, along with a badly stained maple dining room table with claw feet and no leaves, and a microwave that had a dial controller for the timer, which only went as high as ten minutes.

"Sit still," I said to James, teasing him.

It was a peculiar thing, sketching someone. I *had* to look at him. That was the point. But the model could look anywhere. My downstairs neighbor watched her "stories" on television. But James looked straight at me with a very nice mix of cerulean and cobalt blue eyes, rimmed in black, with a few flecks of mainly chromium-oxide green. I considered pulling the paints out but he was starting to fidget. It was an acquired skill, sitting for an artist. I liked to give amateurs a break every ten, fifteen minutes. Looked like James wouldn't make it five.

When we broke, James immediately took my sketchpad and tried to draw my portrait. I squirmed around pretending to be him.

"I'll draw you with fat thighs and upper-lip hair if you don't stop," he threatened.

I sat still and looked at his forehead wrinkle in concentration.

"This is hard," he said. "Give me a tip."

"Just concentrate on shapes," I said. "Pretend everything you're looking at is on a flat plane."

He nodded, bit his lower lip. "I go to the park with my little brothers, they're twins, ten years old," he said, still looking at me and then down. "Once an artist drew them playing on the jungle gym. It was really good. I tried to draw after that but I'm no good at it." He slashed the charcoal across the page and slapped the pad down on the coffee table between us.

"I'll teach you," I told him, looking at what he managed to draw before getting frustrated. Yikes, poofy hair and bugged-out eyes. "Try doing an outline without taking your pencil off the paper and without looking at the paper." I handed the sketchpad back, and he enthusiastically grabbed a pen off the table.

"You just got frustrated too quickly. That's what teachers are for."

"To get frustrated for you?" James stared at me and pulled the pen slowly across the paper.

I felt self-conscious and silently reminded myself not to smooth my hair down. "One of my art teachers in high school used to walk around our tables when it was quiet and sing in this spooky low voice, 'Today's the day the teddy bears have their pic-nic.'"

"What kind of song is that?" James asked.

"A kid's song. You never heard it?"

James shook his head. Then he held up his drawing. "You like?"

I took it. As I suspected, the outline of my hair was ridiculously big. But it wasn't supposed to be accurate. "It looks cool. Sign it," I said, and handed it back.

"I think I need more lessons," he said, looking at it.

I was willing. I hoped I could teach him a few things besides art. I considered his good points as far as I knew them. He was an athlete. He was open to new things. And he was the kind of guy who took his brothers to the park. I firmly believed that men who chose to have kids in their lives were patient and silly. These two things were key elements for the "lessons" I had planned for James. Okay, I was getting ahead of myself.

But James was a far cry from the usual encounters I had with men. On a typical date I generally heard complaints about everything from the speed limit to the price of gas. And these were first dates, best-behavior dates. James didn't complain about anything. Granted, we weren't on a date, but it was looking as if it could get romantic. Although the thought of making out with him and then giving him money for his truck was a little unsettling. No, actually, I sort of liked the thought of that.

He wondered if I did caricatures because he did impressions. Who did impressions anymore, besides Rich Little? He did his shtick for me—Bill Cosby, Rodney Dangerfield, and Moe from the Three Stooges playing golf. It wasn't half bad. Okay, maybe I was smitten. Sure I was. Any woman who likes the Three Stooges is either under eight years old or over twenty and trying to get into some goofy guy's pants.

I got more beers and James looked through my sketches.

"You have to give me one of these for my mom," he said. "I don't want any money, I just want this one," he said, ripping the sketch from my pad.

I didn't object. His mother? Very sweet. Look at how a man treats his mother and waitstaff and you'll see how he'll treat you. Waitstaff might not be a part of that motto. But I know you're not supposed to date people who are mean to waitron. It showed bad character.

James was showing good character. We never went back to work. We sat on my porch in the cool fall air that made my hair bristle when it blew through the knit of my threadbare gray wool sweater. James pulled out two cigars that said, "It's a girl!" on the wrappers and offered me one. We puffed on them. Oh, I knew I was smitten, because that thing was gross and I still smoked it. I asked him if he liked country music. I figured I had an easy opener with that. But he told me he wasn't much of a country fan. His parents were. He liked R.E.M. and the Foo Fighters. His favorite football team was the Giants and he believed in the death penalty. We argued about that for a minute, but I let it slide. Of course I did.

"Do you have a girlfriend?" I asked. So much for being subtle. Beer, the great social lubricant.

James said no but put his fingers to his temple.

"Ah-ha," I said, "your body language tells another story." What the hell, I never was good at being coy.

"I had a girlfriend, but we broke up. She started dating someone else, actually."

"Was she blind?"

"We'd been going out since we were kids. She hates football and was always nagging me about it—practice, workouts, games—it takes a lot of time. I don't care. I just hate seeing her with him."

"You still see her?" I was surprised. "Do you have classes together?"

"I didn't want to tell you," he said and took a deep breath. He squeezed his eyes shut, opened them, and looked at me with his face pinched and tense.

I imagined all sorts of scenarios in those few seconds. She was pregnant with his baby. They were really married from a drunken Vegas junket. She was the other half of his nightclub act. She swallowed swords, which I'd never be able to compete with. She left him for the guy who did the ventriloquist act.

"I'm a . . . senior . . . in . . . high school."

Ouch. The shower ran cold. My car blew a tire in the boondocks in the middle of the night. I was hit in the gut in the middle of my "hills are alive" twirl. Or, I was a twenty-nine-year-old soon-to-be-law-school-dropout, making the moves on a high school kid. There were times when an eleven-year age difference didn't matter. When you were out of high school, for one. When you were a celebrity, for two. And when you were a successful man, for three. Otherwise, it was something of a scandal.

I was sure he was at least twenty-one. Couldn't he have been just a few years older? Hadn't he told me that he was twenty-one when he carried my pumpkins? I even remembered thinking that twenty-one was a little young.

"Why didn't you want to tell me?" I managed to ask. Good

recovery. I was sure I'd have a hard time disguising my disappointment. My mind raced through our evening retrofitting all of our conversations to this new reality. He talked a lot about his family because he *lived* with them. *"Mom and Dad like country music. I take my twin brothers to the park."* Hello. Stupid, stupid, stupid. I wondered if he'd ever been to Nepal, indeed. He probably just started shaving last year.

"I knew you thought I was in college," he said, "and I figured if you didn't find out you'd consider dating me."

What could I say to that? The only reasonable thing, of course. A lie. "I don't consider dating anyone until I get to know them well."

Right. I had practically imagined him in all of the positions of the *Kama Sutra,* for God's sake. One more beer and I might have suggested some nude modeling, or nude wrestling.

"I might be seventeen, but you look seventeen," he said in some sort of desperate attempt at flattery.

"Oh, thanks," I said. "That may be because I was born yesterday." Ugh. He wasn't even eighteen. Make that a twelve-year age difference.

It was getting late and James left. Early football scrimmage on Sunday and then work at the farm stand. Ah, to be in high school again.

After he left, I slumped on the couch where he'd sat and smelled his cologne. He wore too much, like high school boys tended to do. When the phone rang at midnight I was watching *Saturday Night Live* getting looped. I was on beer six, seven, eight—who was counting?

"Lucy? It's James."

"I thought you'd be in bed by now. You've got to get up

early." I slurred my words a little so it sounded as if I said, "Thought you'd be a bed my now. You god a ged up rr-lee." I was trying to sound bright but I felt wretched. Drunk and cranky.

"I can't stop thinking about you."

"Very sweet." Maybe I should come over and tuck you in? No, I didn't say that.

"Before I told you I was in high school, were you considering me for even a second?"

"James, I told you—"

"I know. Not until you're friends," he said.

Only a high school boy would believe that crap. I had come on so strong I was surprised my pheromones hadn't overpowered his cologne.

"We could be friends," he said. "You're awesome and interesting and beautiful."

"Oddly, I don't believe that being beautiful is generally a criterion for friendship." I had no idea what I was doing. Uncharted territory. Get the map. A handsome guy liked me, and I was turning him down.

"I still think you should date me," he said.

I wanted to ask what we'd do on those dates. But I wasn't cruel. I had been in high school myself, after all. "We *are* friends," I said. "Remember, I gave you beer and you gave me tobacco. We're practically kin now." That was the best I could do.

James was a caller. I forgot about that from my high school days. I was regressing. He called me almost every night. This kid was persistent. I didn't have anything else going on in my life, so I enjoyed it. And not in some self-punishing way. I just fully enjoyed his attention. And since I had firmly laid out the ground rules—just friends—my pleasure wasn't tainted by guilt. There had been times when I craved attention and took it under false pretenses. But this was not the case with James. Plus, without him, those days would have been dark indeed. I had stopped going to class and knew it would be only a matter of weeks before I admitted it to my friends and family and officially joined the ranks of the starving artists.

Deciding against law school wasn't simple. I knew what people would have thought of me if I had become a lawyer. I would have had the respect of a professional woman making it in what was still a man's world. The female lawyers had it made in the status department. Male lawyers had to prove they weren't sleazeballs and female lawyers had to prove they were. Instead I would be a "starving artist." It wasn't a cliché for no reason, although I wasn't sure that my hips were benefiting from the poor man's diet of peanut butter and white bread.

The starving artist and the fat-cat lawyer said a lot about our cultural values. I suppose it was a justified caste system. I'd be the first to admit that a good number of lawsuits had improved my world. My speech was fiercely protected. I had artistic, religious, and political freedom. And lawyers were on the frontlines of bettering world conditions, alleviating the suffering of others, fighting for justice. I was struggling with the disappointment of knowing that I would never make that kind of a difference in the world.

What was I doing? Focus: I was painting. I needed more green over here and I couldn't afford the cadmium.

I didn't have a problem letting go of the idea of my clientele and the opposing counsel. The litigious mentality was so ugly. I'd found that most people who sued were the kind of folks that were rude to retail clerks or the poor tech-support guy who was just trying to help—hey, *you* called him. People with entitlement complexes who thought that confrontation would get them what they wanted. And it usually did because all they really wanted was a fight. The business of law supported ugly behavior and perpetuated a whole variety of levels of fighting. But my choice meant that I'd never be on the Supreme Court. I'd never stare down the face of pure evil in court and have him admit that he shouldn't cut down the old-growth redwoods in Northern California. I wouldn't be Atticus Finch. Damn. But I had no focus for law anymore. It was now a fantasy path untaken, where I brokered art, saved the whales, and replaced Sandra Day O'Connor.

I held off telling people I'd dropped out. I didn't take calls during the day while I stood at my easel in the window of my sunny studio. I wanted people to think I was going to class. Eventually, after I confessed, I still let the machine pick up, because I was busy. Painting, however unrespectable, was work, since I was trying to make money from it. *My* work. The kicker was that I liked it. I was beginning to believe that I was good at it.

Usually when James called he got my answering machine. I said he *called* almost every day, but I didn't say I talked to him every time he called. I let him reach me once or twice a week. I had other friends. Okay, I wasn't taking their calls either. I was a little depressed. I had the no-money-no-sales-rent-due-drop-out gloom. But James's messages helped. He was my most creative friend with the answering machine. He told jokes or left the score of the Giants' game. Like I cared about football. But it was nice that he included me in what he cared about. I always appreciated that. Once in a while Bill Cosby or Rodney Dangerfield called. Oh, man, was he a dork. Impersonations? Sheesh.

So we did become friends after all. It was nothing short of a miracle. Go figure. Rarely did a man say that he wanted to be friends and mean it, not to mention that the only reason I suggested it was to scare him off. That "just friends" thing was a repellent, for better or worse. I mean, I had male friends. Some had always been platonic, some had been lovers, and some had been romantic interests. But none had been rejected outright. Actually, that wasn't true. It had happened, but only with boys I went to high school with. Naturally.

James and I went to the movies on Sundays after he earned enough money for his truck tires and quit the farm stand. It was no big deal, just matinees. One week he'd pick and pay and the next week I'd pick and pay.

"It's your week to pick and pay at the plata-plex," he said into my machine. "Say it three times fast."

Plata-plex was his name for our cineplex. It came from a discussion about the *plex* ending. James asked rhetorically, "What's wrong with *cinema*? Or *theater*?" He started ending as many words as he could with *plex*. The auto dealaplex. The supermarkaplex. Zion United Church of Christaplex. Who knew how *plata-plex* came out of all of it? I think it started with the duck-billed plata-plex. James would probably remember. He remembered everything, including what I was wearing the first time we met and what I said to him on the phone, verbatim, last week. He was a sweet kid.

I went to one of his football games with his parents. Imagine. They told me they were glad James was getting exposure to some culture before he went to college. Me? Culture? I wasn't sure if they really believed it, until his mother introduced me to a fellow PTA member as "James's private art instructor." I guessed that was how he explained me. And I finally understood how he had money for the movies without having a job. This kid was smart, or at least opportunistic. He was getting money from his parents to pay for "private" art instruction and was getting paid to do odd jobs for me.

I painted James without his shirt on. He wanted to pose nude. He badgered me about it, but I told him I wouldn't contribute to the corruption of a minor. He laughed, took a swallow of beer, and said he wished I would. I couldn't help that he drank beer. He brought it over himself after I refused to keep any in the fridge; I wasn't the only one who thought he looked older than twenty-one. Besides, I drank when I was seventeen, which didn't seem that long ago and at the same time seemed like it was so long ago that I might as well have been frozen in ice.

Along with talking about posing nude, James typically steered the conversation, at some point while we were together, to sex. Could you blame him? He was a horny teenager without a girlfriend and I was a woman who had sex, enjoyed it, and admitted to both.

He told me he slept with his ex-girlfriend twice but her mother caught them and made them go to church together for months—to the Zion United Church of Christaplex, of course. After dumping James, the little heartbreaker went on the pill and had sex on a regular basis with her new boyfriend. Her mother put her on the pill. James knew all of this private information because the new guy played football and apparently nothing was sacred in the locker room. In fact, tormenting your teammates was part of the rules of engagement in that world. I was curious to know what percentage of trial attorneys were once high school football players. I imagined this type of initiation made for good litigators.

James got a scholarship to Syracuse. Thankfully it was not for prelaw. Maybe he was listening too closely to me. Who was I kidding? He remembered everything I said. Actually, he was premed and proud of it. He had been fascinated by the stories of my injuries. He read up on fractures and told me what to do to rehab. He claimed that he had always wanted to help people, and my injuries allowed him to see that more clearly.

At that age, life was like a carnival ride. You just had to hang on and enjoy. You could make a decision based on a fleeting fascination. You never thought that a screw could come loose from the Tilt-a-Whirl and the whole thing would come crashing down. I realized even *I* wasn't old enough to know the true tragedies life could bring, but I'd screwed in my share of loose bolts. Buried some good friends, lost jobs, a fiancé, lovers, faith, and direction. And I'd had it easy.

The night before James left for college we pulled out the sofa bed, made popcorn, and watched *Animal House* on TV. During a commercial James told me he was scared to leave.

"To leave you," he added.

I could have told him he was just scared of the unknown and he would have a great time. Instead I told him that once he went to college he'd realize I was a crazy artist who never even listened to the Foo Fighters.

"I'll always love you," James said.

"Good," I said, trying to sound as if I was joking. "But don't forget, I know you," I said. "You confuse love and desire, like those kids in all of those teenybopper, *Pygmalion*-rip-off movies you made me watch this year."

"So do you," he said. "Anyway, romantic love *is* desire. At least it is in all of those artsy movies, I mean *films,* you made me watch."

He put his arms around me and in a terrible, fake French accent said, "I du love yu and ah du want yu, ma cherie."

I knew he wanted me to laugh, or at least call him a dork in a fake French accent, but I wasn't in the mood to humor him. I just exhaled dramatically and tried not to melt into his arms. Stiff. I remained stiff. I could do that.

"You can't hold on to someone by having sex, James," I told him. "I think you already learned that the hard way from your ex-girlfriend."

"Below the belt," he said, letting go.

Stiff and cold. I could do that.

"You're still leaving tomorrow," I said, feeling like a pouting child. I hoped that when he got older he wouldn't realize how immature I'd been.

I went to bed and, despite myself, cried a little before I fell asleep. I told myself it was because I felt sorry for being nasty to him on our last night together. But the truth was that he would soon be a lost love, however unconsummated. Ah, but wasn't it true that the best loves were the ones we imagined? They didn't have the same trappings as real love.

I told myself that I got tangled up with James because I was helping him become a better person. Giving him the wisdom of my experience. But the truth was that I might have learned something from him about being myself. He was the only person who knew me as an artist. I was too afraid to try it out in the real world, so I experimented with this poor soul whose only flaw was that he had a crush on me.

He left before I got up in the morning. That day, too depressed to cook, I went to the bar across the street from my apartment, drank beer, and made little thumbnail sketches of everyone who walked in. I drew one of the bartender. He liked it so much he grilled me a burger while I made him a full-sized sketch.

The next day, on the bartender's recommendation, I went back and sold a painting to the owner for sixty bucks. He talked me down from a hundred, but I would have taken forty. Now James, without his shirt, hangs in the ladies' room of a funky jazz bar where the lawyers go for happy hour.

Chairs in Black and Blue
(Oil on Canvas, 2001)

Ben was redecorating his house. It used to be our house. He bought it. But we shopped for it and I stayed there until I felt like I was being crushed by the same pressure that turned carbon into diamonds like the one on my finger. Who could blame me? Um, pretty much everyone.

I heard about this redecoration project from Tami. She was marrying Ben's best friend. We had fixed them up, and we were both going to be in the wedding. Was that a problem? No, absolutely not. There weren't any hard feelings except that I was sure he hated me. But we'd be fine. We were both adults.

Generally when engagements ended, there were things that had to be sewn up. You get this, I get that. "Take back yer mink. Take back yer pearls. What made you think that I was one of those girls?" Yeah, the marrying type.

But with Ben, I just left him everything. My paintings, my clothes. My rubbing alcohol, face wash, hair-shining serum. I suppose it was cruel to leave those things. He would have to pack them up, throw them out, give them away. But I figured that it was better than his facing me carting my insignificant junk out of the house. Or maybe it was worse for him to think that I considered the things I moved into his house, our house, insignificant.

They really weren't. The hair serum, I could buy more of that. But the paintings were a part of me. I felt that I needed to suffer their loss as punishment for leaving him. Okay, I was too chicken to go back and face him. But I cared deeply about the paintings. Some were my own, some I bought, some were gifts. I kept them to remember people I'd known and people I'd been. My bulky photo album.

I began painting when I was a teenager. I'd adopted the studio behind the house I grew up in and did angry, painterly abstracts until my dad taught me some technique. I got a potter's wheel and kiln for my sixteenth birthday and made a thick, lumpy dishware set. I got better. I set my mind to decorating our cabin in the woods. I adorned the outside with elaborate, colorful gingerbreading. I made and attached a polyurethane icing to every conceivable edge. I made rock columns at every entrance. I painted murals on the walls inside and hung mobiles from the trees. I wanted to be everything—installation artist, potter, sculptor, painter. If I heard about it, or read about it, I dabbled. I strained egg whites from yolks for egg tempera. I melted crayons and etched with it. I gathered fallen leaves and strung them together to ornament the tree they fell from. I made tents of Moroccan fabric I'd quilted. I built sculptures to guard the property. And I painted everything. There wasn't a surface left untouched. No one told me, not until Ben, that draping yard-sale scarves from the bedroom ceiling was an unusual design concept. I thought it was fancy.

Ben had seen the gingerbread cabin once. He liked it and affectionately called it "Crazy Cabin." It really was a wonder that he ever wanted to cohabitate. We were two distinct types. I saved the best for last. Ben did not. Best-for-lasters liked

anticipation and delayed gratification. Of course this was because we were afraid that things would end. And they did.

In real-world terms, this meant that I was a collector and
Ben was a cleaner. I saved everything. I didn't just save useful
junk, like glass jars and coffee cans. I also saved what even col-
lecting types would consider junk, like broken glass and plastic
soda caps. I had ideas for them. Sometimes I even executed my
ideas for them.

Ben was an organized, sentimental saver. He had pictures
framed and shelved or put into tidy albums. He had his old
yearbooks, on a top shelf, the spines dusted. And there were a
few cards from family and friends in a tin box, tucked away in a
drawer. I had piles of garbage, and he had cleaning supplies.
While I imagined what I could epoxy to the outside of the house
to spruce it up, he trimmed his bonzai and manicured the lawn.
I strung white lights on the porch and he gave me the thumbs-
up while he slaughtered my garden.

"You mowed over the purple flowers," I wailed.

"Lucy, those are weeds."

It stood to reason that the cleaners had to be more tolerant
of the savers.

After I ducked Ben's last hug and abandoned my paintings, I
had the honor of playing a "lady-in-waiting" for several
friends. Each wedding gave me a pang. Just ever so slightly, of
the I-would-have-had-a-colorful-chuppah-for-an-altar variety. There was another pang, a Ben-related pang, but I stuffed
that as quickly as I could. Then, after running from pillar to
post with each bride-to-be, eating cake, trying on dresses, and
squeezing my stepsister-like feet into Cinderella slippers, my

smug self-satisfaction returned. I didn't want to get married. I may still have wanted Ben, but like they said, it's all about the timing. A romantic sentiment indeed.

While I never considered myself an exceptionally good friend—I didn't send cards or bring soup to sick pals—I was nevertheless asked to stand up for more couples than I felt I deserved. I was of the opinion that one good friend, mine was Kate, was enough for any single human. But after Kate got married, she was effectively removed from the kind of single-girl recreation that I was still engaged in, or engaged to. This included bars and shore houses and trips to exotic places where there were bars and shore houses. And men. Don't forget the men.

And those very men were how the single friends I ran with became couple friends I rarely saw and then became engaged friends I stood up for. I was there the first night they met in Key West at the raw bar. I was there the night they fell in love, you remember the one, when we all drank red-death shots. That was a hoot. It just made sense that I'd take a place of honor among the best high school friend, the sister, the sister-in-law to-be, and the best college friend.

There were rules to being a good bridesmaid, and I followed them to the letter. They included, but were not limited to:

1) Don't be the bad bridesmaid.
   You don't have to try very hard, just hard enough not to be the worst of the group. Brides remember bad behavior and nothing is worse than going down in wedding lore as the person who ruined the wedding. You'll know if you're the

worst one because you'll be asked to stand at the end of the line in wedding photos. This is so the photographer can easily crop you out of the portrait that will forever hang in the couple's living room. Curious guests will ask about the wedding party and they might even remark that it's unusual to see more groomsmen than bridesmaids. Your former friend will give her husband a look and ask if anyone wants more mini-quiches.

2) Don't say, "When I get married, I'm going to . . ."
No bride cares about your imaginary wedding. This is her real wedding. Get with the program.

3) Never say, "This is just like what so-and-so did."
Each bride is unique and her wedding is proof of her individuality. All weddings are not the same. She may not be the only one who ever thought to dance with her father to "Daddy's Little Girl," but it's a fine choice. Their decision not to shove cake up each other's nose is innovation to be proud of. Always praise this idea.

4) Do what you can, spend what you can, bow out gracefully when you have to, and call for updates on a sliding scale depending on proximity to the wedding or related events.
Keep one rule in mind when bowing out: even if you won the lottery, cut off your hand in a freak boating accident, and got an audience with the pope all in the same day, do not ever talk about yourself on the update phone calls. Only talk about yourself if asked, and even then, try to deflect attention back to the wedding. Your hand is gone. There's nothing you can do about it now. Only mention it if gloves are *not* part of the bridesmaid ensemble. And even then, try to be delicate about it. "What do you think about

gloves? I see them a lot in these bridal magazines you sent me."

5) Only if you've cut your hand off and want to disguise it should you make any fashion suggestions to the bride.

Keep all opinions about the wedding style positive. You love the dress. You love the tuxes. Even if your wardrobe is completely wash-and-wear, and your idea of a tux is the polyester kind from the seventies, you approve of, and wholeheartedly support, the bride's choices. Parasols? Grand. Lollipop centerpieces? Fabulous.

6) Dance at the wedding, talk to the goober they want to fix you up with, stay until the reception hall manager kicks you out, and go to the after-wedding party until the bride and groom go to their suite . . . finally.

Be amiable. Do what they want you to do. It's only one night, so even after your feet start to bleed, hang in there. You can ice and bandage them at 2, 3 A.M., at the very latest.

When Tami and Max asked me to be in their wedding, the first thing I thought was, Shit, Max is Italian. The first thing I said, of course, was yes, and hugged them both. "How did you ask? Were you surprised? Did she actually say yes or just weep a lot?" because you should really get a definitive answer to that question. I assured them that I'd be fine with Ben and his girlfriend. I didn't say, "What's she like? Do you think he wants to marry her? Does he ever talk about me?" No. Come on. That was years ago. We were not talking about him anymore. There was a time limit on regret and pining. I told them I was honored. I was touched. I was thrilled. I couldn't wait.

Now, I'd had some experience with Italian weddings, being half-Italian myself. They were big. Not just the wedding; that was a piece of raspberry-filled, buttercream-iced cake. The whole mess was a yearlong event. Additionally, Max and Tami were all personality, the sort of people you wanted to celebrate for no reason, people you wanted to hug even if you weren't a hugger.

The first event was an engagement party. My own engagement party was an impromptu thing. It was the high five of engagement parties. It said, "Hey, way to go." I was in shock at the time, but in retrospect, it was really nice.

Max and Tami's engagement party was the stadium-wide, full-participation wave. It started with the foot-stomping rumble, the low murmur, and then with a big "whoa" everyone was up, arms a-waving. And down. Get ready, because here comes the shower. Whoa. And another shower. Whoa. And the bachelorette party. Whoa. (Is anyone getting sick of this yet?)

I was working as a fine artist and cursing myself for not choosing to starve as an artist earlier in life. Rather, I chose to starve as a corporate slave first. Dumb. Ben had told me to quit back then, become an artist. I didn't listen. I was stubborn. I was an idiot.

When I finally came to my senses, I moved into Crazy Cabin. I ventured out only to go to galleries or to my mother's for dinner. She brokered my work, so I didn't even have to interrupt my schedule to muck around with buyers and gallery owners. Okay, so sometimes I cleaned up and met people. That was part of it. My mother was great, though. She'd been selling art for years and had a method for marketing her artists. "You're not always available. You're working," she'd tell me when I asked if I really needed to meet clients.

I was actually doing pretty well having an insider working for me. The only reason I was starving was because, being back in the hometown, I was terrified of the overly long supermarket hello. "How've you been? / You're an artist now? / Yup, these are my two kids. / Mom has diabetes pretty bad. / Won't give up smoking. / Oh, sorry to hear about your dad. / That long ago already? / Kids, get off of that goddamn shelf, it's going to break and you'll have to goddamn pay for it. / Do ya have kids? / You never married? / No, me neither."

Conversely, I enjoyed the bridesmaid lifestyle. At parties I was talkative and sociable. I was available for midday wedding chores and enjoyed shifting my painting schedule. It helped creativity. And since I lived in relative solitude, I saved up all of my daily charm for these outings. It was different from the supermarket. I couldn't bring up to the "supermarket somebody" that I was currently fascinated by the FBI's most-wanted list. It was actually encouraging. One of the top criminals was a man who helped some others escape from Folsom. This had to mean that the people who'd committed worse crimes were already in prison. Plus, I had the Italian-family thing down. Hug people. Help out! Cry at the sentimental parts. So, I scrubbed charcoal off my hands, put some on my eyes, and drove to Max's hometown in north Jersey for the engagement party.

I braced myself to see Ben. I gripped the steering wheel of my mother's old Mercedes convertible, which she'd essentially given me. She had always been scared of it, and I loved it. I thought I looked cool. At thirty-one, I still thought a convertible had some secret power over people. Even if Ben and his new woman were in bliss, the top down on my car would drive the tiniest festering wedge between them.

As it happened, I psyched myself out for nothing. Ben wasn't there when I arrived. I entered the kitchen, the epicenter of all Italian wedding activity, and immediately introduced myself to the table of high-ranking elders. Then I hugged friends and strangers, and was put to work by Stacy, Max's sister and head project manager. I enlisted the help of the friends, and eventually Stacy and I had given everyone a job. The margarita machine needed to be fixed. We needed more ice. Someone on the phone needed directions. Stir the sauce! Put the tablecloth over the gift table. Make sure the tent legs are secure. Get Grandpa a chair. Under the tent. In the shade, for crissake.

By the time Ben arrived, the party was in full tilt and I was in charge of the meet-and-greet. "Hi, thanks for coming. I'm Lucy, one of the bridesmaids. / Nope, not a matron yet. / Oh, sure, I'd love to meet him. / Can I take your gift for you? / The bar is right over there. / So nice to meet you." I barely registered that I was planning on feeling nervous when I saw Ben. He was talking to some of the groomsmen and I had an armful of gifts.

"Goosey. Hi," he said.

"Oh, Ben, I'm glad you're here." I held the gifts out to him. "Would you mind taking these to the gift table for me? And, Jon, would you go take the gift from that lady in the pink top? The one who looks confused. Introduce yourself. Point her to the bar." I scooted him off.

Ben walked back from the gift table and scooped me into a hug. I wouldn't say the weak knees were from nerves. He was just a nice hugger. It may have been a combination.

"Busy?" he asked into my hair, and I got the impression that he was smelling it.

"There are lots of important people to welcome, so I'm

glad you're here," I told him, and gave him the upper-arm pat that is universally accepted to mean, You got the job, buddy. "Do you think you could take over?" I wanted to clarify that it was universally accepted. I may have lingered on his biceps for a little too long. He smiled at me. So did his brown eyes and hooded lids that said *love* to me so intensely. And—

"I hate to tell you this," he said, "but you've been greeting people with a big black smudge under your eye."

My hand went to my face to cover it.

"Oh, Lucy, it's much too late to hide behind your hand. You might as well live it. Pretend you just came in from football practice," he said, licking his thumb and wiping my cheek. He studied my face. "All better."

"Are you sure?" I looked at my watch. I had to be on the porch with a camera in one minute. Tami's request. There was something special going down and I was to be there.

"You look," Ben said, then took a deep breath. "I'll tell you when I see you next."

I tippy-toed up and kissed his cheek quickly, perfunctorily even, and ran off. Okay, maybe I lingered long enough to smell his clean smell, like new books and saddle soap. I floated across the yard and touched my lips with my fingertips. I stopped and turned, just to sneak a peek, and Ben was looking at me. I shot my hand up in a little embarrassed wave, then Max's brother pulled me into the fray.

Tami gave Max her deceased father's silver pocket watch. He gave her a Saint Anthony medallion from Rome, blessed by the pope. There were tears. Some were mine.

Then food. Then drinks. Then more tears and food. Food. Food.

Before the wedding party got too drunk, Tami and Max asked us to gather in the living room for a meeting of the "advocati," also known as the wedding party. "Where do we go from here? Are you all prepared to hug and kiss our relatives for a year?" I was just glad for the respite from Big Uncle Carmen, who had been badgering me to do shots of grappa.

It was a big wedding party with ten on each side. Max had brothers and sisters, Tami had brothers and sisters, and both had loyal friends from all three decades of life. Best of all was that Max and Tami incorporated their friends. So even though I was gathered in the last half of the third decade, I had not only met but had somehow come to know everyone in the wedding party. Her sisters had come to the shore with us. I had gone to a concert with two of Max's brothers. There were dinners and parties and trips. Tami and Max were the sorts of friends who made your life bigger. So we all cheerfully crowded into the living room together.

"Lucy, you might not want to sit in that chair," Max's brother Angelo told me after I was already sitting in it.

"Will it break?" I asked, leaning up, about to stand.

"No. Sit, sit." Angelo motioned me back. "It's fine. It's just that no one ever sits there."

"Lucy always sits in chairs no one else sits in," Tami said, as if it were a logical explanation.

"I do?" It was a fine chair for sitting, as far as I could tell.

"We went to a wedding," Ben said, "and we were in the hotel waiting for the elevator, and Lucy sat in one of the chairs they always have by the mirrors. The ones across from the elevator doors." Ben smiled at me. His eyes twinkled. He was the only person I knew who made that description, "twinkling eyes," make sense.

"You've got to be kidding?" Tami's sister was incredulous.

"In every hotel we've been to," Tami said, "at some point she'll sit in the hotel lobby."

"Is everyone here yet?" I asked, looking around, pretending to deflect attention. Although, honestly, I found this conversation fascinating. Slightly embarrassing, but interesting. "I know this will be a shock to you all," I said smugly, "but hotel lobbies are designed precisely for sitting. Plus, I sit in them," I said to Tami, "to wait for you because you're always late."

There was a general upheaval over that, the tone implying that everyone in the room had waited at least once for me. Okay, fair enough.

"Normal people," Max said, leaning toward me conspiratorially, "they wait in the room. They watch TV."

"How about at the shower we threw," Trina said to Tami. "Lucy sat in that antique cane-bottomed rocker."

"How do you remember that?" I asked, although I remembered it. It was an elegant piece of furniture.

"Because the B-and-B host practically had a heart attack."

"It was comfortable," I said, and shrugged.

"You're the only one in this century who would know," Trina said.

"In a related matter," I said, "I don't like getting my chair pulled out for me. I have a vague fear that the man's attention is going to wander and I'm going to land on my butt in the middle of a restaurant."

There was some laughter and stories about falling off chairs, which I was happy about. Ben looked at me. Not smiley

Ben. Not cheerful, storytelling Ben. But Ben who felt sorry for me. Interminably sad Ben. It would have been better if he just said, "That's why you left me, you can't trust anyone," and stormed out of the house. But this pity. It was too much to bear.

I don't know what came over me, but I mouthed to him, "I'm sorry."

He shook his head at me with an expression I couldn't decipher. Was it "I don't forgive you?" Maybe it was pure confusion—he had no idea that I had regrets. Or maybe he was confused because in his mind, and everyone else's, we were ancient history. He wasn't sad for me, he was thinking about how he forgot to lock his car. He was wondering what the hell I was apologizing for. He was thinking, She's still a lunatic, thank God I'm not strapped to her for life.

Finally, Tami and Max began their "thanks for being here for us" speeches and I let myself get overwhelmed by their love. Sentimental people like me are the worst. We're just freeloaders.

Tami called me the day after the engagement party to thank me for all of my help and for the serving platter, which I'd made ages ago and dug out of the Crazy Cabin cupboard and washed, thinking it would be perfect for them. "You're welcome, I'm glad you liked it." I didn't say I was especially glad since I'd made a whole set of accompanying pieces that I would be giving them over the course of a year's worth of parties.

"Was it awkward seeing Ben?"

"No, not at all," I said. "I bossed him around just like the old days."

"Did you meet his girlfriend, Allison?"

"No," I said. "Oh, wait, Allison. Yes, I did meet her." My stomach sank. She'd shaken my hand. Yep, she took my hand, with its paint-crusted nails, into her smooth one with ringed fingers and perfectly polished tips. "You're Lucy. It's nice to finally meet you." She was slender. Refined. The kind of woman people described as elegant.

Tami also called to see if I wanted to look at reception locations. "Trina's coming too. It'll be fun." I was in the midst of painting a commissioned piece in black and blue for a collector my mother had lined up, so of course I wanted to get out of the house. I was already depressed enough about Ben without adding bruises to it. Plus, location scouting was my forte. I'd make sure I didn't have charcoal on my face.

That was great, Tami said, and she was off. Running, running, running. She and Max were meeting their sponsor couple for dinner.

Now, most engaged couples go to some sort of training through their church conducted by priests or long-lasting married couples who probably should have divorced. In these sessions, they split the couples into rooms for boys and girls and showed them each a different movie. Each group learned that there would be changes that their bodies would undergo. On the day of the wedding, both would be in the best shape of their married lives, and then they would get softer and rounder with each progressive year. There were diagrams, time-lapse simulations, and before-and-after pictures of people in outdated clothes. They also learned that there would be mental changes caused by hormones. This was normal and they should embrace their new feelings of both sentimentality and entitlement.

Because the men weren't supposed to tell the women what

their movie was about, I couldn't say for sure what their list included. But some things the women were told to keep in mind, roughly, included the following:

1) You deserve to be happy. Deliriously happy.
2) You are the most important person in your life (and now his life too).
3) Candor gets things done!
4) Reminding unmarried friends to get married is your responsibility now.
5) It's your day, do it your way (applicable to every day here on out).

I joke. I really am a fan of love. Falling into it is terrific fun. And there was the self-exploration that it brought about which had nothing to do with Ben, whom I'm not even talking about. But I'd read literary fiction and I knew that men didn't really like wives all that much. They complained about how women acted once the kids came along, as if these kids were her relatives staying in the guest room too long. They complained about how she'd changed. How her skin didn't glow in the moonlight anymore. And how she'd bitched because he'd given the kids too many cookies and now they were up crying. And she was fatter than she was at twenty. These were the candid musings of the literary man, the honest man, the thinking man. Sure, sometimes the woman was more than a prop for his frustration. She had a name and wit. She pointed out that all he ever talked about was "the way it was." But the literary man didn't look at this too long because there was her bedtime attire to criticize and her new short haircut to lament.

As I headed toward a day in Tami's wedding world, I tried to imagine Max bitching about these things. Yup, I could see it coming. Nah. I was only thinking that way because I had indigestion. My real problem was not with disillusionment, it was with a pile of lox and onions that I'd eaten before I left the house. The lox was soft and buttery, but slightly bitter, as lox could be. It was left over from a sandwich I'd bought at the overpriced organic food store I wandered through, coffee in hand, after buying art supplies in town. I could have eaten half the amount I did, but it was too late for those kinds of regrets. Now, my only regret was that I didn't know if I had any antacid. I dug in the glove box and found two tablets, inevitably wedged in the corner with glove box lint on them. Some people preferred to call "glove box lint" dirt. I tried not to think about it. I blew on them then chewed them up. Immediately, I belched three fishy, oniony burps.

I was grateful that I was single because I was sure that fishy, oniony burps would be one of the things that made the thinking man wonder why I didn't wear sexy nighties. And of course, these were the thoughts that meant the beginning of the end, because anyone who couldn't understand that humans sometimes burped fishy onions is an idiot with unrealistic expectations. Of course, I knew that my own expectations in this scenario were unrealistic as well. It was certainly acceptable for someone to dislike something about me and have regrets and neurotic expectations once in a while, because we all did. Some of us more than others.

I met Tami and Trina at a reception hall in a traditional, 1980s-style wedding factory. These never caught on anywhere but

north Jersey. Who knew why? It was basically a replica of
Monticello on the outside. Inside, there were ten or so reception halls and five chapels, so you could pass other brides on
their special day and smugly remark to your bridesmaids that
your dress was nicer.

Tami loved it. Trina and I agreed wholeheartedly. Pictures
could be taken outside in what some optimist deemed "the garden," which had an excellent view of the road and the neigh-
boring strip mall.

Tami and the wedding coordinator discussed details and
Trina cornered me. "Did Ben mention your paintings?"

"I hardly got to see him. What about them?"

"Okay, I'm going to tell you this because I know how you
hate it when people hide things that there's no reason to hide."
She took a deep breath. "His girlfriend is redoing the house
and wants you to come and get them."

"Is she living there?"

"It's heading in that direction."

"Should I call him?"

"I'm sorry, Lucy."

"Why? That's fine. I shouldn't have left them there in the
first place."

"I shouldn't be the one to tell you this, though. It's just that
Allison said he's been dragging his feet about calling you."

"Oh," I said casually, "you're friends with Allison?"

"It's just that I'm Tami's best friend and Max is Ben's. I just
see her a lot. You know. And we went on vacation this summer
with them."

"No, that's good. It's fine. She seems nice. I appreciate you
telling me."

"If it would make you feel better, I could tell you something mean about her."

"That's silly," I said, waving her off, then added, "Like what?"

"She's boring?"

"Okay, you said it like a question, so I doubt it's true, but it does make me feel a little better. I don't care anyway."

"Of course you don't."

There's a town in Germany where brides have to pole-vault over a river to prove they're fit for marriage. In a native Guatemalan tribe the male proposes by breaking a water jug over the woman's head. I guess that if she doesn't drown or die from the blow, then it's meant to be. Ben and I had a similar test, which I failed. It was living together. As far as tests went, it was a pretty good one. I hesitated. Stutter-stepped. I was good at hesitating. I had perfected it.

Once, when I was in college, I was at a house party and some of us thought it would be fun to drink a few beers on the roof of the house. Of course. Fantastic idea! When we finished our first beers, I walked toward the ladder to go down to the kitchen to get more.

"Oh no, Lucy, we go down this way," my pal Donny said. He had apparently used the roof spot before.

I walked to where he was standing and saw that he was pointing to a junked mattress and box spring on the ground. It wasn't so far down. It was only a one-story house, a squat one at that. Yet, I didn't know if jumping off a roof after drinking was the best idea I'd ever heard. I wasn't the jumping type.

"No, it's easy," Donny said, sensing my doubt. My reluctance to get too close to the edge was probably what gave it away. He assured me again then leaped like a gazelle onto the mattress. He bounced once, then bounced to the ground. It looked simple enough. But Donny was the kind of guy who skateboarded and snowboarded and seemed to have rubber band legs. I was decidedly less coordinated. I headed toward the ladder.

But then Donny's brother, who got all of the coward genes of the family, squatted into a sitting position and dropped himself off the roof onto the mattress. If he could do it, what the heck? I stood at the edge of the roof. Donny and his brother coached me. "It's easy, you can do it, just drop down, nothing to it." Other people from the party gathered. "Yeah, Lucy, all right," was the general commotion from the onlookers. So I squatted and jumped out a little to hit my target.

I then watched the faces in the crowd go from encouraging to confused. I had actually hesitated in midair. I hit the edge of the mattress with one foot. The other foot hit the ground full force. My neck snapped back and I landed in a jumble. The faces crowded around, now with worried looks. "Are you okay? I didn't know that was even possible. Did you see that?"

It's a disappointment to perform a miracle that is of no discernible value.

I would not hesitate with Ben again. I would call him and take my paintings out of his house so he could move on with his life with the probably-not-so-boring Allison. I picked up the phone and dialed. As the phone rang I looked at the clock and hoped he'd be at work. He answered.

"Ben, it's Lucy, I hope I'm not disrupting you." I smoothed my hair. It was a nervous gesture that I had consciously weeded out of my repertoire, but still indulged in once in a while for comfort. It didn't work so well.

"I saw the caller ID and thought that was your mom's area code."

"Oh yeah, I moved into Crazy Cabin."

"I heard you started painting full-time. That's terrific, Lucy."

"Well, I like city living better. You know how I hate to cook."

"You looked thin at the party. No one's taking care of you," he said gravely.

"They don't call it starving artist for nothing." Taking care of me, indeed. What was I? A toddler? Couldn't reach the phone and order takeout by myself? He was sweet to worry.

"I guess you're calling about your paintings."

"I guess," I said meekly.

"Since you're making a living with them now, you probably want them back."

"Are there any you want to keep?"

"Are you kidding? I want all of them. Hold on a second. I'm getting a call."

I was confused. Did he want them out of his house or not? Call waiting. That was what I'd been reduced to. Someone Ben put on hold. *"Oh, my old girlfriend called today, wait a sec, I never called her back after we got cut off with call waiting. Yes, she was the one I was engaged to. Dodged that bullet."*

"Lucy, I'm so sorry. I have to take this call. My pop's been sick. It's a long story. I'll tell you in person. Do you want to meet me for dinner?"

"Is he okay?"

"How about tomorrow? I'll be up your way. I'll come to Crazy Cabin and pick you up at five."

"Five?" Had he turned ninety since I'd seen him last?

"Sorry to cut you short," he said. "I'll see you tomorrow."

He was going to be up my way? How was that possible? I lived two hours from him. I looked at the phone, not sure what to make of the conversation. When it rang, I jumped and picked it up.

"Did the phone even ring?" It was Kate.

"I was standing right here. I just hung up with Ben. We're going to dinner tomorrow."

"Well, *we're* going to dinner tonight. Or did you forget?"

"Shit. What time was that? Please tell me you're not there already?"

"Yes, I am. And I'm half in the bag and mad as a hornet." She laughed. Of course she wasn't waiting for me.

Since I had stopped working a real job it was generally understood by my inner circle that I needed day-of reminders for any plans I'd agreed to. Kate also reminded me to put shoes on, which was her favorite accompanying joke to the reminder call. I hadn't been very good at remembering dates or making appointments on time when I'd led a conventional life, but then it made sense. I was a busy working woman. Now I was a cliché. Oblivious artist.

I wanted to be the charming and prompt artist type, if there was such a thing. Damn. I made it to the restaurant before Kate and felt proud of myself for this. I gave myself an A+ for punctuality. The bartender flirted with me and I gave myself an "exceeds expectations" in charm.

Since I'd moved out of Philadelphia, my weekly lunches

with Kate had turned into bimonthly dinners at a bar restaurant halfway between our houses. I played with my straw and then picked at the peanut mix. I really did hate waiting. I thought that I might be the type who was late for things not because I was oblivious but because I was secretly passive-aggressive. Maybe I was filled with such self-importance that I didn't think I should ever be put out.

But I had to prepare. Kate would ask about Ben, and I needed to sort things out so we wouldn't have to spend the whole dinner on him. Ben. Ben. I thought he'd be married by the time I saw him again. Or maybe I didn't. But I did think that he'd tend toward the fiercely independent type, not an elegant, cool swan. More the industrious beaver, the sort of woman who hailed cabs and planned vacations down to the last minute. An intelligent sort who would help him strategize his next business move and tell him when to diet and which diet to go on. The sort that men thought were independent, but really were control freaks. I didn't know why I'd curse him with that. This princess Allison gave me a pang, though. What he really needed was someone who thought he was funny. Someone who believed that ideas were reality, not things. Someone who thought he was handsome, fascinating, brave. Someone who was finally ready for him, who had figured out how relationships worked. I'd have to sort it out with Kate. I was getting nowhere.

"I think," I ventured a possibility to Kate, "that I tried to make the wrong guys fit. The implication being there is a right guy, which is a huge concession for me to make."

"You're like that emperor of India who wanted the magicians to make him a magic carpet."

"Don't tell me he slaughtered the magicians who couldn't make it for him."

"No. Well, maybe, but he did finally settle for a tree house."

"Settle? No, we're trying not to settle."

"Lucy, magic carpets don't exist," she said.

"Neither do emperors of India."

"Of course they do," Kate said. "However, the encouraging word here is that there's evidence in your concession, as you call it, that people really can change."

"You're such an idealist," I said.

"Remember that crazy kid we went to school with, the one who only ate peanut butter?"

"Right, I forget his name. We called him Loony something, his last name."

"We called him Loony Lunderwear. And that wasn't his last name. That was because we saw his underwear once when he was having a fit."

"That wasn't very nice of us," I said. "But it is kind of funny in a peculiar way, Lunderwear. Lunderwear." I liked the word.

"Yes, we were comic geniuses. Anyway, I just heard that he's an honest-to-goodness Buddhist guru now. Full of mental fortitude."

"I had a friend in college who was crazy to get married," I said, "and she changed. She accepted that she was probably going to remain single. She plunged headlong into a fulfilling life where she travels and has lots of good friends."

"And then she fell in love?" Kate sounded so full of hope.

"No," I said, annoyed. "See, that's where all of you marrieds are wrong. Being happy as you are isn't a ploy to find a man. It's about being happy as you are."

"Okay, are you happy as you are?"

"I'm elated. I'm doing what I want. I have great friends. I get along with my family. It's one miracle after another."

"Maybe you're like a woman you knew in college. The one who was terrified to get married? One day she accepted that she didn't have to have any more relationship angst."

"I only have relationship angst for your benefit," I said. "I know how you miss being single."

"You're a good friend. And since you're being so honest with yourself, you might want to look at why seeing Ben has sent you into a tailspin."

"It hasn't," I said defiantly. And then I tried the line again. "It hasn't." And I felt the change. I settled back into myself. I really did like my life. Okay, so I had some lingering regrets. Who didn't? But they would be resolved in an adult manner. Loony Lunderwear and I weren't so different.

As I drove back to my house from dinner, I took stock. I really had changed. I could feel the difference. In fact, I also noticed it in my driving. Since I'd moved out of the city, I was forced to drive everywhere. Now, I was never a good driver. And I eventually wrapped my car around a tree, which wasn't technically my fault, but probably could have been avoided. But recently I'd realized that I was a good driver. The surprises that used to freak me out had disappeared. I saw a car edging out of the strip mall lot and knew it would pull out in front of me. I could tell when a vehicle that passed on the highway was going to cut me off. I finally noticed deer in the woods and willed them to stay out of the road as I crawled by. I was shocked that these perceptions were new to me. It was as if I had dialed into a set of subtle rules that had eluded me before. I didn't know how this new talent would help me in any other part of my life, but I wanted to call my insurance company and let them know they could lower my rates.

So, the next evening, full of my own mental fortitude, I waited for the crunch of tires down my driveway at five. I hadn't known it when I was trying on the thought, but I felt entirely comfortable seeing Ben. It was confirmed when I didn't do anything to get ready for him. I didn't pluck my eyebrows into a pleasing arch, or paint my lips into an attractive bow, or do whatever else the cosmetics industry wanted me to do. I just tried to finish the underlayer of the black and blue painting so it could dry overnight.

Ben picked me up and before we did a thing I got the full story on Pop. He'd had bypass surgery, it had gone well, he was at the new cardiac center about a half hour away from where I was living, and Ben was sorry for the early dinner, but it coincided with the end of visiting hours.

Then Ben insisted I show him any additions to Crazy Cabin. He liked the freestanding weathervane best, which was made mostly of wrought iron pieces I'd collected and lashed together in the shape of a hawk. I couldn't make it look like a rooster no matter how hard I tried. I liked hawks better anyway.

It was nice to see him. Not comfortable, like the old-shoe analogy people always used upon seeing a former lover they felt no animosity toward. He felt more like a fancy cape, one I could swing around and pretend I was Dracula. Or I could let hang over my shoulders as if I were a sophisticated opera-goer. I wore it with flourish, for fun. He made me feel creative, beautiful, silly.

Ben ordered a bottle of wine at dinner, so I settled in. I

knew what kind of restaurant experience I was in for when someone ordered wine. Nice and leisurely. And waitstaff liked you better when you ordered wine. They encouraged you to linger. Go ahead, buy another. I didn't know much about wine, except that it was always overpriced in restaurants and either the odd or even years were supposedly better. Lacking the key element of that last tidbit made it an essentially worthless piece of knowledge. Anti-knowledge. The whole idea of sommeliers saying that I'd made a good wine choice was ridiculous to me. Wasn't it their job to make the good choices? Who picked their wine list anyway? Was there a secret conspiracy to unload bad wine? Each restaurant had to agree to a few clunkers or they wouldn't get any wine at all.

"I've given our engagement a lot of thought," Ben said. "It was bad timing. That's all it was. And a bad proposal."

"No, the proposal was nice." I hadn't been prepared for *that* sort of long evening. I thought the wine was supposed to lead us to the inevitable, "Gee, we were engaged once."

"No, I know a few things now." Ben leaned back. "The men who get it right are the ones who know what their girl-friends need in the proposal department."

"Is that in the school of science or liberal arts?" I asked.

"See, for you it would be liberal arts." He took a sip of wine. "You're a private person and kind. If I didn't do it in a restaurant, you may have told me that you wanted to wait. Then we could have made it up as we went along."

"You may be giving me too much consideration in this scenario."

"I know you," Ben said and relaxed farther into his chair. "I don't just look at you and see the outline. I see you. I don't know why. I just can. I never squeezed you into some image of who I wanted you to be." He raised his glass for punctuation. "And I love every bit of who I see."

"What's not to love?" I wanted to challenge him. I wasn't sure if anyone could remove his own expectations or experiences from his perception of another, but if anyone had with me, it was Ben. It felt like truth. So I allowed it.

"You have lots of things you hate about yourself. You hate that you think you're not doing enough or that it's not good enough. You hate that you like solitude because you think you should be just as comfortable with yourself around other people. Least of all your fiancé."

"Everyone's like that."

"You think that everyone is like you? That we're all variations on a theme?"

"We're not?"

"You have a quirk, and you shrug and say that everyone has quirks, so you're just like everyone else. I show you a hotel room that's exactly like the last and you jump on the bed and say that it's not the same, this bed is fluffier. The view shows a bigger sliver of the ocean and the water pressure is better. You think it's spectacular for those things."

"Holy crap, you're right. I definitely do that." I really was impressed with this revelation about myself. "So, what about you? What are you like?"

"You also agree with people and then deflect their attention."

"No, I really do agree with you." I laughed. "It's not a ploy," I said, smiling.

"But you're also done hearing about it."

"No, by all means, continue. I'm going to go to the ladies' room, though."

"And then you make jokes."

"Now, wait a minute, I thought you loved every bit of me."

"I do. Who else would spend the better part of five years dissecting the woman who walked out on him?"

"Probably any man who wants to live an examined life. You have a nice girlfriend. She's moving in, right? So you're trying to figure out the perfect proposal for her benefit. So she doesn't freak out and call it off."

"Who said she's moving in?"

"Trina. Tami and Max."

"You know I love them, but you have to take what they say with a whole shaker of salt. Anyway, I told you when you left our house that I would wait for you forever."

"You'd go out with me again?" My stomach flipped and I took a big gulp of wine.

"We're getting married," Ben said matter-of-factly.

"I'm not sure I marked it on my calendar."

"It's tomorrow."

"Okay. See you then."

"I'll tell you what I'm like, since you asked," Ben said, "and I don't deflect. Or I don't deflect for long. I'm everything you think I am. I'm a computer geek who played Dungeons & Dragons until he was eighteen. I'm a brute who mows down wildflowers and likes to watch soccer in pubs. And I'm an over-anxious puppy who jumps all over you when you get home from work and all you want to do is have a moment to yourself. And I'm pushy. I try to fix things that aren't broken, and I try to rush things that are going fine the way they are. And I'm a basket case who is in a perpetual one-upmanship competition with his father, a kind, gentle man who has no idea and just unconditionally loves his Oedipal son."

"Just don't go and have a massive coronary to one-up him this time."

"The thing is that I know you would have liked these things about me if I hadn't pinned you to what was essentially your idea of a life sentence. If you'd decided on your own that you liked them, then we'd still be together."

"I do like those things about you."

"I know you do. I've convinced myself that you do and that I just put you in the fight-or-flight mode."

"But women are supposed to want to get married. How were you to know?"

"I knew. I just put myself first. I wanted you for me. But I really want me for you. I'm like a campaign manager and you're the candidate. I have an 'I Love Lucy' button and a red, white, and blue hat."

"Another four years, Desi?"

"We could re-up every fours years if you want."

"I thought we got to make it up as we go along?"

"Precisely. As you know, I'm a planner. But, as proof of my flexibility, I'll tell you that I was going to have this conversation with you after seven years. So, if I have to wait two more years, I'm prepared for that. But I've gotten this far and you haven't smoothed your hair or run to the bathroom." Ben looked at me with a serious, measured expression. "Actually, you seem different."

"It's probably because I'm happy," I said.

"See, again, you're ahead of the curve. Thirty-one and happy, it's unheard of."

"So, no pussyfooting around. If I agree, then we're in full swing? Without a net?"

"Well, that's what I'd want. I don't know who's hanging around Crazy Cabin these days, but if necessary, I could punch him out."

"You've never punched anyone." Ben grew up in front of a computer. His fist was in a permanent mouse grip. The mouse claw, I called it.

"Now, there's where you're wrong. When we broke up—that's what I call it, because there were two of us and it didn't work out." Ben paused, took a deep breath, and then continued. "Earlier I said that you left me, but I'm responsible too. So, when *we* broke up, I decided that there were some things I should do before we made a life together. Coincidentally, when I was putting this list together, I'd watched *Fight Club* and got obsessed with the fact that I'd never hit another human being. It seemed like a male rite of passage that I'd skipped over."

"Did you have sex with a prostitute before or after the fight?"

"Max taught me how to punch, wise guy. Follow through. Aim for a target behind the actual target." Ben did a mock jab. "At the end of the lesson, he told me to hit him in the stomach. He tightened his abs, he's a strong guy, it would be fine. So I aimed and fired. Only I was just slightly off target and I hit him in the sternum. Dropped him to his knees."

"I think that's how Houdini died."

"He had a huge bruise for weeks. I joined a boxing gym after that."

Ben went through his list of "rites." He studied tae kwon do after he broke his nose boxing. He went to Tibet, it was beautiful. He got a dog, Spoons, a pound mutt. He shot a gun, he liked it. He did some drugs, not worth the money, in his opinion. He learned some Spanish. *Me llamo Ben. Soy de Philadelphia. Te amo.* He volunteered for Habitat for Humanity and built houses one summer; he'd do that again, although some days they just had him clean up the site because he hit his thumb too many times with the hammer. He surfed. He reconnected with his extended family by organizing a yearly canoe/camping trip.

He wanted to know everything I'd done since we'd been together. Start with boyfriends. He'd heard a few stories. "Actually," Ben said, "I want to know about everyone you ever dated, before and after me. Somehow we skipped over that, and I want to know everything about you."

So, I told him about Gary, the one who was spending time with me but who really loved Carol. And Todd, whom I dated when I hated myself. And Keith, just a bad choice. Nobody liked him. And there were dates that went only so far. "Kate likes to tell a story," I said, "about how I locked my last date in the car by accident and had to break a window to get him out. Of course that was after I poked him with the bent coat hanger."

"That guy Gary with Carol, that's like me with Allison. The one I'm dating until you decide to love me again."

"Oh? Does she know that?" Ben was always straightforward. An admirable quality, I thought, but Allison might not agree.

"She knows. She might be hoping for that to change. But she knows. I like to think I've always been an honest person. But I see now that real honesty is only as good as the truths, or lies, I tell myself."

"Yes, I think it's those pesky lies that have gotten me into trouble."

"What's an example?"

"I think the biggest lie I tell myself is that my life has compartments, which is unusual, because I'm pretty messy for the most part. But with personal relationships I categorize—what I want, what I need. But there aren't categories. Relationships may be delicate, but they're also organic. They change as people change. There just has to be bedrock to allow for the messy movement of the stuff on top. I don't know. I'm still working this out."

"The delicate balance in intimate relationships isn't as delicate as you may think." Ben raked his fingers through his hair and smiled a terrific smile. "Call me Fred Flintstone," he said, "because I'm *from* bedrock."

I settled into the soft seat of Ben's car. It smelled like him in the car. Leather and the ocean and cedar. Clean smells. Ben. I closed my eyes and inhaled.

"What do you like about me?" Ben asked.

Of course, that question was at the essence of my decision. There wasn't anything else to ask. I was happy alone, and now I had to decide if I could be happy *along*. It seemed to me that most people coupled because it made their lives easier in some way. But for me it had become easy to be happy alone.

I didn't need my life to be easier, but I accepted that it could be richer.

"I like that you can handle any situation," I said. "I have complete confidence in you."

Ben puffed out his chest a little when I said that and it made me feel good. I wanted to like the same things about him that he did. And I wanted to love the things he didn't like to help him see that they were also lovable.

"I like that you're thrilled by whitewater rafting. And you're serene on a canoe ride on a still pond."

"Yep, that's you. A whitewater ride as still as glass."

"And I like that you see metaphors in everything I say and do and you translate their into words so we're both clear about what I really mean."

Ben laughed and it made my stomach feel warm. His laugh was like a favorite chorus. It made me understand why people got obsessed with music. For this feeling.

"You have the kind of intelligence I enjoy. There are those people who are smart but grim about it. Like the only benefit to being smart is that they don't ever have to suffer the humiliation of looking stupid."

"I love looking stupid," Ben said.

"Yep, you're a goof," I said. "You're the kind of smart that knows looking foolish is part of the fun of living."

"And I don't mind looking foolish about you, which is the general consensus with the people who know that I've been waiting for you all of these years."

"Ouch," I said. "Speaking of that, what makes you think I won't freak out and do the same thing to you again?"

"You may, but I know I've got enough inside me to handle it or anything that's thrown at me. I don't need everything to be perfect and I don't need everything to be a mess—because some people are like that."

"You know, you really are great."

"I love you too," Ben said.

We held hands, and when we got to Crazy Cabin I invited Ben in. I used to think that there was some secret to the order of things. I had rules for how I approached each relationship. If we met in a bar, it was doomed. If I told my friends too much about him too early, it was doomed. If I divulged a private moment between us. If I was attracted to someone else. If I slept with him too soon or was overly eager in some other way. Doomed, doomed, doomed. But that night I took Ben home with me.

My sheets needed to be washed.

My house was a wreck.

I hadn't shaved my legs in weeks.

I slipped the watch off my beauty-marked arm. He touched my skin. It was cold and his hand was warm. An old lover returned. I'd forgotten how we were together because there were others in between, and time, and we were different people because if it. But I didn't forget how he tasted, how he smelled. I melted into myself in a way that had nothing to do with anything but myself. And I enjoyed his body. I held his hands. I kissed his cheeks, the corners of his mouth. I held on to his biceps, ran my hands through his hair. I enjoyed his body for my own pleasure. It was delicious. And I loved my body with his. I forgot I hadn't shaved and when it crossed my mind, I realized I didn't care. My legs were glorious.

A favorite moment had nothing to do with any of that. In the morning, he got out of bed and I watched him button up his shirt in the doorway while we talked. It was cold. He didn't want to walk to the bathroom without his shirt, he told me. He started out of the bedroom then stopped, turned, and asked me if I wanted to use the bathroom first. Then, the man I always loved, the man who returned to me, the most considerate man I ever knew, in a button-up shirt, with no pants, walked to the bathroom. Those were the things I never wanted to forget.

There were other things. There was the kiss after he dressed. He looked taller than before in his crumpled clothes with his messy hair.

There was my tingling flesh as we held hands and I walked him to the door.

As we stood kissing on my porch, I tried to put my hands in his sport coat pockets. He'd never cut them open. I wanted to get in there with a seam ripper and make his jacket more useful.

"I'll call you today," he said. "After I call everyone I know first," he said and kissed me on my swollen lips.

"I'm happy too," I said.

I knew about the relativity of time. It defined my life. I painted for hours that only lasted minutes, and I waited at stoplights for minutes that lasted hours. With Ben, those two things collapsed. With him I got a peek at infinity. Events were layered on an endless spindle of time. I watched Ben walk to his car forever, and he was gone in an instant and he was gone forever, although he'd never left.

When I saw him later that day I think my cheeks were still

flushed from the night before. "Hi, you," I said. He looked so perfect in his jeans and boots and sport coat. "My God, are you really for me?"

Ben hugged me and he smelled like sweet pipe tobacco on a warm breeze. I opened wine and he leaned against the countertop watching me.

"So, what's happening in the outside world that I'd be interested in?" I asked.

"Well, you might like to know that the outside world was missing you and wishing you well all day."

"Is there evidence?"

"I brought the biggest supporter of the movement to see you." Ben straightened and held his hands out as if to say "ta-da."

I hugged him.

"I've got him outside in the car if you want to meet him," he said into my hair.

"Did you crack the window for him?" I went back to the wine.

Ben pulled glasses from the cupboard.

"I can tell you the results of my daily experiments in human nature," Ben said.

"Not tested on animals," I said.

"I was picking up a movie for my dad at the video store near the hospital. He has a VCR in his room. Anyway, inside the store they have one of those big cylinders with colored liquid inside and a little pedestal. You drop the quarter in the top, and if it somehow manages to float onto the pedestal, you win a free year of video rentals."

"Right," I said, "one of those games that's impossible to win."

"It's highly unlikely. Like placing the hard-way bets in craps."

"You're basically giving your money away."

"Anyway," he said, "there's this kid whining for a quarter from his mother to play and she tells him no, especially not for that ridiculous thing. He asks and asks and she's getting sort of mad at him. She gets into the 'that's final' stuff. Anyway, he made this little sound of disappointment, the kind with a 'darn it, Mom' inflection. And that's all I can take. I give him a quarter. I just want to see what happens. Will the mother scold me, scowl, approve? Will the kid be happy or guilty? What's going to go down?"

"You've done this before?"

"Oh yeah. I've got tons of variations on this theme."

"In the name of social research, of course," I said.

"Naturally," Ben said. "In this type of situation, involving a whining kid and wasted money, I find that about seventy percent of the mothers disapprove and either outright tell me off or give me a dirty look. The rest say thanks or shrug. And almost all of the kids reveal a combo of happiness and guilt."

"How did these subjects behave?" I asked, trying to sound the way I thought a serious scientist would sound.

Ben laughed. "You're using your computer-dork voice to represent the scientific community, Lucy. Not all geeks have the same vocal quality. I think you might be stereotyping."

"I could be like the token female TV detective. She's always about twenty-five, dressed in short skirts, and made up like she's just come from her pole-dancing job," I said. "What happened out there?" I said in my worst sexy-baby voice.

"The mother gave me a shrug and the kid was happy at first."

"Let me guess," I said. "He dropped the quarter in the impossible game, lost, and then went running back to his mother a little embarrassed?"

"Very good guess, grasshopper. You know your subjects well. But this time a point goes to the weaker statistic."

"He hit you up for more money?" I asked excitedly.

"Guess again."

"He kicked you in the shin when he didn't win?"

Ben laughed. "You're getting close. It has something to do with winning."

"He won?"

"Yup."

"I've never heard of anyone winning that game in my whole life."

"He won, and he started freaking out," Ben said. "His mother came over, shaking her head. He was practically jumping on her. It was so damn funny. He high-fived me. The mother thanked me and said that he had two older brothers and he never won anything. It was awesome."

"It's amazing how one simple decision can make all the difference for some poor kid," I said.

Ben and I raised our glasses and he made a toast to me and to the quarter on the pedestal.

"And to you," he said, "the best prize I've ever gotten."

"To winning the hard way," I said.